KANE

COOPER CONSTRUCTION SERIES
BOOK 2

By Jen Davis

KANE

Limitless Publishing, LLC
Kailua, HI 96734
www.limitlesspublishing.com

Formatting: Limitless Publishing

ISBN-13: 978-1-64034-524-9
ISBN-10: 1-64034-524-8

Dedication

David, Catie, and Michael: You are my life's greatest gifts. I couldn't do this without your love and support.

CHAPTER ONE

Amanda

Nathan's fingers dug into the tender skin of Amanda's inner arm. "How many times do I have to tell you? Fundraisers for my office are not opportunities for you to run your mouth."

She clenched her jaw against the urge to tell him to fuck himself.

"Do you have any idea how many women would give their eye-teeth to be in your shoes?" he hissed, tightening the pressure of his grip.

More than she could count, most likely. In his late thirties, society considered Nathan Shaw one of Atlanta's most eligible bachelors—handsome, rich, and from a political powerhouse family as old as time. His perfectly styled blond hair framed an aristocratic pale face with blue eyes and expertly arched brows. He never left his penthouse dressed in anything less than befit his station. The man was practically Georgia royalty.

He was also an arrogant, entitled bastard.

1

"Actually, Abe," he mocked her voice in a high falsetto, "I think the money would be better spent on a domestic abuse shelter." He shook her so hard her teeth clacked together. "We might as well flush it down the toilet."

"He asked my opinion," she gritted, her head beginning to ache.

Nathan slammed her against the wall, the back of her skull bouncing off the plaster. "*My* opinion is *your* opinion, and you damn well know it."

He let go of her, and she slid to the floor. Hanging his tuxedo jacket on the back of one of the tall chairs he kept tucked under the island in his high-end kitchen, he appeared to be done punishing her.

Her instincts screamed otherwise. She curled herself into a ball, protecting her head, as a vicious kick landed to her lower back.

"If you are going to be at my side, you will behave as your breeding should dictate." His voice no longer betrayed his anger. He locked it down, replacing it with a honeyed cadence of practiced ease. Measured. Controlled. "Do I make myself clear?"

Only one answer would allow her an escape from this. She lifted her head. "Yes," she murmured.

He graced her with a serpent's smile. "Excellent. Now get off the floor. You'll ruin your dress."

Her hindbrain shouted to scoot away from his outstretched hand, but the rejection might set his blood boiling all over again. She fought her instincts and wrapped her fingers around his.

He pulled her to unsteady feet, then released her hand. His fingers tugged on the strands of dark red hair escaping the simple chignon her stylist had created. "Your hair looks all tumbled, pet."

Fuck.

Slowly, he unpinned the rest of her locks, the look on his face growing heated. By the time all her hair rested thick on her shoulders, she could make out the tent in his pants.

She swallowed back the bile burning her throat.

"Gorgeous," he said huskily. "I want to unwrap you."

Before she could move away, he yanked down the side-zipper on her shimmering strapless silver gown. It pooled on the floor at her feet.

So much for his concern about it getting ruined.

The cool kiss of air against her exposed skin made her shiver. All she wore now were her high heels and the tiny scrap of black lace masquerading as underwear.

Getting naked with him was never part of the deal. She bent quickly to grasp the expensive fabric and pull it up. It got as high as her waist before he locked his hand around her wrist.

"I think you need to be reminded who wears the pants in this relationship." His voice dipped lower. "Perhaps what you really need is for me to take what I want and fuck your sweet ass. Maybe *that* will teach you your place."

Gritting her teeth, she shook off the embarrassment of standing there half naked. "No."

He probably could have forced her. Obviously, too many highballs had him crossing lines he'd only skirted in the past. There had been times he'd squeezed her arm too hard or pushed her away with a little too much force, but he'd never hurt her the way he had tonight.

Still, she'd been firm in the past declining any invitations into his bed. Her resolve wouldn't change now. Or ever.

"Let me go." She squared her jaw. "Unless you're willing to do this against my will."

A snarl twisted his face, and he clenched her wrist tighter. She stopped breathing, a cold sweat dotting the curve of her back.

Maybe she'd miscalculated. A dozen worst-case scenarios shuffled through her head. Nathan breaking her wrist. Breaking her arm. Forcing himself inside her.

Should she scream? Run?

Before she could even form a plan in her head, he blanked his expression, then let her go. "You know me better than that." He gave her his back and moved languidly toward his bedroom. "I'm headed to bed. Don't forget to leave the dress."

She didn't breathe until he left the room. Shaking all over, she kicked off the heels still binding her feet, then slid the dress off completely and draped it over Nathan's jacket. It wasn't hers to take home, just a rental he'd made for the night.

Gulping in lungfuls of air, she unzipped the small duffel bag on the counter. She shoved her head into the soft T-shirt, her arms getting caught for a moment before she could cover herself completely. She couldn't get her sweatpants and shoes on fast enough. The idea of being naked and vulnerable with him so nearby made her stomach turn.

God, she hated this place. Hated the man who lived here.

And hated her father for putting her in this fucking mess to begin with.

Closing the door gently behind her, she speed-walked the hall to the elevator from Nathan's penthouse. Her tennis shoes squeaked on the marble floor.

The doorman nodded politely and called the valet for her car. If he noticed the moisture in her eyes or the darkening skin at her wrists, he studiously ignored it.

Nathan had only tried to get her in bed once before, and at the time, he'd accepted her demure rejection with a profession of old fashion values. It fit with his image, even if his southern charm was nothing more than lip service.

Her own condo beckoned from just a few miles away, and though the traffic in Atlanta was usually insufferable, it would be an easy drive this late at night.

She caught sight of a shooting star as she slipped into the driver's seat, and misery thumped harder against her chest.

Her life hadn't always been like this.

There was a time she knew what it was to be loved.

It was a mistake thinking about it. Knowing how much better it could be, knowing she'd never have it again, only made a bad situation worse.

***

13 years ago

July

"Deny it all you want, Mandy, but I know you're only wearing that tiny little dress to drive me crazy."

Kane's dark eyes gleamed as he dragged his gaze over her body. Stalking toward her in long strides, he approached from the parking lot where his brother had dropped him off. His fingers flexed, as though he wanted to touch her, but he held back.

Her blood heated with his regard, and giddy laughter bubbled with the nickname he'd given her. "I'm not denying anything." Tilting her head, she fluttered her lashes. "What other reason could there be?"

She gestured for him to step closer to the grass next to the fountain. She'd arrived at Grant Park a full fifteen minutes ahead of their date so she'd have time to set the scene, though the lush clearing and the water feature provided almost ready-made romance. Her heart beat double-time as he closed the remaining distance between them.

Hello, gorgeous.

Kane Hale had nothing in common with the buttoned-up snobs her father always picked out for her, which was probably part of the attraction. Frays peeked from the hem of his worn jeans, and his Green Day T-shirt hugged his wiry frame.

He wrapped his arms around her waist and lifted

her off the ground before fitting his mouth against hers. Even after three months together, his kisses heated her blood.

Butterflies danced a riot in her stomach as she ran her hand over his damp close-cropped brown hair, then gripped his broad shoulders. He smelled faintly of shaving cream, and her fingertips fluttered over the smooth skin of his cheek.

His tongue swept the seam of her mouth, and she opened eagerly with a small sigh.

She could have forgotten they were in the middle of a popular park if a small dog hadn't started yapping at her feet. Her eyes flew open as a gray-haired woman pulled on the animal's leash and harrumphed, presumably at their very enthusiastic, very public display of affection.

Kane chuckled and took a step back. "See what you did? That old lady was practically scandalized." Laughter danced in his eyes, and her heart swelled fuller than ever.

She ran her fingers over her tingling bottom lip. "At least I know I won't be the only one staying up tonight reliving our kiss."

He stroked her hair and tipped his forehead to hers. "You were never going to be the only one. I'll be thinking about it all night."

It would be so easy to fall into his arms again, but too much distraction would torpedo all her careful planning. Squeezing her eyes shut for fortitude, she broke contact and knelt on the blanket with the picnic basket. Shadows edged the nearby trees, signaling the transition from dusk to dark. The park would be closing soon, but she'd timed their meal to avoid as much of the Georgia summer heat as possible. Even at seven-thirty, though, the thin cotton of her dress stuck to her skin, and she knew her forehead probably glistened with perspiration.

At least she didn't have any makeup to melt off. Kane always made it a point to tell her she was beautiful without it.

"Sit with me. Eat one of these damn hot dogs." She patted the ground beside her. "You know I only packed them for you."

Kane settled on the blanket, but they didn't eat right away. They held hands and watched lightning bugs flit around the trees and laughed at the mom chasing a toddler making a bee-line to the water.

Eventually, Kane fished his foil-wrapped treasure out of the basket. "One day I'm going to get you to try one. It's positively un-American you won't eat a hot dog."

Shaking her head emphatically, she swallowed the bite she'd taken from her PB&J. All the food she'd packed had been simple fare; cooking wasn't one of her strengths. "I may be crazy about you, but I'm not crazy. Do you have any idea what's in those things?" She shuddered.

"You're crazy about me?" He waggled his eyebrows and finished the second half of his hot dog in one bite.

Her face heated. A smartass quip hovered on her lips, but she swallowed it down and went with the simple truth. "Yeah."

His smile widened with her quiet admission, and he ran his hand up the side of her arm. "How crazy are we talking about?" he teased gently.

8

"Somewhere between Nick Nolte's mugshot and Tom Cruise jumping on the sofa with Oprah."

He pursed his lips in mock concern. "Pretty crazy, then." His fingers snaked around the column of her neck, and he pulled her closer, his breath hot on her skin. "It's a good thing I'm every bit as crazy about you."

She leaned forward and brushed his lips with hers. The desire shooting deep into her core felt positively audacious in public. When she pulled away, his stare locked on her face.

"Let's get out of here," he whispered. "I need to be alone with you."

Great minds think alike.

A make-out session in her backseat would not only scratch her itch, but it would provide the perfect inspiration for some toe-curling dreams in the nights to come.

Nodding, she grabbed the picnic basket while Kane snatched the blanket from the ground. Together, they speed-walked to her car.

She stopped short when he grabbed her shoulder.

"Look. A shooting star. Make a wish."

Glancing up, she caught the tail end of the light blazing across the sky.

I wish Kane Hale would be my first. She blinked. *And my last.*

"What did you wish for, baby?" He tucked her hair behind her ear. "I wished nothing will ever come between us."

She slapped his shoulder. "No. If you say it out loud, it won't come true."

Taking the picnic basket from her hand, Kane

put it in the trunk, then laced his fingers with hers. "Hush. We control our fate. Not luck. Not the stars. So, you'd better get used to this face, because it's never going to change, and there is nothing in this world that's going to take me away from your side."

She hesitated. "What about the club?"

His father wouldn't stop pushing for Kane to join the MC where he was a founding member. Not only were his parents deep in the life, his brother, Scott, was too.

As much as she adored Kane, she wanted no part of his world. Those guys treated women like crap. Even the "old ladies" like Kane's mom were second-class citizens, considered barely a step above talking blow-up dolls.

The guys she'd met from the crew? Rude, crass, and violent. Probably criminals. And they were Kane's family.

"I'm not going to join. I told you. I've never wanted that kind of life." He kissed her hand. "I want a real relationship. I want a home and a job and kids who aren't embarrassed by their dad when he comes to their school to pick them up."

He said all the things she wanted to hear, but based on everything he'd told her before, she knew rejecting the club could drive a wedge between him and his family he may never overcome.

"I don't want you to lose your parents or your brother and resent me one day for it."

"It's never going to happen. With you or without you, I'm never going to join." His voice hardened with resolve. "I promise, Mandy. As long as I live, I will never be part of my family's MC."

***

Kane

Present Day

Blood and gore stuck to Kane's boots as he tromped through what was once the city's most notorious drug den. Now it bore the hallmarks of a slaughterhouse. Bodies littered the floor, all members of the crew once run by Sucre de la Cruz.

All dead at the hands of the Skulls MC.

His gaze met his brother's across the dimly lit room. Scott's tongue peeked out of his toothy grin. No doubt, he reveled in the carnage.

Kane only came for his friend, Brick. Well, Brick and the ten thousand dollars the man had promised the MC to help him take out his drug dealer boss and the bastard's crew. The violence didn't excite Kane like it did Scott. He considered it a necessary evil to protect his club.

They were his family.

When everyone else had started killing, his job had been to hold a weapon at the drug lord's head, so the piece of shit could watch his empire crumble before his eyes.

He found it immensely satisfying. De la Cruz and his organization had been a stain on Atlanta for years. The guy ruled through violence, fear, and death. Now his reign was over. Not only did Kane have a hand in the takedown, he did his part without taking a single life.

His brothers were another story. They ripped

through Sucre's men like they were made of tissue paper, and they loved every second of it. All the crazed smiles and laughter would have given it away even before they'd raided the bar and started toasting with tequila shots.

In his years with the club, Kane had seen plenty of violence up close and personal, but he'd never had to kill anyone. Maybe it was a cop-out, but he didn't want to start a body count now.

He swiped one of the tarps piled right inside the front door and dropped it next to a body. Nobody could skip clean-up.

Holding his breath against the stench of viscera and human waste, he grabbed the dead man's arm and slid him onto the black sheet of plastic. He had to plant one foot on the tarp to keep it in place. Stealing a quick gulp of air through his mouth, he knelt and rolled the man up like a burrito. Blood coated his hands and speckled up his arms over his sleeves of tattoos.

He climbed to his feet to repeat the process with the next body. There were about forty to dispose of and only fourteen brothers to get the job done.

Cue Ball lugged each drug-dealer-burrito to the pickup parked out front. Once they were all loaded up, the brothers would take them to Sucre's own dump-spot, the one Brick had told them about, ready-made with barrels of sulfuric acid. Not only was it convenient, but he could appreciate the poetic justice in it.

A playful slap landed on his shoulder as he finished wrapping his third body. "Fuckin-A, man. You really came through with this job tonight. We needed this money in a major fucking way."

Scott didn't exaggerate. Ten thousand bucks was less than a lot of crews would demand for a job like this, but right now they needed it like water in the desert. The club hadn't been making the same kind of cash it once had. Sure, they brought in enough to get by, but the profits from running guns declined more every year. The demand was still there, but the weapons were easier to come by these days. Buyers weren't willing to pay as much for a middleman anymore.

Most of the guys made ends meet with a second job. Scott worked on cars. Kane did construction.

He didn't mind his day job. In fact, he preferred it. He never had to wash blood off his hands after a day nailing up sheetrock.

"I'm glad to do it." The old scar on Kane's cheek tugged when he smiled. Even at thirty-two years old, it felt good to have Scott's approval. He loved his brother, even though they didn't always see eye to eye.

He gripped the backpack Brick had left behind after the massacre was done. No telling what Scott would do if he suspected there was another forty thousand dollars in arm's reach. "Are you heading out with Cue Ball or staying here to bleach the place down?"

"Are you serious?" Scott barked out a laugh. "You think I'd miss a chance to drop bodies in vats of acid, so I could stay here and play housemaid? Fuck you, man." He chuckled as he walked toward the front door.

Kane pulled the elastic from his hair and

gathered all the stray pieces back into a ponytail at the back of his neck, then surveyed the bar. All the bodies were gone, but it would take hours to mop up all this blood. Half a dozen members of the crew had left with Scott to dispose of the bodies, while the other half of the team stayed behind to manage the mess.

It was after midnight by the time they'd erased the evidence of the massacre. As much as he wanted to go home, he had to head back to the clubhouse to meet up with the disposal team and divvy up the money they'd made tonight.

He gave his hands a final wash in the sink behind the bar before he strapped on his helmet and settled on his bike. A Harley Davidson Dyna Super Glide Sport. Black, it was only a few years old with a matte finish.

The engine purred to life, and the rides around him did the same, creating a humming chorus. Kane pulled onto the dark street, and the others followed in a single file line before sliding into a staggered riding formation.

Anemic yellow light shone through the windows of the wood-framed clubhouse when they arrived. Without the sun to illuminate the outside, shadows hid the fading paint and sagging shutters, which both betrayed its age.

All curves in a nearly indecent little black dress, Charlene greeted him at the door the minute he walked in. She wrapped herself around him like a cheap suit, all itchy and ill-fitting. The smell of nicotine wafted off her skin. It even overpowered the bleach and stink of the night still clinging to him from the job.

"I was starting to worry about you, baby." She stuck out her painted bottom lip in an exaggerated pout and twirled a strand of bleached blond hair around her finger. "I've been here all night."

"I had a job." The words came out gruffly, but he didn't have it in him to pretend he cared.

Unfazed, she cupped his jaw with her hand. "It's cool, you—" Her nose wrinkled as she peered at his beard. Using her middle finger and thumb, she pulled something from the unruly coarse hair on his face.

Oh, Christ. Was that a bone shard?

His stomach roiled, and he pushed her away. "Go home, Char."

"But—"

"Go. Home."

He didn't bother to watch her long enough to see if she listened. In truth, he didn't care where she went, as long as he didn't have to deal with her. Rubbing the back of his neck, he trudged to the back room where they held all club business, the room they called the chapel. He was the last to arrive. All but two of the fifteen chairs were taken. They were situated along an oblong table, the seat at the far end noticeably vacant.

The guys cheered at his arrival. Some clapped; others knocked on the worn wooden table.

Forcing his burning eyes to acknowledge his brothers, he dropped heavily into his chair to the left of the president's position. "C'mon now, y'all did the work too. We all earned it."

"But you brought in the business." The booming

15

voice from the door prompted every man in the room to scramble to his feet, even Kane, who wobbled a little when the blood rushed from his head. "I'm proud of you, son."

Despite his sixty years and decades of hard living, Malcolm Hale still cut an impressive figure. He matched Kane's six feet, one inch, and probably came close to his two hundred pounds of muscle. Even though he didn't ride often with the MC, he started the club with his brother, Wes, and as president demanded the respect he considered his due. He also demanded his sons call him Malcolm, just like everyone else did.

Stepping to the head of the table, the man lifted the stack of hundred-dollar bills already waiting in the center. "Ten thousand?"

It wasn't really a question, so Kane stood silent.

Malcolm cracked a wicked smile, a lot like the one Scott flashed in the middle of the bloody bar. "To take down Sucre de la Cruz, it would have almost been worth doing it for free. We helped make that fucker a king. I'll bet he never thought we could break him just as easily." Amid catcalls and cheers, he dropped the money back to the table. "Five hundred dollars a man. Twenty-five hundred for the club. Now, get the fuck out of here so I can get myself a blow job."

Biting back a sigh, Kane swiped his share and made his exit quickly. There was no telling if Malcolm's dick would be getting sucked by Kane's mom or some piece of club property tonight. Neither possibility was one he wanted to think about.

He only had to drag himself a few blocks to his apartment, and he couldn't wait to get inside to close the door on this long and nasty day.

Too bad he couldn't close the door on this life. As deeply as he loved his brothers, the way they lived turned his stomach sometimes.

Closing the distance to his private space on his Harley, he kicked off his boots on the porch before heading inside. No need to track DNA evidence through his home. The blood had dried, but it could still mark up his carpet.

He stopped in the bathroom first, hiding Brick's bag of cash under the sink. Then, leaving his filthy clothes in a pile on the floor, he climbed into the shower and tipped his head forward into the spray. The hot stream sluiced through his hair, and the water at his feet threaded with the rust-colored remnants of his violent night. Once it ran clear, he grabbed the soap and made quick work of his body.

He'd shower again in the morning—right after he bagged up his clothes to burn them—but he wouldn't be able to sleep covered in death. Satisfied he was clean enough, he squeezed the water from his hair and toweled off, then padded naked to his bedroom.

Charlene was spread out nude on his king-sized bed. When he'd told her to go home, he meant for her to go to *her* home, not his. He didn't invite any women into his private space. Ever.

She had some fucking nerve.

Thank fuck she was asleep. He'd lay next to Charles Manson if it meant getting some rest. Sliding beneath the sheets, he gave the woman his

17

back.

How the hell did she get in here?

He sure as fuck never gave her a key. Charlene was not his old lady, and he'd never pretended otherwise. He wasn't interested in calling any woman his own. He'd tried it once and had never regretted anything more.

A flash of dark red hair and sea-green eyes scratched at the back of his brain, but like he'd done hundreds of times before, he shoved the memories down, squeezed his eyes shut, and fell into dreamless sleep.

CHAPTER TWO

Kane

The happy buzz Kane associated with a new day on the construction site took a hike without his best friend there. Unfortunately, Brick had earned himself a little R&R at the wrong end of a gun after the showdown with Sucre, and he wouldn't be back for at least a week. Another guy on the team was hurt even worse, so it was basically a skeleton crew working to catch up on a project already hemorrhaging money for the company.

The man who commissioned the build had decided he wanted major modifications to the plans. It would've been fine, except he didn't make up his mind until after the work had already started, and he flat-out refused to pay for the cost of the changes. It meant a mad scramble for the team to make their deadlines, while their foreman weathered major pressure from the higher-ups to satisfy the client.

If it were up to him, he would've told the buyer to go fuck himself and put the damn house on the market, but nobody had asked for his opinion.

He'd barely strapped on his hard hat when a gangly guy clutching a clipboard darted between him and the front door. "Have you seen Brick?" the kid asked breathlessly.

Robby was the foreman's assistant and had imprinted on Brick like a baby duckling. The young man blew his floppy brown bangs out of his eyes and blinked rapidly.

"Sorry, kid. Not yet." He softened his voice at the disappointment on Robby's face. "He texted me, though. Told me he's out of the hospital. His girl Olivia is taking good care of him. Don't know much about Will, though."

Will was Olivia's brother and the other member of the construction crew who had been shot Saturday night. One of Sucre's goons snatched her before all the killing started at the bar. Brick put the punk down, but not before the fucker put bullets in both Brick and Will during their rescue operation.

Robby's eyebrows scrunched down. "It doesn't feel right for us to be here worrying about this stupid house while they're hurt."

"I hear you. But we've got to make sure they have jobs to come back to. We can't get any further behind on this build." He firmed his jaw. "Are the other guys here?"

Inclining his head toward the entryway, Robby sighed. "Yeah. They're just getting started. You can head in." He stepped out of the way but called out before Kane made it to the door. "I know you're his best friend. You'll let me know if you get any updates, right?"

A lump formed in his throat. He couldn't remember the last time he had a friend outside of the MC, but Robby was right; he and Brick had become tight. "I promise. I'll go see him before the end of the day. Now I'm gonna get to work. This house isn't going to finish itself."

***

Amanda

"Are you shitting me?" Perry's voice rose in pitch with each word. She sat rigid and straight in her seat. "Which ones?"

Amanda paused at her receptionist's desk. She'd never heard the woman curse on the business line before.

"Well, are they going to live?" Her hand covered her mouth and the bottom of the phone. "Okay, okay. They'll be in our prayers, Xander. I'll let Miss Griffin know what's going on."

Did she say Xander?

Her heart stuttered. Xander was the foreman of Kane Hale's crew. Kane. Her first love. Her only love. The man off-limits to her now and forever.

Is who *going to live?*

A hundred questions swarmed in her head, but she couldn't make her mouth form any of the words. She stood frozen, trying to force herself to breathe.

Perry set down the receiver with a stunned expression. "Two guys on Xander's crew got shot over the weekend."

21

The words pierced through her heart like a poison-tipped arrow. Staggering back, she stumbled over her too-high heels and landed gracelessly in one of the chairs ringing the perimeter of the room. The Cooper Construction lobby was easily five hundred square feet with stylish hardwood floors and soothing mint green walls. Walls now closing in on her.

Her eyes burned; her mouth ran dry.

The fucking biker life finally caught up with him.

"—Barlow and Will Turner. He said Brick is out of the hospital, and he's visiting Will today." Perry's words didn't completely register.

She licked her dry lips and croaked, "What?"

"Brick and Will," the receptionist repeated slowly. "Are you okay, Miss Griffin? Do you know them? I know your brother usually deals with Xander and his team."

She nodded absently, relief wreaking as much havoc on her body as the fear had. Now tears threatened.

But she'd never let them fall.

She searched her memory for faces to match the names, but Perry was right. She didn't normally handle Xander's builds, but since her brother's car accident, she was responsible for everything. Frankly, she'd already forgotten the names the receptionist had supplied. It only mattered neither of them was Kane.

Perry looked at her expectantly. Oh yeah, she'd asked a question. "No. I don't know them, but every member of our team is important to me. Do we know if they're going to recover?"

"I'm not sure, ma'am."

She gripped the arms of her chair and forced herself up. "Are the members of the board here yet?"

"Yes. They arrived a few minutes early."

Of course, they did. They thought they could intimidate her, put her on the defensive by forcing her to walk in the room last.

Amateurs.

If people could dick her around so easily, she wouldn't deserve to run this company. Her irritation helped her find her center. Thrusting her shoulders back and lifting her chin in defiance, she walked into the conference room like she owned it.

Which she did.

"Gentlemen," she crooned, and the six men seated around the mahogany table sprang to their feet like their chairs were electrified. "Please, keep your seats. All our time is valuable. Let's get straight to it." She picked up the iPad Perry had ready for her on the table and swiped it to life. The screen mirrored on the monitor mounted to the wall. The image showed a line graph in decline.

She jumped in briskly. "Obviously, we've seen some decline in the past quarter, but—"

"*Some* decline?"

She didn't have to turn her head to identify the voice of Tom Poole. The pompous prick never missed an opportunity to be a thorn in her side.

"Let's call a spade a spade. We're bleeding money out of our asses, sugar."

The men at the table gave a collective chuckle, and she bit the inside of her cheek at his insincere endearment.

"Hardly. We've had a few setbacks, but nothing we can't rebound from." She swiped to the next slide. "In my opinion, we need to branch out. Go bigger. If you look at these projections—"

"*Bigger?*" This time it was Samuel Levine. "Darling, what we need to do is scale back. Cut the fat, as it were."

"I disagree, and I would appreciate it if you hear me out."

Samuel shot her a placating smile. "I appreciate your step-daddy started this company, Amanda, but I think it's time you let the board do its job. We've been doing this a long time."

That doesn't make you any good at it. Gritting her teeth, she bit back the retort. "The board's job is to advise me. Ultimately, I need to decide our best course of action."

Tom stood. "What you mean is, the president of the company decides the best course of action. Maybe it's time we elect ourselves a new president."

She should've known.

"I suppose you're willing to offer yourself up for the position." Hard as she tried, she couldn't keep the bite out of her tone.

"As a matter of fact, I am." Shooting her an oily smile, he stroked the silk tie resting against his rotund stomach. "All those in favor?" Every man at the table raised his hand.

It was a coup. Or at least an attempt at one.

She smiled, but it didn't reach her eyes. "Sorry, Tom. You don't have the votes."

"I beg your pardon?" he sputtered. "I have every vote in this room."

"Too bad for you, they're not enough. My brother and I have fifty-one percent controlling interest in this firm."

His self-satisfied smile returned. "But Mike isn't here."

Leave it to this flock of fucking vultures to try and use her brother's car accident to take control of their company. She should have never agreed to let outsiders invest in Cooper Construction in the first place. Thank God, she wasn't the kind of woman who ever left things to chance.

Now it was her turn to smile. "It doesn't matter. I hold his proxy." She navigated to the copy of the notarized document on her tablet and left it up on the screen. "Does anyone need me to zoom in on his signature? Do you need the name of the notary on the seal?" She didn't wait for an answer.

Her voice hardened. "This is my company, gentlemen. You don't want to hear my ideas, fine. You know your way to the exit."

Tom's round face grew red; the blush even peeked through the strands of his ambitious comb-over. "Arrogant bitch. President or not, you can't expand without money, and I refuse to fork over one red cent to finance your ridiculous little fantasies."

"Then it's a good thing I have my own money." Even if she hated herself for how she got it. "This meeting is officially adjourned. Don't let the door hit you in the ass on the way out."

***

She waited until the last board member was off the property before she hopped in her car for the short drive to her father's office. It was a shot in the dark since she didn't make an appointment, but it was a conversation she didn't want to have over the phone.

Eleven stories high, Atlanta City Hall loomed in familiar majesty in front of her. Her father had told her stories of its history so many times, she knew them by heart. The high rise was built back in 1930 on the site General Sherman took as the headquarters of his occupation before his March to the Sea. It was on the National Register of Historic Places and served as the headquarters of Atlanta City Government.

Including the mayor's office.

Her heels clacked across the ornate lobby with its pillars, cornices, and marble wainscoting. She no longer found it impressive, if she ever had. Only a fool would ever reveal such a thing to her father, though. He lived for the pageantry of it all.

She rehearsed her speech in the elevator. It had to strike exactly the right balance of strength and vulnerability, independence, and deference. And even then, there was no guarantee he'd give her words any more credence than he'd give to the average constituent. Maybe less, since he didn't think he needed to curry her vote.

Her father's secretary gave her a stiff nod when she stepped through the double glass doors, and she walked straight to the small settee on the right. It was the most comfortable seat in the room, and she could be here waiting five minutes or five hours depending on his schedule and the mood he was in.

She went over the points in her head again. One: she was ending things with Nathan. She'd promised her father six months with the guy so he could use a private connection to cultivate political gain. Her part of the bargain was fulfilled. Two: she was going to spend Thanksgiving with her brother. Holidays at the Griffin estate were more about pomp and circumstance than family bonding anyway.

Maybe she should lead with the Thanksgiving thing. Rip the band-aid off.

"Miss Griffin?"

She lifted her head and locked eyes with the sour-faced woman at reception.

"The mayor will see you now."

He stood from behind his thick oak desk as she walked into the room. Beauregard Griffin oozed southern charm and class. His charcoal three-piece suit was impeccable, his smile warm and practiced. An article in *Atlanta* magazine said he was reminiscent of Gregory Peck in his *To Kill a Mockingbird* days. He liked the comparison so much he had the article framed and hanging on the wall in his study at home.

His appearance was like the fancy lobby downstairs. It was cultivated to impress and intimidate, but it was really all window dressing.

"A surprise to see you, darling."

She stepped into his embrace and offered her cheek before taking her seat. "Thank you for seeing me. I know how busy you are." Polite bullshit, and they both knew it.

His eyes narrowed, and she pressed forward.

"I need to give my regrets for Thanksgiving. It's important I spend it with Mike and his family."

"Absolutely not." He folded his arms in front of his chest.

A hint of what she was really feeling seeped into her words. A tactical error, but she couldn't stop herself. "Dad, he's going through a difficult time right now. You know how badly he was hurt in his car accident."

"Last I checked, he had a devoted wife to cut up his carrots. He doesn't need his stepsister to do it for him."

She gritted her teeth. She never called Mike her step anything, but her father always made the distinction. "I want to be there, Dad."

"Of course, you do." He shot her an icy glare. "Even when you were a girl, you acted like they were your *real* family. You've always chosen them over me."

She wouldn't argue over what constituted a real family. Her father thought no one should come before blood. Or maybe it would be more accurate to say, no one should come before him. "I'm not choosing one over the other—"

"Right. I'm making the choice for you. I've already invited Nathan, and I can't very well spend the holiday with him, without you."

She took a deep breath, sucking back the venom she wanted to spew at the mention of his name. Things were delicate with her father; he still hadn't entirely made good on his end of the bargain they'd struck. She tugged back on the Ice Queen veneer she wore like a second skin. Letting it slip in the first place had been a stupid mistake. "We never discussed Nathan joining us."

Her father waved her clipped words away. "Do I need to get your approval for the decisions I make? This is an excellent opportunity to solidify the support of his political action committee."

The thought of spending another minute with Nathan made her skin crawl, but he would be the perfect gentleman in front of her father. He always was.

Her dad kept speaking, oblivious to her masked frustration. "Besides, we'll be done by nine. Plenty of time to visit your other so-called family afterward." Looking down pointedly at the papers on his desk, he dismissed her. "I'm very busy, Amanda. Perhaps anything else you wish to discuss can wait until a more opportune time."

Fine. One more dinner. She would nod and smile, give her father this last chance to secure his political support, but no more. Then he'd make good on his promises, and the deal would be done.

Then, she could put this madness behind her and get back to the shreds of her life she hadn't managed to ruin quite yet.

***

13 years ago

September

AC/DC piped in through the speakers mounted in the backyard for her parents' Labor Day barbeque. Though technically speaking, Charlie Cooper wasn't her father, he never treated her as anything less than his daughter. As soon as she and Kane cleared the patio door, he swept her up in a hug.

"I'm so glad to see you, Baby Girl. You know it's not a party until the family's all here." He smelled like Old Spice and barbeque sauce, home and safety.

Her mom bussed Kane's cheek and accepted the KFC bags in his hands.

"I hope you don't mind my contribution is store bought."

Mom peered into the bag and grinned. "Why would I mind? Corn is corn."

Kane let out the breath he'd seemed to be holding, then slid his hand around Amanda's. The heat of it warmed her even more than the late summer sun.

Is this how Charlie makes Mom feel?

She couldn't imagine her father ever inspiring warmth.

The knowing look on her mom's face made her cheeks burn brighter.

Mom cleared her throat. "Your brother is already in the pool with his friends, if you two want to go join him."

Sure enough, Mike waved like an idiot from atop a giant floating yellow duck. "Come on in, y'all. With you two, we'll have enough people to play water volleyball."

Kane's forehead wrinkled. "I don't really play sports," he said into her hair.

She wrapped her arms around his trim waist. "It's not a real sport, I promise. It's only an excuse to splash around in the water and get the girls to jump up and down in their bikinis. No one cares how well you play."

"If you say so." Or at least that's what she thought he said. Her attention was frozen on all the skin he flashed as he pulled off his shirt. Flawless and tan, it stretched across his wide shoulders to a tapered waist. A trail of hair led from his belly button to the treasure hidden beneath the button fly of his jeans. Her breath caught.

Hell, yes.

She couldn't resist the urge to touch him. "Maybe after this, we can sneak back to my dad's house. He's out of town." Her fingers slid down his arm before entwining with his.

He winced. "Your dad hates me."

"My dad hates everyone he doesn't personally select to be part of my life." She rolled her eyes. "I don't care what he thinks, and neither should you. This is my real family, and they think you're awesome."

Kane opened his mouth, but whatever he was going to say got lost in the whoosh of air her brother knocked out of him when he tackled Kane into the water. The sneaky bastard had managed to maneuver himself out of the pool and onto the deck without her noticing.

Now Mike and Kane were splashing it out while the girls around them protected their faces from the flying water.

Warmth bloomed in her chest seeing how easily he fit into her world here. She glanced over her shoulder, quickly spotting her mom's red hair resting against Charlie's broad chest.

That's what love looked like.

She rubbed at her sternum.

And this *is what love* feels *like.*

She could have it. What they had.

She didn't have to endure a society marriage simply because her father expected one. Half of her friends from the upscale private high school she attended were already engaged, their buttoned-up fiancés, each an heir to his father's fortune. Their marriages virtually guaranteed to be loveless, lifeless, and devoid of laughter.

Amanda knew her father considered this a rebellious diversion from her real future, but *it doesn't have to be.* She could have this forever. The realization made her sway on her feet.

As Kane and Mike wrestled and dunked each other underwater, she could see dozens more holidays, exactly like this one, sharing them with Kane and her family. Maybe one day, *their* family. She swallowed against the emotion rising in her throat.

How did I get so fucking lucky?

A hand on her shoulder made her jump. "You've got it bad, sweetheart." She hadn't even seen

Charlie coming.

Laughing at herself, she didn't even try to hide the truth. "Beyond bad." She sighed as Kane blew her a kiss. "I think he could be The One."

Charlie lifted his thick, dark eyebrows. "The One, huh? Does he feel the same way?"

She didn't even have to think. The answer was in a hundred secret smiles and gentle touches, whispered words and shared dreams. "He does."

"Well, nothing else matters."

"You're not worried about his family? My father—"

Charlie held up one of his big, calloused hands. "The things your father finds important aren't the same things I do, and you know it."

Understatement of the year.

"Your mom's parents weren't too keen on me either." His gaze sought his wife across the yard and softened when she blew him a kiss. "It's about more than where he comes from. He can't help who his daddy is any more than you can help who yours is. All I care about is whether he loves you and he treats you with the care and respect you deserve. From what I see, you're getting everything I'd want for you."

"I wish you were my father." She'd thought it a hundred times, but this was the first time she said it out loud.

Charlie's brown eyes grew suspiciously damp. "Aw, Baby Girl, in my heart, I am." He looked over at Kane and Mike, now fighting over sovereignty of the giant floaty-duck, and he grinned. "If my blessing is what you're looking for with Kane Hale, you've got it. You're old enough to know your own mind and your own heart. Any man worthy of your love is welcome in this house and in this family." He swatted her butt. "Now get your ass in the pool before lover boy drowns my only son."

CHAPTER THREE

Kane

The club didn't do much to celebrate the holidays. Kane's parents weren't what anyone would call domestic. He'd only observed a handful of festivities in his entire life; all of them had been with someone else's family. This year, though, Cue Ball got a wild hair up his ass to fry a turkey for Thanksgiving.

He'd never seen the big, bald bastard cook anything in the fifteen years he'd known him, but it wasn't like he had a bunch of better options busting down his door, so he agreed to help. He tilted his head at the deep fryer set up in the carport.

Wait. They were doing this over an open flame?

Cue Ball's deep laugh drew his attention away from the vat of oil. "You're looking at that thing like it's gonna jump up and bite your ass, K." His arms flexed in his sleeveless-T as he used the netting to lift the two turkeys in curls with each hand.

"Save all your showboating for the girls, brother. No need to flex for me." Kane grinned and covered his heart with his hands. "I'm already a fan."

"Go fuck yourself." Cue Ball smirked and deliberately lifted one of the birds, his bicep bulging. "You know you wish you had guns like these." He kissed the muscle with a loud smack.

A set of feminine arms snaked around his buddy's waist. "I hope you're saving some of those kisses for me, baby."

Cue Ball turned toward the husky voice. "Maybe I have some better ideas for what you can do with your mouth."

He turned away as his friend made a spectacle of himself with his Flavor of the Moment. Watching another man's conquest did nothing to light his fire.

A quick Google search on his phone about frying turkeys raised about a hundred red flags. "Hey, Cue, those turkeys aren't still frozen, are they?"

"What do you take me for, an idiot?" If the man could talk, it meant the woman was finished swallowing his tongue.

He chanced a look up from the screen and caught sight of her tight jeans as she sashayed back into the clubhouse. "You asking a trick question?"

Cursing under his breath, Cue Ball dropped the turkeys on the folding table next to the propane tank. Then, he pulled a wicked-looking knife from the scabbard on his belt. "Help me cut the packaging off, ya prick."

They kept up their good-natured ribbing as they cleaned and dried the birds. He was trying to attach the hooks inside his turkey's chest cavity when his senses recognized the unmistakable combination of secondhand smoke, Aqua Net hairspray, and a knock-off version of Chanel No. 5.

Mama.

"Well, I'll be goddamned." Her pack-a-day habit gave her voice a hint of rasp that never went away. "Desiree said you were out here cooking, but I thought she was full of shit."

"You come out to help us, Mama V?" Cue Ball couldn't hold back a chuckle.

She only had two natural born sons, but almost every man in the crew called her Mama, never Vivian. Even Malcolm did it sometimes, though it made Kane shudder if he let himself think about it. Sadly, it wasn't even close to the most disturbing thing about their dysfunctional relationship.

She chuckled. "You know damn good and well—"

He finished along with her, Cue echoing too. "Mama don't cook."

Never had. Never will.

He and Scott grew up on an assortment of fast food and any kind of meat they could throw on the rusted old charcoal grill cemented to the ground near the back door.

His mother smiled. Her boys knew her well.

Cue Ball squatted at the base of the fryer and lit the propane. "We're more than happy to cook for you." He lifted his eyebrows. "Right, K?"

"Assuming we don't burn down the carport, sure."

The turkeys were ready to go in, just as soon as the oil got hot enough. Unfortunately, there was no sign of a thermometer, which meant they would have to wing it.

Mama V pulled a Kool Menthol from its green and white pack and lit the end. She took a deep drag, and the smoke escaped on an exhale as she spoke. "Charlene was in the clubhouse looking for you, KC."

KC. Short for Kane Charles. His mother called both her sons by their initials. Kane's brother was SP. Scott Paul. She thought it was cute, but it didn't feel genuine. It never caught on with the rest of the men.

"You plan on making her your old lady?" His mother smoothed the top of her bleached hair, where a hundred broken pieces stuck out before her ponytail holder. Her long red lacquered nails were a sharp contrast to the washed-out color.

He shook his head. "Nah. I think Charlene and I have run our course. There wasn't much there, even in the beginning."

His mother smiled with satisfaction. She was one of only two old ladies in the MC, a privilege she was in no hurry to share with anyone else. Even if it didn't mean a whole hell of a lot. "Well, I'll just tell her to go on then, shall I?"

A sigh escaped him. "No. She should hear it from me." He'd put it off too long already. As many times as he warned women it was only sex, they always thought they would be the exception to his rules.

No commitments. No feelings. Just fucking.

He wasn't cut out for anything else. More to the point, he'd never put himself through loving somebody again. It hurt too much when it went away. He'd rather invest his heart in the bonds of friendship. Something he could rely on. His brothers would never abandon him, and no matter how crazy their world was sometimes, he'd never leave them either.

Allegiance was the least he could give those guys for the loyalty they'd shown him over the years.

Leaving Cue Ball to figure out when to drop the turkeys in the fryer, he strode past his mother into the clubhouse. The back door led to the kitchen, and beyond there, a common room featuring a scarred pool table in the center with green felt so worn, it was almost completely smooth. A Budweiser lamp they rescued from a dive bar hung over it, spilling yellow light onto the table.

Scott played against a prospect, while Charlene leaned against the wall, watching and nursing a longneck.

He stopped and studied her. Like his mother, her blond hair was out of a bottle. Even if the brittleness didn't give it away, he knew firsthand the carpet didn't match the drapes.

Her red dress was flimsy, revealing, and too tight, showing off the bony hips and hard lines of her thin frame. She couldn't have been more than twenty-five, but she wore a thick mask of makeup. Even though he'd surveyed every inch of her skin, Kane had never seen her without her foundation and false eyelashes. It was simply another barrier between them, though to be fair, it was the only one she'd built. The rest were his.

He tried to imagine her with a clean, fresh face, brown hair, and an extra ten pounds on her frame. She'd probably be a knockout.

Too bad she'd never believe it. Wholesome beauty didn't go very far around here.

He nodded toward the closest bedroom, not doubting for a second she would follow. Sure enough, she appeared a step behind him when he cleared the ten-by-twelve room, and she closed the hollow, fake-wood door once she crossed the threshold.

"Want me to give you something to be thankful for, baby?" She batted her thick fringe of lashes, but they both knew her heart wasn't in it.

He didn't have the patience to beat around the bush. Besides, it was kinder to put his cards on the table. "I think it's time we make a clean break."

She blinked, then lowered herself to sit on the rumpled sheets atop the double bed. "This is because I let myself in at your place."

Speaking of which. "How did you even get inside to begin with?"

Her fingers tangled in the sheets, and she stared at them like they held the secrets of the universe.

"Charlene." His sharp tone issued a warning, and her eyes flashed up to meet his.

"I took Scottie's key." She cleared her throat. "Off his keyring."

Heat climbed his neck. He fought the urge to lose his shit and simply held out his hand. "Give it to me," he said quietly.

Biting her lip, Charlene reached down the top of her bodice and pulled a long chain from between her generous, unnaturally round breasts. The key was threaded at the bottom. She frowned as she lifted the chain over her head and put it, along with the key, in his waiting hand.

"I knew I was losing you," she whispered. "I thought if I could be there when you needed me, you might see how good it could be between us."

He shoved the key into his jeans' pocket. Any sympathy he might've had for the girl evaporated the moment she admitted what she'd done. "Geez, Char. It's only been a few weeks. You can't lose something you never had." Deliberately, he turned his back on her and headed out the door.

Scott glanced up from the table. "Quick work." He snickered. "You know they make pills that can help if you're having trouble in the bedroom."

Wisely, the prospect busied himself rubbing chalk on the end of his stick. Getting between two brothers was a lose-lose proposition.

He lifted his middle finger. "If you're worried about how well my dick works, feel free to suck it, brother."

Scott raised his thick, dark eyebrows. "Maybe if I could find it, I'd take you up on your offer."

They pretended to glare at each other for a few seconds before they both relaxed into smiles. A few feet from his brother, he leaned his hip against the table. "It was time to cut her loose. She was getting too attached."

"So? As long it's her mouth attached to your junk, who gives a shit?"

Scott's bedroom door policy was wide open, with a welcome mat for any woman who wanted to come inside. His brother wouldn't understand the way Charlene's longing looks made his mouth dry up. But the man did understand the concept of respect. Maybe too well.

"I found her in my bed the other night. Uninvited."

Scott lifted one shoulder in a half-hearted shrug, then turned his attention back to the table, lining up a shot.

"She stole your key to my apartment."

The shot went wild, the white ball bouncing hard on the table. "The fuck, you say?"

He dug in his pocket and tossed the key and chain onto the table. "The only women I want in my bed are ones I invite there."

"You toss her out of the clubhouse?" Scott pressed his lips together. It was a whole different ballgame when she crossed one of his lines.

"Nah. I just told her we were done." It seemed cruel to excommunicate her from the club simply because he didn't want to fuck her anymore. Frankly, he had no idea why any woman wanted to be Property of the MC anyway. It was a life lacking in respect from anyone you shared your body with, but hell, it was their choice to make.

Scott's expression turned sly. "Maybe I'll let her work off her transgressions on her knees."

"Knock yourself out." The smell of frying meat wafted in from outside. He had forgotten about the turkeys. Turning toward the door, he tightened the ponytail at the base of his neck. "I'm gonna go finish helping Cue. Take better care of my key, asshole."

Scott's belly laugh followed him as he returned to his post at the fryer.

***

Amanda

The Griffin house was more of a showplace than it had ever been a home. Amanda's father lived upstairs, but the downstairs was designed to invite, impress, or intimidate, depending on the guest.

As she walked in the door, she gave the interior a detached once-over. The walls were an icy white, with thick ivory trim. They contrasted starkly with the dark wood floors. The entry boasted a high ceiling all the way to the second floor, where a curved staircase drew the eye. Much of the ground floor was an open plan, which was great for the shock and awe her dad loved so much. She could see all the heavy, expensive furniture, thick rugs, and crystal chandeliers in a single sweep of her gaze.

Terrence escorted her deeper into the house, though she knew the way. The older, soft-spoken butler had been with the family since she was a kid.

She smoothed her hands over her black pencil skirt before approaching the two men standing by the fireplace. Both Nathan and her father were sipping off glasses filled with amber liquid. Fifty-year-old Scotch, no doubt.

Her heels clicked on the oak panels as she advanced toward them. They both met her society mask with practiced, insincere smiles. Terrence disappeared silently into the background.

"You're late, darling. I hope you didn't encounter too much traffic on the way here." Her father's lie dripped off his tongue like honey. He had told her to be here at five o'clock and it was four fifty-five. Still, she knew better than to argue.

"I'm terribly sorry for keeping you waiting. You know how we women like to make ourselves look perfect. The time must have gotten away from me." Rolling her eyes inwardly, she kissed her father's cheek, then nodded at Nathan. "Happy Thanksgiving."

His eyes slid appraisingly over her body, from the loose twist in her hair to her pale pink silk shirt, all the way to her counterfeit Louboutin's. They were fakes—good fakes—but she had no doubt Nathan would know the difference. Her feet weren't where his eyes lingered, though. "Don't worry yourself, pet. You were worth the wait."

She smiled tightly. "Shall I check on our meal?"

The men wouldn't talk business while she was here, and she knew damn good and well their wheeling and dealing was the real reason for this dinner. Without waiting for an answer, she slipped away to confer with the chef. The heat of Nathan's gaze nearly singed her skin, and she fought the urge to shudder.

Thank God, she wouldn't have to endure him much longer.

The double doors offered no sound or resistance as she made her way into the kitchen. Quiet and compliant, like everything else her father surrounded himself with. The chef was putting the finishing touches on the tray of carved turkey. His head shot up as he sensed her approach.

"We are ready to serve, Mademoiselle."

"Thank you, Jacques. We'll be in the dining room."

She'd hoped for an excuse to linger, but she should have known her father's staff would be punctual to a fault. He would accept nothing less. Forcing her chin up, she returned to the fireplace where the men still had their heads together. She kept a respectful distance until her father nodded subtly for her to return. Even though he'd ignored her for five minutes, she had no doubt he'd been aware the instant she'd returned to the room.

Leading the men to the dining room, she took the seat left of her father's place at the head of the massive table. Nathan sat to his right. The servers immediately poured out of the kitchen. The wine came first.

Nathan swirled the dark red liquid in his glass before taking a small sip. He prided himself a wine connoisseur. One of a hundred ways he excelled in pretension and pomposity.

"Mmm. Goldeneye. Pinot noir." He rolled the flavor around on his tongue. "2014?"

Her father nodded sagely. "Always nice to share a meal with someone who appreciates the finer things."

She sipped from her glass demurely, the perfect society accessory, nodding as they waxed on about wood smoke and cherries. White zinfandel would satisfy her any day of the week.

The meal rivaled any she'd tasted in a five-star

restaurant. In addition to the lemon-herb turkey, Jacques prepared a sweet potato and butternut squash soup, cornbread dressing, and a cranberry-chocolate tart.

The men spoke in hushed tones as Amanda moved the food around on her plate. Her father really hadn't needed her here. The only purpose she served was to help them pretend this meal was something other than a business meeting on a holiday. The ticking of the grandfather clock only accentuated the lack of warmth or laughter at the table.

Eventually, the staff returned to clear their plates. Nathan drew to his feet and nodded at her father. "It's been a pleasure, Beau. I think you'll be able to do some great things for the party. You have our full support. My secretary will reach out to yours at the beginning of next week. Amanda." He said her name as an afterthought, but there was heat in his gaze when he nodded his farewell.

She waited until the front door closed completely behind him before she spoke. "Shall we return to the sitting room?"

Her father was rarely one to grin, but right now he clearly fought the urge. And lost. He rubbed his hands together as they moved toward the pristine white sofa.

"You look pleased."

He schooled his features. "Yes. This evening has been a productive one."

Allowing her shoulders to relax, she leaned back into the seat. "I'm glad." Finally, she could breathe. "I am so ready to end this farce of a relationship with Nathan. I don't think I could've forced myself to keep it up much longer."

Her father narrowed his eyes. "You will not be ending anything with Nathan Shaw."

It took a moment for his words to sink in, but when they did, she sat up straighter. "What?" Panic fluttered in her chest. "No. Our agreement was for six months. You have no idea—"

"*You* have no idea." He slapped his hand on the arm of the sofa. "Our association with Nathan has been very productive, and I will not have you upset the apple cart."

"*Our* association? Easy for you to say. You're not the one who has to endure his company or get treated like a piece of property." Apparently, the three glasses of wine she'd downed at dinner were loosening her tongue. "After all, what's the benefit to having a daughter if you can't sell her off to seal a business deal?"

Her father's face hardened with every word. "You will not speak to me that way in my home, Amanda Grace."

"I won't do it anymore, Dad." She shook her head, climbing unsteadily to her feet, defiance pumping through her veins.

"You will if you want my money."

She stopped.

"Ah. Right. Let's not forget, you aren't dating Nathan out of the goodness of your heart. You want my money to save your little construction company."

She whirled around. "I only asked for a loan. Parents give loans to their children all the time. *You* were the one who put strings on it. The terms said I would date Nathan for six months, and you would grant me the fifty thousand you had for me in trust. It's not even really a loan. It's my money. And those six months are done. I held up my end of the bargain."

Her father peered at his fingernails. "It's your money when you turn thirty-five. Let's not forget."

"A deal is still a deal. You gave me twenty-five thousand at the beginning. I need the other twenty-five thousand now."

He rolled his eyes. "To save your precious Charlie's company."

"It's my company now," she growled. "Mine and Mike's. And you know it."

"Be that as it may, I need you to stay on Nathan's arm a little bit longer."

Her voice rose. "Those weren't our terms."

"Our terms have changed!" His shout echoed in the cavernous room. He breathed deeply and clenched his jaw. "Nathan finds you a pleasant companion. He and his connections are going to support my run for governor. I can't have you upsetting the balance of things right now."

"But he hurt me," she whispered, balling her fists. "The last time we were together, he hit me, and he kicked me when I was down." She thrust a fist against her thigh. "Don't you care?"

"Of course, I care." Nothing in his voice indicated he was surprised by her admission. "I'm not asking you to let him hurt you. I'm simply asking you to extend your association with the man for a little bit longer. Really, what can he do to you in public?"

When she released her tense fingers, tiny half-moons marks indented her palms. She swallowed back the sob lodged in her throat. Reaching for her Ice Queen veneer, she met her father's level stare. Her feelings didn't matter to him. Why would she think otherwise? This was a business deal. "How do I know you won't change the terms on me again?"

He held up his palms. "I give you my word."

"I no longer find your word carries the weight I thought it did," she said formally. "I suppose I inherited my sense of honor from Mom's side of the family."

"Honor," he spat, and his face contorted in a sneer. "Was she honoring me when she ran off and left us? When she married another man?"

She stuffed her outrage down. Why was she even surprised? Her father had never thought of anyone but himself. Her happiness had never been his priority. Neither had Mom's. It was the reason she'd left, and she'd been right to do it.

Her mask slipped a little. "Mom didn't leave us. She left you. I should've done the same thing years ago."

Why hadn't she? Was she still worried he'd betray the agreement they'd made all those years ago? Or was it because she was so hollowed out, there was nothing beneath the masks she created to hide her true self?

"You're being overly dramatic. Whether you recognize it or not, I've done nothing but look out for your best interests." He walked to the fireplace and poured himself two fingers of scotch from the decanter on the mantelpiece.

"Sure. As long as I did things your way. Dated the men you wanted. My happiness never mattered then any more than it matters now."

He slammed his drink on the mantle, sloshing the liquor over the rim. Only the thickness of the high-quality crystal kept the glass from breaking. "You are not talking about the ridiculous infatuation you had in college. We always come back to it. That boy—"

"Man." Her voice shook, all signs of the Ice Queen melted. "That *man* meant everything to me. But no. I'm not talking about Kane. I'm talking about Nathan. I won't date him anymore. I won't sleep with him. And I won't let him hit me ever again. I will be cordial to him and be an escort to a few more events. But I swear, Dad, in two more weeks, I'm done either way." Empty as she was, she'd reached her limit.

"Four. And I'll send a bodyguard with you everywhere you go."

She considered his offer. The money was essential for her expansion plan at Cooper, and though she'd probably qualify for a bank loan, the debt would make the company look weak. The man she wanted to do business with will have done his homework, and she had to approach him from a position of strength.

"I know your stepbrother really needs that business of yours to stay afloat. Even with insurance, his medical bills must be quite draining."

Bastard. Mike, his family, and their business were the only things left she cared about. "Fine.

Four weeks. And I'll take you up on the bodyguard."

Her father's smile was the same practiced one he'd given Nathan. "It may actually work out for you better in the end. Even if he is a bad egg underneath it all, Nathan Shaw can only help your social standing in this town. You never know, maybe some time on his arm will help you land a man worthy of the Griffin name."

CHAPTER FOUR

Amanda

Walking through her brother's small foyer, the weight from Amanda's stressful day finally lifted from her shoulders. The Cooper house represented everything she wanted her own home to be one day. Never mind the fact it would fit four times over into her father's place. She'd take warm and inviting over cold and pretentious any day of the week. She loved sinking into the plush suede sofa, and she always wanted to kick off her shoes the second she walked in, just to squish her toes inside the fluffy throw-rugs.

It's what her niece, Aliyah, did now, standing barefoot on the thick fabric. Her pudgy, eighteen-month-old fingers held on to the coffee table for balance.

"Mana!"

She swept the little girl into her arms for a gentle hug and was rewarded with a wet kiss to the side of her face. Her heart ached. She'd held out for years, unwilling to raise a child if she couldn't do it with a man she loved. At this point, though, she was ready to be a mom, even if she had to do it all on her own. Lots of women did it.

She could have done it with Joshua, but when he was born, it seemed easier to let him go with her brother and his wife.

A new baby wouldn't happen while Nathan was in the picture, though. She would rather cut out her own tongue than to tie herself to a prick like him for the rest of her life.

She breathed in the lingering baby-smell on Aliyah's light-brown skin. Soon, all of her toddler traits would vanish, leaving a rough and tumble preschooler in their wake. She'd seen it happen before with Joshua, even if it had been from a distance, more than a decade earlier.

"Is your Auntie-Manda covering you with kisses?"

The little girl squirmed at her father's voice, and Amanda released her to toddle toward her daddy's wheelchair. Mike looked frailer than he had the last time she'd seen him. It seemed counter-intuitive since he was supposed to be healing, but it's not like he could hold on to his muscle mass with two broken legs, a shattered pelvis, and a punctured lung.

Her heart eased a little when he flashed her a smile. He was still here. Still Mike. Even if he couldn't lean over to pick up his daughter.

His wife stepped from behind the chair to lift their daughter in her arms. Cindy and Mike had been together for so long, she was more of a sister than an in-law.

"We saved you a piece of pecan pie. I figured your dad wouldn't have any at his house."

Leave it to Cindy to remember it was her favorite. "Thanks. I wish I could have been here for dinner." She rubbed at her forehead as Cindy sat beside her on the couch. "You know my dad. Couldn't miss the chance to turn a holiday into a political opportunity."

Aliyah twisted her little body in her mother's arms, determined to get back to her daddy. When Cindy refused to let her down, she started to cry.

"It's almost her bedtime," Cindy murmured. "I'm going to go give her a bath."

Mike's smile fell as his girls left the room, and Aliyah's cries echoed down the hall. "I'm not strong enough to hold her. She doesn't understand."

"How could she? She's only a baby. But it's not forever. You'll get stronger, and you'll hold her again. She won't even remember all this."

She wished she could forget too. The memory of Mike so quiet and motionless in his hospital bed after his accident still took her breath away. Her brother had always been larger than life, her rock after their parents died more than ten years ago.

"Let's talk about something else," she said brightly. No sense in dwelling on the past. "What's with the beard? You look like Sasquatch."

Mike ran his hand over his scruffy cheek. "You don't like it? Cindy says it makes me look kind of like Chris Pratt in *Guardians of the Galaxy*."

A bark of laughter escaped her mouth before she could stop it. "They say love is blind. All I can say is your wife must really love you." Mike may have had the same coloring and dirty blond hair, but no one would mistake him for a blockbuster actor. His features were far too broad and blunt. He wasn't a bad-looking guy, but pushing forty, he looked like, well, what he was, a hard-working, blue-collar husband and father.

He joined in her laughter, then rubbed at his chest. "Are you trying to kill me? Don't make me laugh." When he caught his breath, he rolled closer. "What happened at the meeting with the board?"

Reliving the failed coup killed any urge to laugh. "They tried to force me out." She held up her hand when he started to sputter. "They tried and failed. I had proof I was your proxy. Guess all our planning paid off."

"Fuck them for even trying," he growled.

"They didn't even let me pitch the plan." Suddenly, she was very tired. All she did anymore was fight losing battles.

"Have you brought it to Xander yet?"

"What? No. You and I haven't officially decided to move forward yet."

Mike rested his elbows on the arms of his chair and folded his hands beneath his chin. Despite his lighter hair, he looked so much like Charlie right then, it was almost like her stepdad was in the room. "Bullshit. You were afraid of running into Kane."

"Fuck you. I saw Kane the last time I went to one of Xander's sites. I'm still standing. Things have been over with us for a long time."

Her brother always saw straight through her bullshit. "Things will never be over for the two of you. I still don't understand why you broke things off."

No way. They weren't going there. "You want me to talk to Xander? Fine. I could see Kane a hundred times, and it wouldn't change ancient history."

"You're not happy," he said solemnly. "You haven't been for a long time."

"Being here makes me happy. Spending time with Joshua these past few years has made all the difference...and now Aliyah." She cleared her throat against the rising tide of emotion. "You've always made me feel like a real part of this family."

"Because you are." He wrung his hands, his eyes fixing on a spot behind her shoulder. "Sometimes I think you regret giving him to me."

"Never." Her answer was immediate and unwavering. "I love him, but I could never have done the job you and Cindy have. God, Mike, I was such a wreck back then, and I was alone. The two of you had so much to offer him. You still do."

He flicked his eyes to hers then back over her shoulder. "He knows Cindy's not his mom." With her dark skin next to Joshua's pale white complexion, it would have been a tough sell. "We've told him the truth. It was past time, really. I'd always planned for you to be there, but when he asked, I couldn't put him off. I'm sure he'll want to talk to you about it."

Her heart froze. She should have been there. But Mike was right; they should have dealt with this ages ago. But it hurt so much. "If you thought it was best, you know I support you. It doesn't have to change anything. You're his parents in every way that counts."

Heart heavy, she forced herself off the comfortable couch and rose to her feet. She spoke carefully, infusing her voice with a lightness she didn't feel. "I'm sorry I didn't catch him before he went to his buddy's house. Tell him I love him, and we'll talk soon." She kissed her brother on his scruffy cheek. "I'll meet Xander on Monday, but you'd better shave before I see you next. You know how much I hate kissing a man with a beard."

***

Kane

As much as it irritated him in the summertime, Kane was grateful for his heavy beard in falling autumn temperatures. Though Atlanta wasn't known for cold weather, it did get chilly a few months out of the year. And riding a motorcycle, the wind could be a sharp slap in the face. He arrived bright and early at the build site in Decatur and switched out his helmet for a hard hat.

Robby waited with his clipboard in the shell of the double garage, ready to start the new workweek. The kid wore his regular khakis and a button-down shirt, but an Incredible Hulk T-shirt peeked through underneath.

He warmed to the kid despite himself. Robby looked younger than his twenty-three years, with his floppy dark hair and guileless puppy dog eyes, and the superhero shirt made Kane want to take him out to a baseball game or—no, not that—*a strip club* and load him up with dollar bills.

Shit. Maybe a male strip club. Robby was batting for the other team.

Whatever. The kid needed somebody looking out for him. He was pretty sure Robby had no one except Brick, who'd become his surrogate big brother.

"Love the T-shirt, kid."

Robby gaped as he looked down over his white Oxford. Obviously secondhand, the fabric was thin from too many washings. His cheeks colored. "Oh no. You can see it?"

"The Hulk? Yeah, but don't sweat it. Who isn't into Marvel?"

Frowning, Robby plucked at his button-down. "You're missing the point. Graphic-T's aren't very professional."

"So why did you wear it?" He'd never seen Robby dress down, even the one time they'd been out at the same bar.

The kid toed at the sawdust residue on the concrete.

He was sure an answer wasn't coming when Robby finally looked him in the eye.

"For Brick. I, uh, I think about him like the Incredible Hulk sometimes. I'm worried about him. I miss him, you know? The shirt..." He shrugged. "I guess it's my way of rooting for him to get better. Guess it sounds kind of stupid."

If Brick were here, he would have lifted his eyebrow the way he did when he was trying to look badass, but Kane suspected Robby's words would have chipped one more layer of ice from the man's frozen exterior. It had been melting a little bit more every day since he met the love of his life.

Love.

Relationships.

It always seemed to come back around to the same shit.

"It doesn't sound stupid at all. In fact, I think it would mean a lot you're rooting for him. I saw him over the weekend, and I think he'll be able to come back to work soon. Maybe next time I go, you can come with me."

The hope shining in Robby's eyes reminded him of a character he'd seen in a Japanese cartoon. "Really? You don't mind? You don't think *he* would mind?"

"I think it might be exactly what he needs." He dropped his palm on Robby's shoulder. "In the meantime, we've got work to do. Who am I with today?"

"It's only you and Cyrus." Robby frowned. "Brick and Will are still out, and Matt has some kind of family emergency."

The way Robby rushed through the last part...even if he didn't already know about the guy's king-sized crush on Matt York, he'd sense something was up. But Robby clearly wanted to keep those feelings under wraps, so he resisted the urge to tease him. Instead, he focused on the impact of what he was being told.

"How in the hell are we going to get the work done with just the two of us? We're already behind on this house. Cyrus is good, but it's going to take more than two guys to do all this sheetrock."

"Only the two of us?" Cy had moved in so quietly, he hadn't heard him approach.

"We're not on the battlefield, brother. Make a little noise when you come up behind somebody."

The slight lift to the corner of Cy's mouth was the closest he had ever come to seeing him smile. "I'll take your suggestion under advisement."

Robby lifted his hand in greeting before peering down at his clipboard. "I know it's not really fair to put all this on you, but we don't have a lot of options. If it helps, Xander is here today to be an extra set of hands. He's already working out back."

Cyrus nodded, his placid demeanor already back in place. "We should probably get started."

Several sheets of drywall were already piled in the garage, giving them a head-start. They set up the small scaffold, and he held the first sheet in place against the ceiling joists as Cy screwed them in with the drill. The labor made his arms burn, but the strain felt good. He and Cyrus worked in companionable silence, taking turns switching off throughout the morning, one bracing the plaster, while the other secured it.

Back aching, he called for a break around eleven, and Cy offered to grab some water bottles from the ice chest. He pulled off his hard hat and yanked out the elastic from his hair. The cool air was a welcome relief after working up a sweat.

He sensed her before she said a word.

"Kane."

His name on her lips still made his chest tighten and expand at the same time. It was a silken caress—and broken glass shredding his soul. He closed his eyes and let her nearness sink in for a heartbeat before he turned around.

"Twice in one month. Before you know it, you'll be sending me fruitcake at Christmas."

The tiny lines around her eyes tightened. "I'm here to see Xander."

"I figured. He's out back."

Indecision flitted across her features.

He smirked.

That's right. You either have to walk past me or tromp around in the mud in your fancy high heels. What's it going to be?

She pursed her lips as though she could read his thoughts. Lifting her chin, she moved toward him. To a casual observer, she would seem completely unaffected, but he recognized her moves when she was faltering inside. Time hadn't dulled his memories of Mandy Griffin. They were sharper than ever, which made sense, considering how often he'd taken them off the shelf of his heart and examined them over the years.

It didn't help her name was inked in his skin. And he made damn sure she'd never know it.

"How's Mike?" The words came unbidden.

She stopped with only a few feet between them. Her perfume was new. Subtle, it reminded him of fresh linen. Not the lavender scent he associated with her for so long.

"He looks…small." Her soft reply reminded him of a time she wasn't afraid to show him her vulnerability. It had been more than a decade since he'd seen anything but the hard shell of a businesswoman she wore like a second skin.

"The wreck. What happened?"

Her brow furrowed, and she started to shake her head, but he spoke before she could brush him off. "Don't worry. We can go right back to hating each other afterward."

"Some asshole was texting and driving. He didn't stop at a stop sign and smashed right into the driver's side door of Mike's car. It flipped him over. Broke his legs, crushed his pelvis. It messed him up really bad." Her voice shook at the end. "And the asshole from the other car is walking around without a scratch on him."

He fought the urge to comfort her, to pull her into his arms and stroke her beautiful red hair. But she wouldn't appreciate it. It would only upset her more if she realized he saw her hard shell cracking. "Is any of the damage permanent?"

She lifted one shoulder halfheartedly. "He says no, but I'm not sure he would tell me if it was. You know Mike; he takes the whole big brother thing seriously."

He had always respected the way the man treated his sister. "Maybe I'll visit him, see if I can find out how he's really doing."

This time it was Mandy who lifted her hand like she might reach out, but she dropped it quickly and smoothed her skirt.

Another tell.

"I would really appreciate it." She bit her bottom lip. "He always liked you."

"I always liked *him*. Thought he was going to be my brother, too, one day." He regretted the words as soon as he said them. Surely, the reminder of how close they'd come to a happy ending would make the sharp-edged version of his ex return.

Only, it didn't. Her eyes looked far away as she nodded. "We all did."

What is going on here?

She'd barely spoken to him in years, and she certainly never acknowledged their shared history.

Her gaze snapped back into focus. "I think a visit from you would be good for him. Maybe you could take him to a Braves game." She smoothed her skirt again. "I really need to talk to Xander."

His mouth dropped open as she slipped past him to the interior of the house.

Take him to a Braves game.

Was she fucking with him? Tugging off his hard hat, he tossed it on the ground and rubbed at his temples.

He hadn't been to a baseball game in ages. Even thinking about Turner Field held his heart hostage, though maybe it would be better now since the team played somewhere else.

Who was he kidding? It didn't matter where they played or how much time had passed. Braves baseball would always be a link to his past. A punch in the gut.

Associated forever with the first time he met the woman who'd break his heart.

***

13 years ago

April

The parking lot at Turner Field was filled to bursting with cars. It would have been impossible to find a spot if they hadn't come on Scott's old Harley. Kane's brother always managed to find a place to park, even if it wasn't always strictly legal.

"Thanks again for giving me your extra ticket." Scott had won them in a Last Man Standing beer-drinking competition hosted by the hard rock radio station. "I've never seen a game in person."

Scott puffed up. "It's your birthday, K. That's what big brothers are for."

The crowd parted as they approached the entrance. Scott cut an imposing figure with his old Army Surplus boots and the leather vest proclaiming him a brother of the Skulls MC. His long, dark hair was down, and he had a red bandana wrapped around the top of his head.

It didn't garner the kind of attention Kane wanted, although he was used to it. His father had started the stupid biker club, so the family had gotten wary looks his entire life. Scott thought it was respect he saw in people's eyes. Kane recognized it was fear.

If he were walking by himself, he could've disappeared into the crowd. He could've been a regular guy with jeans and a vintage Guns N Roses T-shirt. But even if he kept his vow to stay out of the MC, he would never be a generic face in the crowd when walking with his brother.

When they made it to the front of the line, Scott presented the winning tickets and shrugged uncomfortably. "Sorry, we're in the nosebleed section."

"Are you kidding? Being here at all is a trip." The energy from so many people was like a live-wire. His senses were on overdrive, from the smell of popcorn and grilled burgers to the din of the crowd. He'd never experienced anything like it.

"I've got a couple of bucks on me. You want a Coke?" Scott made the cash working a side job loading boxes at a warehouse. His brother had the kind of muscle mass he never expected to achieve.

It didn't bother him, though. If he managed to finish his accounting courses at night school, he wouldn't need bulk, only brains. He'd be the first one in the family to finish college. Hell, he was already the first to get his high school diploma.

He flashed Scott a thumbs-up, still soaking in the sights and sounds of the stadium.

"I thought you were supposed to be a good time, but all I'm seeing right now is a stuck-up bitch." One man's voice rose above the cacophony of sound.

He scanned for the owner of the disembodied voice.

"The only reason I agreed to come to this godforsaken pit is for your father's box seats. The least you can do is make it worth my while." There he was. The snobby shit couldn't have been more than five-foot-nine. He had gelled-back blond hair and a white sweater vest over a short-sleeved button down. The guy stood only a few inches taller than the pretty redhead he was berating, but he was in her space. His face inches from hers.

The girl's cheeks flushed pink, but she lifted her chin a fraction higher with every venomous word the man spat in her direction.

Without a second's hesitation, he shouldered his way between them. He was taller and broader than the other man, but more importantly, he was harder, used to the kind of rough life Mr. Country Club had probably only seen on TV. "You got a problem, buddy?"

The asshole's eyes widened, and he knew instantly no one had ever called the guy on his bullshit in his life.

A haughty look replaced the shock. "Do I know you?" As if he were the dirt on the bottom of the man's shoe.

Ha. If a look was all it took to rattle him, he would never leave the house. "If you don't adjust the way you're talking to the lady, you're about to know me better than you ever wanted to."

He had very little patience for guys who refused to regard women with respect. His dad had always treated his mother like yesterday's garbage, and though he learned the hard way there was nothing he could do about their relationship, it didn't stop him from speaking up now. An unexpected wave of protectiveness rose toward the woman behind him.

The guy spoke over his shoulder to her. "Oh, this is rich. Are you slumming it, Amanda? Don't want to give it up to me because you're too busy getting it from Mr. Thrift Store Reject over here." He turned his cruel gaze to Kane. "Tell me, Reject, does she spit or does she swallow?"

He didn't hesitate. He balled his fist and slammed it into the asshole's still-flapping jaw. It knocked the guy flat on his ass.

The woman stepped forward and curled her arm around his, startling him with her touch, then making him puff up in pride. "Don't ever call me again, Chip. And if I find out you're spreading rumors, trying to ruin my reputation, I will crush you. You think you've got clout in this town? You think you can take on a Griffin? I learned from the best. My father eats toads like you for breakfast."

Stepping deftly around the still-blustering Chip, she led Kane down the aisle. She didn't stop moving until they got to the reserved seating. "You didn't have to do that…step in, I mean."

He rubbed her hand, which was still locked around his bicep. Her skin was soft and smooth. Delicate. His protective instincts swelled. "Yes, I did. That guy had no right to talk to you like he did. You deserve better."

She shook her head, her red hair swishing across her shoulders. "You don't even know me."

"*Every* woman deserves better than the way he treated you." It came out a little more forcefully than he intended. "Still, I'm sorry I kind of lost it. I probably could have found a better way to handle the situation." He cleared his throat. "My name's Kane, by the way."

Her smile was like sunshine on his skin. "I'm Amanda, and it appears I'm going to be watching this game alone. Unless…you'd like to join me?"

Scott's face flashed for a moment in Kane's

head, but if anyone would encourage him to accept an invitation from a beautiful woman, his brother would. He fired off a quick text of apology, then gave her his most charming smile. "I can't think of a better way to spend my birthday."

"It's your birthday?" She raised a perfectly arched brow. "Well, Kane, let's make it one you never forget."

CHAPTER FIVE

Amanda

As she stepped back onto the construction site, Amanda wondered what her stepfather would think of the way she was running things. A love of construction prompted Charlie to start his company, and his hope for a legacy inspired him to give it his name. He'd told Amanda dozens of times over the years how satisfying it was to watch a crew build something up from nothing. He passed the same joy onto his son. Mike liked to drop in on builds just to see the parts come together in a whole.

She was a businesswoman. And while she liked construction as well as any other thing, creating the strategy behind the company's success really got her blood pumping. Though Charlie would have rolled over in his grave if he knew, the exquisite home coalescing around her barely even caught her eye as she searched out the foreman in the backyard.

Of course, her indifference could have something

to do with having her first real conversation with Kane in more than a dozen years.

Oh, she'd caught a glimpse of him a few times now and then. With him working for the company, it had been inevitable. She still couldn't get over the changes in him, though. The long hair, the beard, and the scar cutting across his cheek. He'd grown bigger, too, bulkier, which made sense when she factored in the manual labor he did every day. From the outside, he'd become the very thing he swore he'd never be: a biker in his father's club.

But his voice.

His voice made it hard for her to breathe.

He sounded exactly the same as he always had. Time had done nothing to change his husky baritone. Even worse, though, was the way he looked at her when he spoke. Like he considered her precious.

The man had every reason to hate her—and maybe he did—but there was no denying he still cared. It was a blessing and a curse. A small flame, a candle burning in the window of a home she could never return to. Maybe it would be easier to live without him if the candle ever burned out. Or maybe it would extinguish whatever part of her soul that still burned for him.

Not likely. She'd probably take that to her grave.

Shaking off her melancholy, she stepped into the backyard where Xander Karras was cutting drywall. The foreman was at least a decade older than she was, but he wore it well. Silver threaded his nearly jet-black hair, and his olive skin glistened with a sheen of sweat. He didn't have Kane's bulk, but his muscles were clearly defined, even through his thin flannel shirt.

She waited for the high-pitched whine of the saw to cut off before she called out his name.

He visibly flinched when he heard her voice, but after their last conversation, she couldn't blame him. The delays from this build were costing the company money, and even though none of it was his fault, he'd borne the brunt of her frustration.

She held her hands up in surrender. "I'm not here to give you a hard time. I swear."

His tense shoulders relaxed, but only a fraction. "What can I do for you, Miss Griffin?"

"First, I want to apologize for the way I behaved the last time we spoke. None of the delays and complications on this job have been your fault."

He finally looked her in the eye.

"It's no excuse, but the truth is, my behavior was more about my brother's accident than the money we've been losing." She leaned against one of the pillars supporting the patio overhang. "The money's important, but Mike means everything to me."

"I know." He pulled a handkerchief from his back pocket and wiped his lined forehead. "We're all worried about Mike. He's a good man. If there is anything I can do to help while he's getting better, all you have to do is ask." His steady eyes spoke the truth of his words.

She took a deep breath and let it out. "Mike and I want to expand."

"Expand," he echoed.

"There's a new development going up about five miles from here. Sandpiper Run."

Xander nodded. "Yeah. A Berringer Homes project. I've heard of it."

"They're looking for another subcontractor. Their old one went under."

"New development like Sandpiper, a lot of the houses will be on spec, and you know it takes a minimum of five months before we can turn a property around from an empty lot to a home."

She stood up straight and closed the distance between them. "Yes, but Berringer is taking the lion's share of the risk. The beauty of working with a developer is we get paid the same whether they sell the houses or not. As long as we do quality work and finish on time, we have a steady source of income."

Xander swiped a half-full water bottle from the ground at his feet and unscrewed the cap. "What's the downside?" He took a healthy swig before replacing the top.

"We'll need to hire more men. I know it's a particular challenge for you since you're down two guys. Obviously, we'll need to pay them as they work, which means I'll need some upfront cash for payroll and for materials, but I've got it covered. It's—Mike and I both respect you. We believe this is the right course for the company, but we—I— want to know what you think."

She threaded her fingers together to keep her hands steady while he considered his answer.

Xander wasn't the company's only foreman. There were four others, two junior and two senior, but Xander never promised more than he could deliver, and his crew always did top notch work.

The man knew this business like the back of his hand. There was no single employee she or Mike trusted more.

"It's this or downsizing. Am I right?"

She nodded.

"I'd have to hire at least one more guy to pull my weight. I'm not sure when Will and Brick will be back at full capacity." He paused. "I imagine you heard what happened to them."

Her brow creased. "Perry told me about the shooting. It happened offsite, right? Do I need to be worried about any blowback at one of the work sites?"

"No." Neither Xander's face nor his tone belied even a hint of doubt. "Those men have never done anything but work hard for me. There's always a place for them on my crew." His eyes flashed, almost as if he were daring her to argue.

She didn't. "Your crew, your call. If you need to hire another set of hands, you have my blessing. Forward me all his information when you have it, and we'll get him on the payroll."

His face relaxed. "Thank you." He rubbed at the back of his neck. "For what it's worth, I think you're making a good call. Berringer is a reputable developer, and semi-custom homes are a lot easier than full custom jobs once you get used to the plan options. You've got my support."

She let out a breath she hadn't even realized she was holding. Xander wouldn't tell her it was a good idea unless he really believed it. "Excellent. I'll get the ball rolling." She started back toward the direction from where she came.

"Amanda." He spoke softly, but the hard undercurrent in her name stopped her in her tracks. "Why don't you go around the side? I can't imagine it would do Kane much good to run into you twice."

His unmistakable admonishment squeezed her chest.

Was their history so obvious? Did everyone view her as the villain in their doomed romance?

She shoved down her questions and her doubts into an impenetrable place inside her, then smoothed her skirt and lifted her chin before escaping around the house, through the mud, back to her car.

***

Kane

The scent of fresh linen still teased Kane's nose hours after he ran into Mandy at work. Back at the clubhouse, he imagined he smelled it even amid the thick odor of second-hand smoke clinging to his brothers' clothes.

He took a deep pull from his longneck. If only he could drink his thoughts of her away. God knew he'd tried for years, but he'd never even come close.

How many nights had he sat on this very same recliner and tried to figure out what went wrong? How often had he choked back the waves of grief threatening to drown him?

Not tonight.

He backhanded the empty water bottle off the

rickety table beside him, and it bounced off the wall with a satisfying thwack.

Why the fuck did she think it was okay to show up where he worked? Did it mean so little to her? Was she over it now?

He drained his Budweiser and reached for another from the cooler at his feet.

Who was he kidding? She'd been over him a dozen years ago.

He downed the second beer even faster than the first.

Before he could twist open a third, a flying wad of crumpled paper bounced off the side of his head. He growled as his brother's cackle carried across the room from the far end of the pool table.

"What the fuck, man?"

Scott ignored the acid in his voice. "Stop sulking. Life is too short for all your broody bullshit." He tossed his stick to Frank, the club's resident Casanova. With his perfectly maintained stubble and wavy blond hair, the guy looked more like an actor than someone who would take MC life seriously. He brought in more pieces of ass than Hugh Hefner probably got in his heyday. But when the chips fell, he never let his brothers down. Not once.

Scott stalked toward the recliner, then toed his foot with a heavy boot. "Seriously. What the fuck do you have to mope about?" He squatted down so they were eye level. "You've got your brothers. Money in your pocket. More pussy than you could ever fuck in one night." He slapped the arm of the old vinyl chair. "Life is good."

Kane knew better than to bring up Mandy. His brother didn't like her, not from the day he introduced them after the first Braves game, to the day she left him with a broken body and heart in a hospital bed. "I'm not moping." It didn't even sound convincing to his own ears.

Pulling up to his full height, Scott scoffed. "The fuck you ain't. Come back to the chapel. I've got something to take your mind off your troubles."

Knowing Scott, that could mean anything from two women fucking on the table, to a midget stripper or a clown standing by to pie him in the face. Except for the fact they were headed to the club's private meeting room; it was as close to sacred space as any of them had.

The chapel was empty when Scott led him to the big table. Intrigued, he took his customary seat, folded his hands, and waited as his brother paced the paneled room. The flimsy, dusty blinds were closed, as always, and the halogen lamp standing in the corner did little to relieve the room's ever-present shadows.

"We have an opportunity, Kane. *The club* has an opportunity. We need to jump on it now."

He cocked his head to the side, in a silent invitation for Scott to continue.

"Sucre has been dead for—what—a little more than a week? Shit on the street is already falling apart." He loped from one end of the room to another then turned on his heel and paced the other way. "Say what you will about that sick fucker, he kept things straight."

"Yeah, because people couldn't so much as fart

for fear he'd shove something up their asses." Sucre had run Atlanta's streets with an iron fist and unyielding consequences for failure. His methods and his brutality were legendary.

Scott flapped his hand like he was swatting away a fly. "Fear is the only thing guaranteed to motivate criminals and drug addicts, brother, and it's got to be scarier than a slap on the wrist. Otherwise, what's gonna work? We're talking about people who already deal with terrible shit. They've got roaches on the floor and kids they can't feed or pimps who slap them around. It's got to get worse than what they're used to if you're gonna make them pay what they owe."

His brother finally stopped moving and faced him. "It doesn't matter right now anyway. Bottom line, the man is gone. Where are all these junkies getting their fix? You know how desperate they've got to be right now? They'd probably pay anything—do anything—to get their hands on a stash."

His stomach churned as he followed the train of thought. "You want us to take his place."

Biting his bottom lip around a wide smile, Scott spread his arms wide, palms up, then spun around. "It's perfect. Who else is gonna do it? We've got the men; we've got the reputation."

"We don't have the money. Or a supplier." He could tell by the faraway look in his brother's eyes no argument was going to register. Once he had an idea stuck in his head, it played over and over like a song on repeat.

"We'll put a second mortgage on the clubhouse."

"No." He sprang from the chair. "We only paid it off last year. We're not pulling in enough cash to start making payments again."

Scott rested both hands on his shoulders and brought their faces so close together, he could smell the bourbon on his brother's breath. "That's exactly why we have to do this."

He shook his head. "But we don't have any connections to score us a high volume of product. Drugs don't just fall from the sky."

"Malcolm's already working on it." Scott's smile was pure pride.

"Malcolm—so this is already decided?" The unease churning in his stomach solidified into a pulsing mass of anger. Guns were bad enough. Drugs would take the club down a path of no return. They'd all end up the same kind of scum as the man they took down—if they didn't end up in jail first. "Did I miss some kind of vote, brother? Because I know you and Malcolm wouldn't start making decisions for this club without giving everyone a say in what we do."

Scott scowled. "Calm your tits, K. We're only putting a few preliminary things in motion. The club will vote in a few hours."

After Scott had a chance to set up all the pins for a strike.

"I don't like it."

His brother's usually smiling, congenial face soured. "I don't care. Make your case at the vote this afternoon, but don't think you're gonna stop this."

Kane thumped his fist on the table. "This is

78

gonna blow up in our faces." He was far from done, but Scott was already stomping out the door. His only chance to stop this was to convince the rest of the club.

***

The air positively crackled with unspent energy as the brothers took their seats around the heavy wooden table. Even the prospect attended the meeting, leaning against the far wall. He wouldn't have a seat unless they made him a member.

Kane had no doubt his brother had planted the seeds for support with most if not all the guys already, but still, he had to try to talk them out of this plan. They spoke among themselves in a low hum, but all talk ceased the moment his father walked into the room. Of course, Scott went for the big guns.

Malcolm walked to his chair, but instead of sitting, he stood behind it. "When I founded this club thirty-five years ago, it was only me and three other guys with a love of the open road and a big fuck you to anybody who wanted to tell us what to do."

The men knocked on the table in a show of support. Malcolm winked and waited until the noise stopped to continue. "Case and Bender are gone now. We all know what happened with Wes." He scowled, then shook it off. "But as I lost brothers, I gained sons. Sons who still embrace a life lived on two wheels and raise their middle fingers to anyone who wants to challenge our authority to carve out our own place in this town."

This time the knocking was louder and punctuated by cheers. Malcolm took it as his due. "We have a unique opportunity to take this club to a level it's never been before. No more scraping and scratching to get by. We've already done the hard part. We eliminated Sucre de la Cruz. Now we can step into the void he left behind."

Kane's mind raced as his eyes skimmed over the faces of his brothers, all lit with excitement. His father had them in the palm of his hand.

"I'm so proud of both my sons. Kane, who opened the door to this opportunity by setting up the hit—and Scott for mapping out a plan to turn this promise into reality." More cheers. "Stand up, boys."

Masterful. Now it looked like the whole family was on board.

Scott cleared his throat. "When Kane and I discussed the details earlier today, he brought up some good points, and I want to address any concerns you might have. Obviously, this is going to take seed money. We've got to purchase the products before we can sell them, and we haven't exactly been rolling in cash lately."

The men around the table nodded in agreement.

"Our first impulse was to take out another mortgage on the clubhouse, but the bank isn't making it easy…which got us to thinking. We may not have cash, but we do have something valuable."

No. Don't say the guns, Scottie. Don't say the guns.

"Guns."

You dumb fucking fool.

"I've made some quiet inquiries and discovered the name of Sucre's heroin connection. They're willing to discuss providing our first shipment of product in exchange for a load of semiautomatic pistols."

"Scott." He said his brother's name as a warning. "If we trade the guns for drugs, we won't be able to pay the Russians." Their gun suppliers would expect cash. No excuses. No exceptions.

Scott nodded and smiled as though they were reading from a script. "It's what all of you are thinking, right? But the beauty is, we pay the Russians with some of the profits we make on the drugs and use the rest to buy more. In the meantime, I've got a guy who can show us how to make our own meth. It's fucking cheap like you won't believe. You can do it with cold pills, lye, fertilizer, and some shit we have right here in the clubhouse. If you dumb fuckers can follow the instructions I found on the internet without blowing us up, we can be in business tomorrow." He poked the tip of his tongue through his toothy smile. "Play some more Devil's Advocate, K."

"The Russians are going to be pissed, Scott. Even if we can pay them back—"

"You mean *when* we can pay them back."

Scott's arrogant tone was digging under his skin like the needle of a tattoo gun. "If, when, it doesn't matter. It's their money, not ours, to gamble with."

"Kane is right," Malcolm boomed. "This is why any move we make must be done with complete discretion. I know most of us don't socialize outside the MC, but if you do, it's more important than ever for us to keep club business inside the club."

"That's not—"

"All in favor of taking over the cash flow we wrestled from that bastard bottom-feeder?"

A chorus of "ayes" shook the rafters. Kane was poised to vote no, but his father didn't give him the chance.

"The ayes have it." Malcolm nodded. "Meeting adjourned."

Laughing and slapping each other on the back, the men filed out of the room. All but Malcolm and Scott were completely oblivious to his objections.

"You really thought you could push them against my wishes?" He fought the urge to jump at his father's words behind him. "This is my club, Kane. Or have you forgotten?"

He faced his dad, who wore his club cut, the "President" badge on full display over his heart. The man lived and breathed the MC, and the brothers treated him like a god.

"I haven't forgotten anything. But it sure seems you have. Like what happened to Kip's club in Raleigh when he pissed off Sergei. They made him eat his own fucking eyes."

"Kip was an idiot. He deserved what he got."

"Yeah, because he was dumb enough to cross the goddamn Russians."

"No!" Malcolm roared. "Because he was dumb enough to get caught."

He clenched his fists at his sides. "I'm not willing to bet the lives of my brothers on the hope you're right."

His father's eyes glittered with malice. "Then it's a good thing it's not up to you, isn't it?"

Without another word, he went searching for Scott. He had to try one more time to make him understand.

He didn't have to look far.

Scott stood in the hallway right outside the chapel door, leaning against the wall. Jeans bunched around his thighs, he leisurely pumped his hips toward the open mouth of the woman on her knees at his feet.

"You need something, K?" he asked, his rhythm never missing a beat.

Charlene looked up, her gaze challenging, as her cheeks hollowed around his brother's cock.

"Nah." He shouldered past the spectacle they both designed in an effort to get back at him for their perceived slights. They were wasting their time. It was just another Monday night at the clubhouse. "Knock yourselves out."

Gritting his teeth, he stepped out the front door and nearly tripped over the prospect lighting up a smoke on the porch. The kid struggled to his feet, an apology falling from his lips.

He waved the guy off and kept heading to his ride. "Not your fault, man. Forget about it." He stopped when the prospect put his hand on his shoulder.

"Kane?" The man shrank back when he turned to face him but found his nerve after a moment's pause. "In the chapel, Malcolm said something I don't understand."

Trying not to take his frustrations out on the new

guy, he simply raised his eyebrows.

"He said, um, everyone knows what happened with Wes. But I don't. Know what happened, I mean. Is it okay for me to ask?"

Ah. His uncle. Everyone knew what he did, but no one talked about it. "He patched out."

The prospect gasped.

"He got arrested, I don't know, maybe twenty years ago. His probation officer rode him hard about the club, threatened to put him back inside if he didn't cut ties. So, he made a choice. He chose his freedom."

The prospect said nothing else; he shook his head as he walked away.

That was the thing about patching out. A brother didn't just leave the club, the club left him. Walking away made Wes dead to them all. He hadn't seen his uncle since he was a kid. He didn't know if the man was even still alive.

It was why he never thought about leaving, even when he knew the club was on the wrong path. Those men were his family. They'd been there for him when he needed them the most. They laughed together, partied together, and picked each other up off the floor.

Patching out was the ultimate betrayal. If he didn't like what was happening in the club, he'd need to fix it from the inside, or else he'd be left with no family, no friends, and no hope of ever getting them back.

CHAPTER SIX

Kane

The back of Kane's leather jacket pulled in Robby's clenched fingers, as the man scrambled for purchase on the back of his motorbike. No chance in hell the guy would fall off, not with the death grip he had going. If this was how hard he held on now, God knew what it would be like once the engine started.

"Nervous?" Kane turned his head to the side, catching a glimpse of pinched features on Robby's normally cheerful face. "Is it the bike, or is it me?"

"Scared of you?" Robby scoffed, the tension melting from his face. He relaxed his hold a fraction. "Okay, maybe a little. When I first met you. Other than Brick, you're probably the biggest guy I've ever seen in real life. When you mix in the tattoos and the scar..."

Yeah, the scar was kind of hard to ignore. But it was a part of him now, just like the ink covering both arms from shoulder to wrist.

Robby shrugged. "Then I realized, you can't be all bad."

He grunted, his finger hovering over the ignition button. "Gee. Thanks."

"No, I mean it. Brick wouldn't have chosen you as a friend if you were a bad guy. He doesn't hang around with people like that anymore, you know?"

If Robby only knew how true his words were. Not only did Brick keep *bad guys* out of his life, but the man had also led the execution of every one of them who posed a threat to him or the woman he loved. He and Robby were probably the only people Brick had given a peek behind the curtain of his tough guy shell. Well, them and his girlfriend, Olivia.

"If Brick thinks you're good people, I trust his judgment." Robby had the voice of a true believer. "So, no, I'm not scared of you. I'm just—not great on two wheels."

"I'll keep you safe, kid. We'll be there before you know it."

True to his word, he got Robby to their destination in one piece. Brick now lived at Olivia's apartment, since he'd left his old place—and his old life—behind.

He climbed off the bike, the rumble from beneath his thighs still echoing in his muscles.

As unsure as his passenger had seemed before they left, now Robby hopped off the bike like he'd been riding for years. "Are you sure he's up to having company?"

Unbuckling his helmet, he pulled it off and hung it on the handlebars. Robby followed suit.

"I'm sure. He's looking forward to seeing you. C'mon." He led Robby to the closest door and rapped on the heavy wood, his hands still sheathed in his black fingerless gloves.

Hopefully, Brick's recovery was going as well as he'd promised. His skin had looked a little gray when Kane had dropped by to return his money this other day. But Robby was worried about his hero, and well, seeing was believing. At least, that's what Brick said the last time they talked.

His hand was balled up to knock again when Brick finally opened the door. His buddy was barefoot, wearing a black T-shirt and gray sweatpants. Instead of sickly or fragile, Brick looked better than ever. His cheeks were rosy with color, his eyes sparkled, and he was…smiling.

Instead of waiting for either of them to step forward, Brick came out of the apartment and dropped his big hand on Robby's shoulder. "I hear you've been worried about me." The deep rumble and cadence of his voice made his Georgia roots unmistakable.

Clearly swallowing back tears, Robby nodded sharply. It was like the kid had been so prepared for the worst, he didn't know how to deal with good news staring him in the face.

Keeping the grip on Robby's shoulder, Brick led him into the apartment, Kane two steps behind. Olivia's place wasn't exactly girly, but it didn't look like a man had ever lived there. The overstuffed blue sofa was covered with a mountain of pillows and a fluffy blanket where Brick must have been lounging in front of the TV.

Brick swept it all up and carried it back to what was presumably a bedroom, then returned empty-handed. "Sit down. It's good to have some company." Robby swiped a throw pillow wedged under the coffee table and hugged it to his chest as he settled on the cushions.

Kane glanced dubiously at the sofa where the kid settled in, then grabbed one of the chairs at the kitchen table and carried it one-handed back to the living room. Straddling it backward, he winked at Brick. "I know how you feel about snuggling up next to me."

Chuckling, Brick rolled his eyes and sat next to Robby. "More like you know the furniture couldn't support both of us at once."

He tried to look innocent, but who was he kidding? "You're looking good, brother."

"I'm feeling good. I put in a bid on the house we wrapped up on Burgundy Street. We close in two weeks."

"I'll be damned. You took my advice."

As Brick raised his eyebrow, he couldn't help but preen.

"Don't pat yourself too hard on the back. You might pull a muscle." With a grin still on his face, Brick turned to Robby. "I'm sure you already knew. Everything seems to go by you first."

Pink flooded Robby's cheeks. "I did. Once I heard, I figured you must be doing better." His knuckles whitened as he squeezed the cream-colored pillow. A moment later, he released it, balancing it on his knees. "I want you to know I...I prayed for you. Every day. I know it probably sounds stupid—"

"No."

"—but I used to go to church all the time when I—before I moved to Atlanta. I always felt really close to God, even when, well, even when my church didn't have a place for me anymore. So, yeah. I prayed for you, and I really wanted to come sooner, but I didn't want to intrude." His eyes dropped to the fingers he'd laced on top of the pillow. "I wasn't sure if you wanted me here."

"Look at me, Robby."

His eyes shot up at Brick's command.

"I don't know what I did to deserve your friendship or your loyalty, but I want you to hear me. You are always welcome." Brick's gaze was unflinching. "You don't have any family, right?"

Robby opened his mouth, then closed it. He was silent a moment before he answered softly, "On paper somewhere, but no, not the way you mean."

Kane locked his legs against the urge to squirm in his chair. No matter how fucked up his family was, he never doubted they would go to bat for him. He felt like an intruder, witnessing the stark look on Robby's face and the answering gentleness from his normally ball-busting best friend.

"No family for me either." Brick rubbed at the scruff on his chin, and a grin broke out on his face. "Now I'm *making* one. A family. Olivia's going to be my wife. And you two jokers," he said, gesturing between Robby and Kane, "you're my brothers." He shrugged his broad shoulders. "If you'll have me."

Robby swiped at his eyes with the heels of his

hands. "I'd like that a lot."

Please, God, don't let the kid cry.

The mood hung heavy. Somebody had to break the tension. He snorted. "Are we gonna hug it out, ladies?"

"Fuck off." Laughing, Brick snatched the pillow from Robby's lap and beamed it directly at his face.

Ha. Too slow. He dodged it at the last second, and it thumped to the floor behind him.

"It was never like this with my real family," Robby murmured.

"Like it or not, we *are* your real family." He was surprised to find that he meant it. "Get used to it. You're stuck with us now."

Robby vibrated with energy as they said their goodbyes. The kid damn near glowed after Brick's promise of family.

Kane hadn't been the object of hero-worship from the young man that Brick was, but he'd be damned if he'd go back on his buddy's word. His family had helped him through some of the worst moments in his life. He didn't know what he would've done if he'd had to face it all alone.

How long had Robby been on his own?

He shook off the question as his Harley roared to life. It didn't matter. He wasn't alone now, and he wouldn't be again.

Family. Fuck. He was still pissed as hell at the shit his father and brother had pulled the night before, but it wasn't like anger was going to help anything now. He'd been outplayed, and the club had voted. Even if he would've had the chance to cast his vote, it would've been overruled. He'd have to live with it. At least for now.

Clearing his mind, he allowed himself the simple joy of the road. He'd had a lot of issues with the MC over the years, but riding had never been anything but a pleasure.

All too soon, they arrived back in Decatur, their lunch hour having stretched well past the ninety-minute mark. It was just as well. No one else appeared to be around either.

His eyes tracked over the house and the curb where the crew usually parked. "Did everybody make a break for it?"

"Nah. I think the new guy is starting today. He's a friend of Cy's. They served together in Afghanistan. I'm pretty sure Cyrus and Xander are picking him up from the main office where he's finishing up his paperwork and taking him for his drug test. All the H.R. stuff."

"A new guy? They're not replacing Brick and Will." He didn't phrase it as a question.

"Oh no." Robby swiped his clipboard from the pile of sheetrock still in the garage. He carried the thing around the site like a security blanket. "He's an add-on. And I think we can thank Brick he's here. It's a big deal he's buying the house on Burgundy. The company really needed the cash."

The information didn't surprise him. He'd heard Amanda ripped Xander a new asshole a few weeks ago about delays and how much it was affecting the bottom line.

"Between you and me," Robby said quietly, "there was talk we might not even make payroll next week. But there is something in the works. I'm not in the loop yet, but I get the impression it's something big."

To take the company from not paying their employees to hiring an extra man. Yes, it would have to be something big. Maybe he should pay the visit to Mike he'd promised and get the low down. He really did need to go see his old friend.

He pulled his attention back to Robby. "That explains Xander and Cy. Where's Matt?"

Robby flinched.

"Listen, I know you have a big-ass crush on the guy, but you have got to be able to keep it together when someone mentions his name."

The kid's face turned crimson. "Wow. Am I so obvious?"

"Yeah," he sighed. "You are. But you're not the only one who feels this way."

Robby's eyes grew as round as saucers. "You have a thing for Matt too?"

He buried his face in his hands and waited a moment. Two.

Aw, fuck it.

His shoulders shook, unable to suppress the laughter bubbling up inside him. It came up from deep in his belly and echoed in the unfinished garage.

He chanced a glance at Robby, but the guy's befuddled expression only made him laugh harder until, eventually, tears streamed down his face. Pulling off the bandana he had wrapped around his hair, he wiped his cheeks with one last chuckle. "Thanks, brother. I can't remember the last time I laughed so hard."

Robby scowled. Kind of like a tiger cub, he was all growly but without a threatening bone in his body. "I take it you do *not* have a thing for Matt."

"No. I don't." He ran his fingers through his hair, trying to unsnarl the knots from the road. "What I meant is, we all have someone who makes us embarrass ourselves. For you, it's Matt. For Brick, it's Olivia. For me—"

"For you, it's Ms. Griffin," Robby finished.

Now it was his turn to scowl, though he doubted there was anything cub-like about it. Most people would've taken a step back, but Robby stayed cool as a cucumber.

"That won't work on me now." The kid had the nerve to smirk. "We're family."

"It's not the protection you think it is. My brother Scott kicked my ass growing up more than anyone I've ever known."

Robby ignored the warning. "Everyone heard the two of you the day she came and yelled at Xander. And you were fit to be tied the whole rest of the day. So, what's the story? Did you break her heart? Did she break yours?" His words sped up with each question. "How long were you together? Did you love her?"

"Enough!" he roared, and this time Robby did take a small step back. "Stop. Please." He rubbed circles into his temples.

"I'm sorry." Robby's voice was small, and he hated himself a little for making it happen.

He took a deep breath. "No. I'm sorry. Obviously, I'm still kind of fucked up about it. But I shouldn't take it out on you. I'm sorry."

Robby nodded, but he kept his distance.

He leaned against the wall and slid down to rest on the concrete slab. The kid needed to feel safe. Maybe he'd be less threatening on his ass. "Yes, I loved her." He gently banged the back of his head twice against the drywall behind him. "I'll probably always love her."

Cautiously, Robby lowered himself to the ground and sat cross-legged a few feet away.

"We dated in college."

The kid's jaw dropped, but he quickly closed his mouth.

"Yes, Robby, I went to college. But I dropped out after we broke up. Not because of her, or at least, not entirely." He sighed. "We were together about six months, and I thought I was going to spend the rest of my life with her, get married, have kids, the whole bit."

Robby squinted his eyes, but he didn't say anything. The poor guy was probably afraid to speak.

"If you've got a question, it's okay. I won't bite your head off this time."

"I thought bikers didn't get married."

He laughed, but there was no joy in it this time. "They don't. I wasn't in the club back then; I wasn't gonna join. I never wanted my dad's life."

Robby inched closer. "Why not?"

To really answer his question would take hours...and several beers. His hand flexed, trying to conjure a longneck. "A hundred reasons." None he should be discussing with an outsider, but he owed Robby some kind of answer. "It's very insular. It's got its own code, which isn't always very evolved. Plus, as you said, it's not much of a life for women and families."

"But *you* grew up there," Robby pressed.

"Exactly, kid." He closed his eyes. "Exactly."

***

15 years ago

December

The shelves at Wal-Mart were stocked haphazardly as shoppers pawed through the After-Christmas Sale items. Strings of lights spilled out of torn cardboard boxes next to footie-pajamas and tins of fruitcake, which apparently had no expiration date. Kane's mom dug through the unsteady piles of almost-garbage, searching for bits of treasure beneath.

This trip was an annual event designed to find the perfect sale-priced gift for his dad. Malcolm's birthday was December 26th, and Mama V prided herself on spoiling her man while keeping to a razor-sharp budget. They had no money for the family to exchange gifts, but she pulled five dollars from her budget every month to put in her man's birthday fund. She didn't do it for her sons, but they never knew any different.

She inspected a grooming kit, then put it back on the shelf. The same treatment followed for a three-pack of DVDs and a bundle of barbeque supplies that would have really made Kane's attempts to cook for himself much easier. He knew better than to argue, though. It's not like his father ever cooked a meal in his life.

Malcolm was a simple man. He liked beer, cigarettes, sex, and his bike. The problem was, there was nothing on an After-Christmas rack likely to support his hobbies. He would have been happiest with a carton of Marlboros and a case of Bud, but those things weren't *special* enough for his old lady.

In the end, she settled for an American flag with slightly battered packaging and an insulated cup with a label promising to keep hot things hot and cold things cold. She used her remaining three dollars to buy a fancy cupcake at the store bakery because God forbid there be enough of a treat for everyone to share.

She intended this celebration for Malcolm and Malcolm alone.

When they got back to the clubhouse, which doubled as their home, she carefully wrapped the presents in the ninety-nine cent, shiny red paper with silver bells. Then, she sat down at the kitchen table and waited. And waited.

He made two grilled cheese sandwiches and set one down in front of her. As he scarfed down his dinner, hers grew cold on her plate. She was sitting vigil for her man. Of course, she wouldn't eat.

Shortly after eight o'clock, the rumble of engines sounded outside. A handful of brothers trickled in. Case, Bender, Scott…but no sign of Malcolm.

"You gonna eat that, Mama?" Scott didn't wait for an answer; he scooped the cold sandwich off her plate and stuffed it in his mouth.

Fifteen minutes later, a crash sounded from the carport out back. Mama V jumped to her feet to investigate, Kane trailing at her heels. He almost ran her over when she stopped short a few feet outside the door.

He craned his neck to see what caused her strangled cry.

Malcolm's body draped over the back of a woman Kane had never seen before. Or maybe *girl* would be more accurate. She couldn't have been much older than he was. Her thin arms gripped the metal column supporting the structure, her exposed breasts bouncing over the top of her skin-tight tank-top.

His first thought was she must be cold, so close to nude on a winter night. Then, his father's loud grunt shook him back to the bigger picture. Malcolm's hand on her back forced her to bend over further as he drove into her from behind. The wet slap of his body against hers echoed into the awful silence.

Mama stood frozen, watching him fuck the girl, his eyes closed and his features slack.

Kane couldn't think of anything more awful until his father opened his eyes and met her gaze. He didn't even break his rhythm. "Get back in the house, Viv. You can join in later tonight."

His mother didn't hesitate. She turned on her heel and went back into the house as instructed.

The next morning, he spied the dark-haired girl leaving his parents' bedroom. Her eye makeup smudged and smeared, she looked like a raccoon or a heroin addict. She walked slowly out of the house, gaze locked on the ground, carrying her chunky heels in her hand.

Mama left the bedroom moments later, her long, silky red robe cinched around her waist, an unlit cigarette between her fingers. Face drawn. Eyes empty. She, too, moved slowly.

He assumed she didn't see him, but she spoke before stepping into the backyard. "Start the coffee, baby, would you?" She didn't wait for his answer, and within seconds, he heard the snick of her lighter right outside the door.

In a small blessing, Malcolm didn't show his face. He wasn't ready to face his father after the spectacle he'd made last night. Sadly, it wasn't anything new. The man did what he wanted when he wanted. Always had. The twenty-something years his mother had devoted to him meant little to nothing. *She* was expected to be faithful, of course, but Malcolm could stick his dick anywhere wet and warm.

With a sigh, he pulled the filters out of the cabinet and got the pot ready to brew. Despite its age, the 1970s Mr. Coffee model worked fast. The kitchen filled with the aroma of coffee right as the ding of the toaster announced his Pop Tart was ready to burn the tips of his fingers.

He had his cup of caffeine in one hand and his breakfast in the other when something red and shiny caught the corner of his eye. His father's birthday presents still sat untouched on the kitchen table. He paused, thinking about the effort his mom had put in to select the right gifts, and dollars to donuts, Malcolm wouldn't give a shit one way or another.

This was club life. And he wanted no part of it.

CHAPTER SEVEN

Amanda

Nerves fluttered in Amanda's stomach as she ran her hands over the darts of her Dior business dress. It was the best she owned, and still, she had to remind herself she wasn't a little girl playing dress up.

Her gaze swept over the building in front of her. The outside of the Berringer Group's main office resembled a scaled down version of an old-money mansion. It stood two stories high, with thick white columns on either side of the dark oak front door. The entrance was decorated with a tasteful evergreen holiday wreath. Wide red ribbons wrapped the cylinders all the way to the top. Tasteful Southern Christmas elegance.

She had an appointment with Jared Berringer, the biggest name in Atlanta development—one of the biggest in the Southeast region—but he was still only a person. She knew how to handle people, and she knew how to handle her business.

She refused to be felled by her own insecurities.

Lifting her chin, she opened the door and walked confidently to the front desk. "Amanda Griffin for Mr. Berringer, please."

The slight man behind the counter glanced up from his computer and tapped the side of his headset. "Yes, ma'am. He's expecting you. Please come this way."

The inside of the building looked even more impressive than the façade. Her heels clicked on the high-grade marble floors, polished to a near-blinding shine, as they headed toward a wrought-iron double staircase that curled up around either side of the reception desk—a desk which, if she was not mistaken, featured her favorite sarsaparilla stain and a white Silestone countertop veined in black.

She followed the young man up the stairs, down a deserted hall to the corner office. He opened the door and gestured her through before nodding his farewell.

The photos she'd seen of Berringer hadn't done him justice. Even a casual observer wouldn't miss those George Clooney good looks. But anyone paying close attention would realize, in him, they'd found the whole package. He broadcasted it subtly. In the quality of his suit, the shine of his shoes. In the way he held himself, poised, serene and with nothing to prove. This was a man at the top of his game.

He greeted her with a congenial smile and a handshake just firm enough to tell her he wouldn't judge her worth on the fact she was a woman.

"Ms. Griffin." He gestured for her to sit in one of

the two chairs in front of his desk. Surprisingly, he took the seat next to her, rather than the position of power behind the heavy furniture.

She liked him already. "Amanda, please."

"And you'll call me Jared. I understand you're here with a proposal from Cooper Construction. I'm intrigued."

"I've heard you've lost your builder in the Decatur development."

His eyebrows shot up. GeorgiaSouth's bankruptcy was very hush-hush. She only knew about it because Mike was good friends with the owner.

"We'd like to step in and take over for them. Cooper isn't the biggest outfit in town, but we have a good reputation and do quality work."

Jared crossed his leg at the knee and relaxed into the soft leather chair. "I met Charlie a few times over the years. He struck me as a good man."

She swallowed. "The best," she murmured.

"You were his…"

"Daughter." She shook her head ruefully. "Stepdaughter, actually, but he never made the distinction."

"And you run the company with his son, correct?"

Jared knew the answer to every one of these questions before he ever accepted this meeting. The man was known for his research. She played along, giving him a patient smile. "Yes. Mike and I are very close. He would be here with me if he weren't recovering from a car accident." She paused, taking a chance by dropping the pretense. "Tell me, Jared, what is it you really want to know? Ask me, and I'll give you a straight answer."

He didn't miss a beat. "If I do business with you, will I be working with Charlie Cooper's daughter or Beau Griffin's?"

No wonder he was working up to that one. She considered her words. "My father—the mayor—has taught me a lot about business. About making connections, managing money, persistence, and perseverance. Those lessons have made me more successful, and I use them every day. But everything else about the way I do business, I learned from Charlie. Honesty, honor, integrity. Those are my core values, and they shape all the decisions I make for the company he built."

"Mayor Griffin is not someone who values honesty and integrity."

It wasn't a question, so she let the remark stand in the space between them. Either Jared could see past her family ties, or he couldn't. Arguing about the merits of his decision would get her nowhere.

"What about Nathan Shaw?"

She tried to keep the challenge out of her gaze. "What about Alexa Bell?"

His eyes widened when she mentioned the name of his paramour. Berringer was largely a private man, but even a discreet affair traveled along the grapevine. "Touché," he murmured.

"I don't mean to be coarse, Jared, but the people who escort us to parties or warm our beds have nothing to do with the deal at hand. I wonder if you would have asked me the same question if I were a man."

Dammit.

She didn't mean to say exactly what she was thinking.

Temper had no place in a business meeting. It was a hallmark of immaturity. How many times had her father drilled it into her head? His lesson had been the catalyst for her Ice Queen persona.

She cringed, waiting for Jared to show her the door. There would be half a dozen other companies he could secure to do the job with a snap of his fingers.

Instead, he laughed. "Oh, you're Charlie's girl all right. Beau Griffin would never let me know I'd gotten under his skin. And for the record, yes, I would have asked a man the same question, though it would have been equally as rude. I simply want to be sure there's no hidden agenda when someone wants to go into business with me."

She held her palms up. "No hidden agenda."

"Okay then. Cooper's financials are good. No outstanding debts for the company or for you." He stood when she nodded and offered his hand. "You've got yourself a deal."

Standing, she shook with her new partner.

"Now let's talk terms."

***

Kane

Kane hesitated with his hand poised to knock on Mike Cooper's door. He'd seen the man a handful of times over the years, but always with the buffer of work between them. Even when he was so desperate for a paycheck that he'd sought his old friend out for a job, he'd approached him through the company.

No telling how Mike would feel about him showing up on his front porch at dinnertime.

Clamping down on the fluttering nerves in his stomach, he clenched his jaw and rapped on the door.

There was a time in his life he considered Mike to be family, as much his brother as Scott ever was. After things went south with Mandy, though, it was too hard to maintain the friendship. Mike and his sister were inexorably linked, and Kane needed the distance to heal.

He held up his hand, poised to knock again, then thought better of it. Maybe Mike wasn't home, or maybe he wasn't interested in a blast from his past. Shoving his fist into the pocket of his faded denim jacket, he turned toward his bike at the curb.

The door creaked open behind him.

"Kane?"

He froze at the sound of the familiar voice. Damn, it brought him back. To barbeques and baseball games. To late night conversations over beers in the Cooper backyard.

How many nights had he stayed up until dawn, talking and laughing with Mandy, Mike, and Cindy? Those memories were as clear as if they'd happened yesterday. It was like nothing had changed.

Until he turned around and got his first look at his old buddy. The curly blond hair had darkened with age; the brown eyes he remembered always sparkling with laughter were now tired and dull. But those weren't the biggest changes.

Mike had always been a big man with an easy smile. Now his broad shoulders hunched in his wheelchair. His skin sagged on his bones, and though he smiled, it seemed forced.

It hurt to look at him. He tried not to flinch.

And Mike had to know it because the smile on his face faded when their eyes met. "Yeah. I look like shit." He sighed and backed his wheelchair into the foyer. "You just gonna stare at me with those puppy dog eyes, or you gonna come in?"

Kane followed him into a cozy living room, then sank into the big brown sofa Mike gestured to. It looked nothing like Charlie's place, but he felt the echoes in all the important ways. Warm colors bathed the cozy space, all the textures, soft and inviting. A baby swing sat in the corner.

No one would doubt a family lived here.

A pang of jealousy zinged through him until his gaze returned to Mike's haggard face. "You look like hell, brother," he said somberly.

Mike barked out a laugh. It wasn't like his old full-belly laugh; it had bite. "At least somebody's willing to say it. The girls kind of pretend like everything is fine in front of me. Then they whisper about me in the other room, but I can hear everything." He scowled. "We have baby monitors all over the house, dude."

He smiled despite himself. "Got yourself another kid, huh?" He'd heard through the grapevine Mike and Cindy had a son not long after things ended with Mandy. He should have come to visit then, but he was still too raw. "Boy or a girl?"

This time when Mike smiled, it reached his eyes. "A girl." He rubbed his hand in small circles over his chest. "She looks so much like Cindy, but every once in a while, she'll get this expression on her face, and I'm looking in the mirror. It's the damnedest thing. When I start to feel sorry for myself about the accident, I look at her, and I remember how lucky I am."

"Is she here?"

"No."

The swift disappointment at Mike's words took him by surprise.

"But she'll be back soon. Cindy took her to pick up some ice cream for dessert." Mike stuck out his lower lip in a parody of a pout. "I'm feeling too bad for anything but Baskin Robbins."

Something else that hadn't changed. Mike had been a slave to his sweet-tooth forever. Kane had personally witnessed the man eat an entire gallon of butter pecan in one sitting. "Don't tell me Cindy can't see through your pitiful-me bullshit."

Mike shrugged with a slight upturn at the corner of his mouth. "A few months ago, she would've. These days, she's so determined to take care of me, I think she forgets who I am under all this plaster." He knocked on one of the two impressive leg casts, the one ending below his right knee. The other extended all the way up his thigh beneath the leg of his cut-off sweatpants. Both were decorated with art of varying skill, from a fair approximation of a butterfly to a skull with crossbones, and some red scribbles, clearly made by a small child.

He also spotted a small heart, marked with the letter A.

Mandy.

He winced, but Mike didn't seem to notice.

"As bad as it looks now, it was worse when all the metal was holding my pelvis in place. At least now, I'm out of the bed." Mike's eyes drifted to the front door as it opened to reveal his wife, a toddler on her hip, a diaper bag on her shoulder, and a Baskin Robbins bag clutched in her hand.

Jumping to his feet, Kane reached out to lighten her load.

Her delicate brows furrowed for a moment, and her grip on her child tightened. No doubt, she was wondering what a grizzly looking biker was doing hanging out in her living room, possibly reaching for her kid.

He raised his hands in surrender. "Sorry CeeCee, I tend to forget my manners when I see a beautiful woman carrying ice cream."

Cindy's tension faded into shock, her eyebrows now climbing her forehead. "K-Kane?"

He waved. "Long time, no see."

She let the diaper bag slide down her arm as she put her squirming child on the floor.

On hands and knees, the kid made a beeline straight to her daddy's chair.

Cindy gaped as her gaze swept over his long dark hair, worn jacket and jeans, all the way down to his Army Surplus black boots. Then she smirked. The expression took him back more than a decade. "I didn't recognize you in your Hells Angels costume. Halloween was weeks ago."

"Still a smartass, huh?" He grabbed her arm and pulled her in for a hug. "Nice to know motherhood hasn't softened you up."

She returned his embrace. "Are you kidding? Motherhood makes you toughen up. *You* try parenting a twelve-year-old boy and see how soft-hearted *you* can be." Pulling back, she wrinkled her nose. "You don't have anything living in your shaggy beard, do you?"

"Bitch."

"Prick." Mike and Cindy spoke as one.

The familiar exchange lightened his heart. He released his hold and returned to his seat on the sofa. "I've missed you guys."

Cindy sat next to him, the light dimming a little on her face. "We've missed you too." She sighed, for the first time looking a little older than the twenty-two year old he remembered from his youth. "You didn't have to cut us off, Kane. Just because you and—"

"I did." He'd spoken more sharply than he intended, so he tried to gentle his tone. "Things were...bad for me. I was drowning."

Her hand rested on his forearm. "Times like those, you need your friends the most."

"But you were her family before you were my friends." He squeezed her hand. "If there was a break, it had to be a clean one." Even now, the memories of their friendship still tasted of Mandy. "I should've come sooner than this, though. It shouldn't have taken a near-death experience to bring me around."

Mike's little girl started crying and squirming on her father's lap.

"I think she needs a change, Cin."

She gave his arm one last pat, then climbed to her feet before scooping up her child. "She needs a bath, too. I'm going to stick the ice cream in the freezer while you two finish catching up." She shot him a warm look. "Don't wait so long before you come back next time."

The crying grew fainter as Cindy moved with her baby deeper into the house.

Mike cleared his throat. "You're not coming back, are you?"

"It's complicated, brother."

Scoffing, Mike leaned back in his chair. "Bullshit. You've got to forgive her. It's been thirteen years, man. You've got to let it go."

"Who says I haven't?" His voice was deceptively mild.

Mike laughed darkly. "Look at you. You joined your father's motorcycle gang. You became the thing you hated most in the whole world. You're the walking definition of someone who hasn't let shit go."

"It's not so simple."

"The hell it's not. She left you, and you turned your back on who you were when you were together. You dropped your friends, your dreams. But you could have it all back. Cut your hair, shave your beard, get your fucking degree. And for God's sakes, walk away from the biker gang. It was never the life you wanted."

Memories of his dreams for a future were a

110

crushing weight on his heart. It was why he usually pushed them down with beer, bourbon, and pussy. None of which were available at the moment. "The club is all I have." Flawed though they were, those men were his brothers.

"You have me," Mike said quietly. "You have the construction job. I hear you're pretty tight with a guy on the crew. It's a start."

"The guys in the club were there when I needed them, brother."

"And I wasn't. Right?" Mike's jaw clenched. A vein pulsed at his temple. "I would have been if you'd let me. Fuck, Kane, I don't even know what happened. My sister never would tell me. All I know is one day, you were there, and the next, you were gone like a puff of fucking smoke."

His fingers dug into the soft, fuzzy fabric of the sofa cushion. "You want to know what happened? Your sister ripped out my heart. When I needed her the most, she threw me away, and she never looked back."

***

13 years ago

October

Scott wasn't as good of a liar as he thought he was.

Kane would have been more than happy to take the bus to the mall, but his brother had insisted on giving him a ride. No way Scott could know he was

111

planning to look at engagement rings for Mandy, and no way was he going to find out. The man couldn't speak her name without a sneer on his face.

Still, accepting the ride on the back of his bike meant he could avoid the twenty-minute wait at the bus stop, and he was anxious to start searching for the perfect ring. It would have to be small, obviously. His job at the bank barely covered his tuition, but he'd put aside enough for a down payment. Now he needed a jeweler willing to let him finance.

He'd been thinking about those things when he'd accepted his brother's offer, and they'd taken off ten minutes ago. Now they idled in front of a shady-looking apartment building in Vine City, nowhere near the mall.

Scott said he just needed to deliver something. He was lying through his teeth. Like always, his left eye twitched as the line of bull came out his mouth. Even worse, a light sheen of moisture dotted Scott's forehead. Octobers in Atlanta weren't exactly cold, but generally not warm enough to make someone break a sweat.

Except for whatever reason Scott was hiding.

"Why don't you come in with me, K? I could use a little backup."

He folded his arms. His brother couldn't even look at him. "You know I don't want anything to do with club business. Why would you need backup for a delivery anyway?" He didn't even mention the obvious. Scott wasn't carrying anything to drop off.

His brother made an impatient gesture toward the apartment building. It was one of at least five large, brick structures looming in front of them. A single basketball goal without a net stood amidst the cracked blacktop. An empty Cheetos bag skittered slowly across the pavement, but nothing else moved in sight.

"I'm delivering a *message*, okay?" Scott's voice held an edge. "I'm not asking you to do much. Just stand there. You don't have to think of it as helping out the club; you're helping out your brother."

A knot of unease tightened in his stomach. "What exactly do you need my help with?"

Scott didn't answer. He advanced on the apartment building, his shoulders tense, hands balled into fists at his sides.

Kane scrambled off the bike to catch up. "Scott—"

His brother's hand flew up, silencing the question. Then he rapped his knuckles against the third door from the left.

It swung open instantly to reveal a tall heavyset black man with two thick gold chains resting against the vee of a black short-sleeved button-down shirt. He had a cigar cinched between his teeth. With a short nod to Scott, he opened the door wide enough for him to enter.

Kane had no choice but to follow.

A thick haze of marijuana smoke fogged the room, giving the illusion of soft edges in a space where none really existed. Three men sat surrounding a kitchen table littered with clear plastic bags filled with white powder, bricks—presumably of pot—wrapped in brown paper, stacks of cash, and a couple of handguns.

If he lived through this "delivery," he was kicking Scott's ass.

The big dude who answered the door stood behind the man sitting at the head of the table and crossed his arms over his chest. The seated guy, apparently his boss, looked sharp in a long-sleeved black dress shirt that managed to appear both soft and crisp at the same time. Black—maybe forty—he wore a fat, round diamond in his left ear.

The man to his left looked younger. Bald and Hispanic, he wore a gold silk shirt and a suit jacket the color of a peacock. The third guy—the one closest to Scott and Kane—was clearly a grunt, a skinny twenty-something with a backward baseball cap.

The boss spoke without looking up from the money he was counting. "Hale." His voice had no inflection. "This isn't your normal neck of the woods."

Scott cleared his throat. "No."

Placing the last bill into the stack in front of him, the man looked up. "Then what are you doing here?" he asked mildly. The question was all the more menacing with his gentle delivery.

Scott eyed the door, then shifted his gaze to Kane before turning back to the boss.

Oh shit. His heart lodged in his throat.

"Just delivering a message." A heartbeat later, Scott had a gun in hand and was unloading bullets into the man in black and the bodyguard behind him.

Kane stood frozen, his ears ringing, unprepared as the skinny guy with the baseball cap sprang to his feet. Everything went in slow motion as the man pulled a wicked blade from his belt and lunged toward Scott.

There was no thought, only instinct, as he stepped between the knife and his brother's throat. The serrated blade sliced into his left cheek.

He threw a punch, and his assailant doubled over, then struck out again with his blade. This time, the metal poked fire into his gut.

More gunshots flew around him, and the punch of a bullet penetrated his shoulder. He dropped like a ton of bricks; his attacker fell a couple of feet away, his dead eyes staring at the ceiling.

The room was silent now. His vision swam, blackness threatening to overtake him.

Peacock-blue slacks and a duffel bag passed his line of sight. "Your money, Señor Hale. You'll find the cash is all there as promised." A Spanish accent. "Now I suggest you see to your young friend. He's not looking so good."

It was the last thing he heard before the world slipped away.

He woke up in the hospital. Everything hurt.

His room was quiet, save for the steady beeping of the heart monitor. No sign of his brother or his parents. He blinked, and the last vestiges of daylight had disappeared. A dim light shone from a panel above his bed. A gentle pressure squeezed against his hand.

He turned toward the small sob from his right.

"Mandy," he rasped. The skin on his face tugged against the tape and bandage as he formed the word.

Tears streaked her face. Her beautiful hair

tangled in wild disarray. He attempted to lean toward her, to comfort her, but the pain of moving leveled him back to the bed. He tried to swallow, but his tongue was so dry, it stuck to the roof of his mouth. A cough shook his body and, dear God, did it hurt. Still, he couldn't stop.

Finally, a straw slipped between his lips, and the cool water helped him settle. Mandy held the glass close to him until he drank his fill, then set it on the tray beside her.

"I'm so glad you're here," he whispered, squeezing her hand weakly. He'd made such a mistake following his brother into a stupid fucking drug den. Never again. He'd cut the cord. His family business was the past. Mandy was his future.

She pulled her hand away from his. "I can't see you anymore."

Her words didn't make sense.

The medication must be messing with me.

He shook his head.

"I can't be involved in this world, Kane." She wiped the tears from her cheeks and hardened her expression. "Do you know how many people died today?"

"But—" His voice failed him. God, he hurt so much.

She stood. "Don't call me; I won't answer. Don't try to see me; you're no longer part of my life." She gave him her back and walked to the door.

Tears spring to his eyes.

What is happening?

Nothing made sense. The only thing he knew was he had to stop her from walking out the door.

He forced himself upright, the pain in his gut burning fire anew. Blood seeped through his sheets. He reached out. "Mandy."

"Goodbye, Kane."

He felt like he was dying. And when his last glimpse of her red hair disappeared from the room, he no longer had the will to fight it.

CHAPTER EIGHT

Kane

Kane couldn't look at Mike as he recounted the night he'd refused to think about in years. In the weeks and months after Mandy left him, he'd dissected the memory in every way he could. He tried to make sense of it, but every time he came up empty. Eventually, he simply stopped trying.

"You never tried to see her again?" Mike's words finally made him look up. "Never tried to call her?"

He blew out a deep breath. "Course I did. But she wouldn't take my calls. You hadn't seen her. She even had a bodyguard for a while to keep me away."

"She didn't come around here for weeks." Mike seemed to be talking to himself. "Wouldn't take my calls either. I figured she needed time." His eyes narrowed as he focused back on Kane. "I always thought you must have cheated on her or something. Nothing else made sense. She loved you."

Heat flashed up his neck. "Fuck you. I would have cut off my arm for your sister. I never even looked at another woman." He rose to his feet, his voice climbing with his outrage.

"So, you're saying she left you because your thug brother dragged you into a shootout?" Mike shook his head like his own words didn't make sense.

He sighed deeply, the familiar weight of the memory settling on his chest. "Something, or *someone*, set the building on fire after I passed out." He rubbed his fingers over the crease in his forehead.

Mike shrugged. "Okay. It still doesn't—" He gasped as the realization hit. "Oh, my God. The big apartment fire in the Bluff?"

"Yeah," he murmured.

The horror on Mike's face punched him in the gut.

"Something like twenty people died. Holy shit, Kane. That was you?"

Growling, he launched to his feet and loomed over his former friend. "No, it wasn't *me*. Were you even listening? I was un-fucking-conscious."

"Step back from my brother. Right. Now." Ice and steel reinforced Mandy's voice behind him.

He whirled to face her, taking in her fiery hair and fierce expression. His pulsing anger muted the effect her nearness usually caused. "Back off. This has nothing to do with you."

A lie.

Her green eyes glittered dangerously. "My brother has everything to do with me. Threaten him again, and I'll wear your intestines as a hat."

"I wasn't threatening him." Thank God furniture stood between them. The urge to shake her overwhelmed him, though he'd never really put his hands on a woman in anger.

She shook her head. "Bullshit. You're up in his face—"

"I am not—" Their climbing voices tried to drown each other out.

"Enough." Cindy's sharp voice cut through the air, silencing them both. The baby on her hip was crying. "Take it outside." Mike gaped in stunned silence beside her.

Mandy spun on her heel and stomped out the front door. He followed at her heels.

The door was barely closed behind them when she poked him in the chest. "This was *not* what I meant when I said you should come to visit him."

"And it's all about what you want, right, Your Highness?" He purposely chose a variation of Scott's old nickname for her, and she flinched.

"Mike is recovering from a serious accident. The last thing he needs is you bullying him over something that happened a hundred years ago."

A hundred years ago? Reliving what had happened at the hospital made it feel more like yesterday. He looked pointedly at the place her finger still rested against his chest, then raised his eyebrow.

She dropped her hand and shook it like it burned, then made a frustrated noise in the back of her throat.

"Is everything okay here?"

He looked over Mandy's shoulder at the quiet question. The first thing that registered was the hair. The boy's hair was the same beautiful red as Mandy's.

"It's fine, Joshua," she murmured. "Go on inside with your parents. I'll be there in a minute."

Parents? No way was this kid Mike and Cindy's. Not with Cindy's dark skin and Mike's dirty blond curls.

This kid had a fiery head of hair and green eyes he could have only gotten from one place.

Mandy.

Had she moved on from him so quickly? He staggered back. "How old are you?"

The kid—Joshua, she'd called him—frowned. "I'm twelve. Why? Who are you?"

He searched the boy's features. Could this be…?

Suddenly, the air felt thinner. His chest grew tight.

Joshua said something to Mandy he couldn't make out, then walked into the house.

"Is *this* why you left me?" The tangle of emotions rising in his chest made his head swim. He leaned against the siding next to the front door.

All this time. He had a kid, and he didn't fucking know it.

He had a son.

"How could you keep this from me?" he roared.

Mandy paled. "He's not yours."

He found his footing again, and the rage bubbled up. "The fuck he's not."

She reached out, putting her hand on his arm, but he shook her off. "He's not even mine."

121

The lie burned like fire. For the first time, things started to make sense. Why she left him. Why she wouldn't even see him all those years.

He'd loved her for so long. Even after she crushed his heart. Even after she ruined him for any other woman. But now? For the first time, he knew what it was to hate her. "I want a DNA test." He shouldered past her, heading toward his bike. He needed to be anywhere but here.

She ran behind him. "Joshua is not our child."

"Do you think I'm blind?" he shouted as he whirled to face her. "You and Mike don't share one strand of DNA. His kid looks just like you."

"He's my brother," she said weakly.

"Your *stepbrother*." The fury threatened to make him explode. He turned back to his Harley before he said or did something he couldn't take back.

"No." She stepped between him and the bike, blocking his path. "*Joshua* is my brother."

He shook his head, his brain trying to make sense of what she said.

She forged on. "We both look like my mom. Joshua is her son with Charlie."

"But…they died." Only a few months after Mandy left him. He'd heard nothing about a baby.

Mandy squeezed her eyes closed tightly. "Mom didn't tell anyone she was pregnant until after her first trimester. She was in her forties; she was worried about a miscarriage. She was about seven months along when their car accident happened. The baby survived; she didn't. I give you my word."

His mind scrambled, searching for a hole in her

story. His knees weakened, the rage giving way to crushing sadness. There was a time he would have accepted Mandy's word without question—back when he thought he knew her. She was a stranger now.

He walked around her and climbed on his bike from the other side. "Your word isn't good enough. Not when it's this important. I need proof." He pushed the ignition button, and the engine rumbled between his legs. "You've got until Monday."

Ignoring her stricken expression, he revved the engine and peeled out into the street.

***

Amanda

Amanda's eyes stung as Kane sped away, his long, dark hair streaming behind him. How far had she fallen in his eyes for him to believe she would have kept a child from him?

Tired and heartsick, she let herself back into her brother's house.

Mike was nowhere in sight, but Joshua sat on the sofa, his thin arms folded over his chest. He stood when she walked in. "I finally got to see the infamous Kane." He frowned. "He thought I was his kid, didn't he?"

She gaped. "Wh—where did you hear his name?"

Joshua rolled his eyes. "Are you kidding me? I've heard his name my entire life. Being a kid doesn't make me deaf, and despite what all of you think, it doesn't make me dumb. Of course, the guy thought you were my mom. I used to wonder the same thing."

Oh no. She rubbed at her chest as she dropped to the sofa. "Oh, honey. Why didn't you say anything?"

"I did, eventually, but for a long time before I talked to Dad, I used to make up stories in my head. About why you gave me up…about how you might want me back someday. About the Kane-guy Mom and Dad whispered about sometimes." His eyes lost some of their fire. "I'm glad I know the truth now. It makes things easier."

"We should have told you sooner." How long had he thought she'd rejected him?

Mike wheeled in from the kitchen. "It's getting late, Josh. Go finish up your math homework."

Joshua nodded and left the room without another word.

Mike waited until the bedroom door closed before he spoke again. "It's time to stop keeping so many secrets."

She'd kept so many for so long, she couldn't imagine what her life would be like without them. Her secrets had defined her for longer than she wanted to admit.

"He told me what happened the night you broke up with him." There was a hint of accusation there. "You should know he had nothing to do with the fire, Amanda. The guy he was then wouldn't have hurt a fly."

"I can't do this, Mike." She needed a drink. Thankfully, she knew where her brother kept the bourbon. A dozen steps to the kitchen, then she had a highball glass in her hand. The familiar burn soothed the shards of ice in her chest.

But Mike was right behind her. He was clearly unwilling to let this go. "He was going to go buy you a ring, for fuck's sake."

She didn't want to know that. More bourbon, more burn. "Leave it alone," she rasped.

"I won't!" he bellowed. "I should have never left it alone this long. What the hell happened, Amanda? I know you loved him, and the poor bastard obviously loved you too."

"Stop." Tears threatening, she pushed them back and drank from the bottle.

"It was your father." He said it quietly, with no hint of doubt. "Nothing else makes sense. He never wanted you with Kane. What I don't understand is how he got you to go along with it."

What difference did it make now? "He would have put him in jail for the rest of his life," she said dully. "He still could. There's no statute of limitations on murder."

***

13 years ago

October

A baby.

Amanda couldn't help but smile as she held up the tiny onesie with the Atlanta Braves insignia. It didn't matter if she was having a brother or a sister, this kid would be a Braves fan. She paid for the outfit and hummed quietly as she left the store.

The sunshine on her face was the cherry on top of the delicious fall afternoon. A cool breeze lifted her hair from her neck. She stood only a couple of feet from the curb when her father's silver BMW pulled in front of her.

The passenger side window rolled down. "Get in."

Ignoring her creeping unease, she climbed inside. "How did you even know I was here?" She'd been at her mom's before she started shopping; she hadn't even seen her dad in weeks.

He didn't answer her question as he pulled back into traffic. It was only a few blocks to his house. He got out of the car without a word, assuming she would follow—which she did, but only after a deep sigh.

Surprisingly, he led her to his study, where he turned on the TV mounted on the wall. The news played; a giant fire blazed through what looked like an apartment building. The words on the bottom of the screen read:

**TWENTY-TWO MISSING,
FEARED DEAD IN APARTMENT FIRE.**

"How terrible," she murmured.

"It's going to send your boyfriend to jail for the rest of his life."

She turned in time to see the hint of a smile on her father's face before it disappeared. "What are you talking about?"

He steepled his fingers beneath his chin. "The urchin you've been seeing. He's responsible for this."

She didn't believe him for a second. "Kane would never start a fire, Dad. Don't be ridiculous."

He entwined his perfectly manicured fingers together and dropped them in front of his waist. "What is ridiculous is my daughter, involved with a member of the Hale family. Those…people…live on the fringe of our society. Motorcycle gangs, drugs, and guns. It's all beneath you, Amanda."

There was a reason she kept her private life away from her father. "Kane isn't involved in any of his family's dealings."

"Really?" he mused, and dread trickled down her spine. Reaching down to his desk, he spun his open laptop to face her. Frozen on the screen was a still frame of Kane and his brother on Scott's motorcycle. He hit the spacebar, and she watched the two of them exchange words before Scott walked away. Kane followed him into the apartment building she saw ablaze on the TV.

She swallowed. "Okay, he was there. It's a pretty big leap to go from stepping on the property to him setting the fire."

"Not when I have someone threatening to testify to it if I don't pay him off." Her father all but hissed. "I don't like being threatened, Amanda. And I don't appreciate you giving someone the means to do it."

"I have nothing to do with you getting blackmailed." Heat climbed her face. "And I don't care what some lowlife says, Kane didn't do this."

"That lowlife…is an undercover cop." He slammed the laptop closed. "If you think his word won't carry weight, you're a fool."

None of this made sense. Kane wanted nothing to do with his father's motorcycle club; she'd bet her life on it. "I know he had to have a good reason for being there."

"It doesn't matter, Amanda. Whether he did it or he didn't, this cop has the power to put him away. Unless I pay him not to."

"How much does he want?" She had some money saved. Maybe she could take care of this herself.

"Fifty thousand dollars." The words fell like a lead balloon. "Your boyfriend had the motive, the means, and the opportunity to set this fire. There's an eyewitness and a video placing him at the scene."

Motive? "He had no motive, Dad. What could he possibly have to gain?"

He raked his hand through his hair in a very un-Beauregard-like gesture. "To benefit his father's organization. The real targets were in the drug trade. They were the men the cop was in deep with. I'm not sure how this change in leadership ties to his family's 'motorcycle club,'" he said, curving his fingers into air-quotes, "but that's the crux of it. Whether the Hale boy is part of the club or not is irrelevant. Some people actually value getting their father's approval."

His little dig hit home. She knew her father loved her, but it was a selfish kind of love. It had been the same way when he was with her mom. If she didn't put him first—if she didn't see things his way—he took it as a personal affront. You were either with him or against him. She sighed. "What are we going to do?"

"We?" He narrowed his eyes and approached her. "*We* aren't going to do anything. *I* am going to pay this bastard for his silence."

She let out the breath she'd been holding. "Thank—"

"*You*," he continued as if she hadn't spoken, "will cut all ties with Kane Hale. Now and forever."

"No," she breathed.

Her father put his face centimeters from hers, so close she could smell the cigar smoke on his breath. "Oh yes. I will not leave myself open like this again. You want to save this young man, give me what I want."

Tears streamed down her face, but her father appeared indifferent. "Decide now." This. This was the kind of thing her mother ran away from, but now Amanda was trapped.

What choice did she have? She nodded.

"He's at Northside Hospital. Go now. Make a clean break."

She turned, her heart in her throat. Her stomach churned, threatening to empty its contents on the Aubusson rug.

"And Amanda, don't get any ideas about changing your mind later. If you go back on our deal, I'll go to the police myself. This stays between us. Remember, there's no statute of limitations on murder."

CHAPTER NINE

Amanda

Mike listened to Amanda's confession without so much as a twitch on his face. But the moment she finished her story, his features twisted. "Your father is a rank bastard."

Not the response she was expecting, but it was true, nonetheless. Beau Griffin was also controlling and narcissistic. His genteel manners and charming smile, the simple tools he used to boost his popularity among the people. Their regard fed his bottomless well of need for respect and adoration. No matter how hard they tried, the simple love she and her mother had to give could never have been enough. They'd been doomed to disappoint him.

The bourbon no longer burned as she swallowed it down, generally a sign she needed to stop drinking. She screwed the cap back on the bottle and returned it to its perch above the side-by-side refrigerator. "Be that as it may, he's the only reason Kane is walking free."

Mike rolled his eyes. "He's the reason Kane was threatened in the first place."

"Ah, but you're forgetting one thing, big brother. My father had nothing to do with Kane going to the apartment building or with whatever went down inside." She dragged one of the kitchen chairs from beneath the round oak table and sat down. "Don't you think it occurred to me he was behind the whole thing? But it doesn't make sense. There were too many factors out of his control."

Mike wheeled to the refrigerator and pulled out a plate covered in Saran Wrap. He lifted up on one heel to stick it in the microwave and hit the start button, then sat back down to watch the plate spin around on the revolving tray.

"I guess you're right, but it doesn't change the fact he manipulated the circumstances to his advantage. He never wanted you and Kane together. Thought he was beneath you, like he thought my dad was beneath your mom."

The timer went off, and he lifted up again to pull out the plate. He placed it on his lap, then grabbed a fork from the drawer and delivered it to her.

Under the cellophane, she spotted two chicken legs, some mashed potatoes, and corn. Her stomach gurgled.

"Eat," he chided.

She pulled off the covering and moved the food around with her fork. It smelled amazing. "You're right. My dad doesn't do anything out of the goodness of his heart." Look at the price she had to pay for his help with the company. Though she had no intention of sharing those details with her brother.

She blew on a forkful of steaming potatoes. "It doesn't matter anyway. Kane and I are both different people now." Carefully, she slid the creamy bite into her mouth.

"For a smart woman, you sure are stupid sometimes." Mike shot her a patronizing look. "It's still Kane. He's still the same guy."

Mike couldn't really be so naïve. She grunted as she swallowed her food. "The Kane I was with would never have joined a biker gang. He hated everything about it. He wanted to be an investment banker, for crying out loud. Now he's right there, living the life with his asshole brother and misogynist father. He lives outside of society. If those things don't make him a different man, I don't know what would."

His face softened. "Talk to him. God, sis, you owe him that much."

"Yeah." She took a few more bites, but she barely tasted her meal anymore. "I need a copy of Josh's birth certificate. Kane saw him tonight; he thinks he's ours."

"Damn," he muttered. "His reaction couldn't have been pretty."

The food no longer held any appeal. "It wasn't." Exhaustion was a crushing weight on her shoulders. "You mind if I crash here tonight?" Tomorrow was Saturday; it wasn't like she had to go to work.

She didn't wait for an answer. Depositing her dish in the sink, she stumbled to the guest room and crashed face-first onto the bed.

She dreamed of kissing away Kane's scars in his

hospital bed, a life free of her father, and a baby with dark brown hair and green eyes who she could call her own.

***

Kane

Kane squinted against the rays of afternoon sun burning his retinas. Though he wore a pair of durable sunglasses, a night with little-to-no sleep had left him sensitive to the light.

He couldn't find any holes in Mandy's story about the kid he'd seen on Mike's porch, but he also couldn't dismiss the possibility it was all a lie. Maybe a part of him *wanted* it to be a lie.

The idea of a child of his own—a son—did something to his insides he couldn't bring himself to examine all at once. There was hope there, but also anger and a deep sense of betrayal. Surprising, since he thought Mandy had already dicked him over as much as one person ever could.

The blaring horn from a car behind him shook him out of his thoughts. The light had turned green. With a sigh, he lifted his hand in recognition before resuming his course to the seedier part of town.

Gone were the streets lined with Wal-Marts and Applebee's. Now he passed small houses long ago repurposed as various businesses. One was faded pink with a rusted air conditioning unit in the front window and a wooden sign advertising a psychic inside. The one next to it was blue with a yard made of mostly short weeds and dirt claiming to be a daycare. A "KinderKare," according to the stenciled letters next to the door.

Some of the houses looked like they'd been abandoned for years. A couple showed evidence of fire; one had no roof at all. Then, an old service station…an overgrown lot with a threadbare sofa on its side and two bald tires…and finally, his destination.

He shuddered as he pulled up to the massive apartment complex. It was the same place where Scott had dragged him all those years ago. The place where a wannabe gangbanger carved a fucking ravine across one side of his face. The place where life as he knew it came to a screeching halt.

He parked next to his brother's Dyna Low Rider and tried to ignore the burned-out shell of Building D as he walked past. After all these years, no one had touched a thing; it was left like a macabre monument to the families who died inside. Or maybe no one had the money or the motivation to fix it.

Rubbing over the scar on his cheek, he ambled to Building E, projecting a nonchalance as real as a three-dollar bill. The last thing he needed was for anyone to smell blood in the water.

The door opened before he had the chance to knock. He didn't recognize the guy who waved him in, but he looked young enough to be in high school, dark skin, hair cropped close to his scalp, jeans, and a T-shirt. But his eyes were older, and the handle of a handgun peeked from his waistband.

He pushed down his misgivings and followed the sound of his brother's voice.

"—won't be any problem at all. We have the men to keep the business running and a reputation guaranteed to give anyone second thoughts before they try to fuck us out of our money." Scott wore his cockiest smile as he talked up the club to a black guy in his mid-fifties wearing an impeccable gray three-piece suit over an open-collared black dress shirt.

The man traced the thin beard along his jaw with the back of his fingers. "Very good, Mr. Hale, because if we go into business together, your money is our money." He turned to a small entourage of three men behind him. "Jay, what do you think?"

The guy who scowled had on black jeans and a white shirt with a leather jacket that had to be stifling in the warm apartment. "You know what I think, Ace. Our focus needs to be on what happened to Sucre."

The guys around him nodded in agreement.

Ace, obviously the boss, shook his head. "We talked about this."

"You asked me my opinion and this is it." Jay broke away from the group and paced the room. There wasn't a lot of space, but it looked way nicer than Kane would have ever expected from the outside. A black leather sofa and chair in the living area to their left. A big flat screen on the wall. And a long glass table to the far right of the room. It had probably been moved to create the empty space where they were standing. In most apartments, it would be the eat-in kitchen.

Something told him no one cooked here; no one shared this space for a family meal.

No. This place was for business, and their visits couldn't happen often. No dishes anywhere. No garbage cans. And a light sheen of dust reflected off the face of the television.

Jay's lips pinched. "Sucre didn't just walk away from us."

Kane's stomach turned. They couldn't know the club took Sucre out. He and Scott were outnumbered. If this went bad, neither one of them would walk out of here alive.

Thankfully, Jay seemed oblivious to his discomfort. "The guy was creepy as fuck, but he never gave us reason to doubt his loyalty. He paid on time. He met his obligations." Jay got more animated as he went on. "He was our *associate,* and whatever happened to him is a reflection on us."

Ace shook his head with the sufferance of a father explaining something to his wayward son. "We have no reason to believe he didn't take his money and move to the Bahamas." It echoed of an argument made many times before.

"Bullshit, man, and you know it." The men who had been standing with Jay nodded with his words. "Someone knocked him off, and whoever did it took out his whole crew. Unless you think they *all* went to the Bahamas."

"Enough." Ace's hand sliced through the air. "I told you this already. If we find out someone killed de la Cruz, we'll handle it. In the meantime, we have a business to run. To make money, we need a distributor. My only question to you now is who it's going to be." He turned back to Scott. "Obviously, we've had a lot of interest in what's only been a short period of time. In my opinion, however, your club seems to be one of the most suited for possible success."

Scott smiled. "We wouldn't ask for the job if we weren't up for it."

The man waved away Scott's reassurance. "Obviously, your club has made a name for itself in weapons. I understand you work on the up and up, and you know how to be discreet. My only concern is the impact of your plan to diversify."

There was a reason this guy was in charge. He asked the right question, and it was the one Scott seemed determined to ignore.

His brother tilted his head to the side like he didn't understand what Ace was saying. Maybe he didn't.

Kane cleared his throat. "We're still committed to our original business partners. Loyalty is important to us too." He gave what was supposed to be a reassuring nod to Jay, who was still pacing in front of the flat screen. "We've worked with those partners for over a decade. Our club has grown over the years, and we have enough men to run both operations."

One of the guys who had been standing by Jay spoke for the first time. His arms were folded tightly in front of him. "Sucre had more than twice as many men."

No one was looking at Scott anymore. Kane liked it better when he'd been invisible. "Like us, Sucre had diverse interests. But unlike us, he had no other partners. He needed more enforcers to collect on the loans he fronted." He shrugged and held up his empty palms. "We have no interest in becoming loan sharks. The startup costs are way too high, and policing the returns requires additional manpower and yields unreliable results."

Ace raised an eyebrow. "Indeed." He shooed Jay out of the room, and his lieutenant returned a moment later with two big black duffel bags, which he dropped at Kane's feet.

"H in one bag, coca products in the other." Ace stepped closer to him, Scott all but forgotten. "You want meth, make your own. Weed and pills, you'll have to get somewhere else. But I will be your only supplier for the products I carry."

It wasn't a question, but he nodded anyway. "My brother has your guns."

Two of the men sat with Scott at the table to sort out the weapons.

Ace stood two feet from Kane. He spoke softly. "One last thing. No matter how unsavory all this is, it is a business. And I am a businessman."

There was no doubt in his mind.

"Your brother is not."

No doubt of that either.

"Before you spoke up, I was prepared to walk away from his proposition. However, you strike me as someone I could work with. This…association between my people and yours is contingent upon your continuing involvement. I assume my caveat is amenable to you."

He glanced at his brother whose jaw was now clenched shut. Ace had spoken softly, but Scott had clearly heard it all.

It didn't matter, though. This was the deal; take

it or leave it.

"It's fine," he agreed gruffly.

"The guns check out." Jay hoisted Scott's heavy backpack onto his shoulder.

Ace smiled and offered Kane his hand. "Then it looks like we have a deal."

***

Scott didn't say a word as they walked back to their bikes, each with a duffel bag in hand. His face was unreadable—at least to anyone who didn't know him—but Kane knew there was emotion simmering beneath his skin.

It only took a few minutes to get back to the clubhouse, and even then, Scott said nothing as he stomped in the door, heading directly to the chapel.

It wasn't until Kane stepped in behind him and closed the door, his brother dropped the duffel and whirled around with an expression on his face loaded with hurt and betrayal. "How could you do that? You knew this was my deal."

Sighing, he set down his burden on the table. "I didn't even want to go at all, Scott. But you and Malcolm made damn sure it happened anyway."

"This is how you get back at me?" Scott raked his fingers through his hair. "You try to undermine me? Make this *your* deal? We're brothers. We're supposed to have each other's backs."

Kane balled his hands into fists. "The *last* thing I wanted was for this to be *my* deal. I think it's a terrible idea, which you know damn good and well. It should have been more obvious than ever when those guys started making noise about avenging Sucre. They find out it was us, they're coming for every brother wearing a cut."

Scott rolled his eyes. "If they were really worried about what happened, they would be looking for us regardless."

"But by approaching them, we drew a big fucking bullseye on our backs." Scott could not be this fucking dumb.

"Nobody forced you to come." Scott grabbed the pack of Camels on the table and stuck a cigarette between his lips. He marched outside the back door, and Kane followed on his heels. "I could've brought Cue Ball with me."

Funny. Scott never mentioned Cue Ball when he told him about the meet. "You think I would have ever chosen to go back there?"

Scott lit his cigarette, then took a long drag. He blew the smoke out defiantly.

It took everything he had not to close the distance between them and knock the cigarette out of his fucking mouth. "The last time you dragged me there, I almost died. Twenty other people actually did."

Scott's eyes darkened, his hurt feelings giving way to something harder. "Who took care of you when you got out of the hospital, huh? This club did. *I* did. Your precious old lady kicked you to the curb, and your family stayed with you to pick up the pieces."

He stepped into Scott's face. "There would have been no pieces to pick up if you hadn't manipulated me into going in the first place." He poked his brother in the chest. "You want me to *thank* you? For almost getting me killed? For ruining my fucking life? *Fuck you, brother*. You'll go to your grave waiting for any thanks from me."

Pain bloomed across his cheekbone before he even realized his brother had taken a swing. But it was fine. It gave him permission to finally let go.

He hit back with a hard punch to Scott's gut. Then, as his brother doubled over, he grabbed his shoulders and wrenched him down until Scott's head connected with his knee. But instead of assuaging the ember of rage inside him, the violence only fed the flame.

It was almost a relief when Scott threw another punch.

He knocked it away with his forearm and with a howl, used his shoulder as a battering ram to knock his brother to the dead grass at his feet. It would be so easy to kick him while he was down. Or to climb on top of him and whale on his face until it was beaten to nothing short of raw hamburger.

But Malcolm grabbed him by the shoulder and jerked him back.

He hadn't even heard him come out.

"What the fuck is going on here?"

For a moment, he was tempted to land his next punch across his father's weathered face, but he forced his anger under control. It was a skill he'd damn-near perfected over the years. "Scott's pissed the supplier wants me to take the lead as the liaison for the club."

"*He's* pissed, huh?" Malcolm looked meaningfully at Scott as he pulled himself to his feet.

He shrugged. "He threw the first punch. I threw the last."

The explanation seemed to satisfy his father. He turned away from Scott to give Kane his full attention. "Do we have a deal?"

"The product's right there." He used his thumb to gesture toward the door behind him, the duffel bag on the table inside. "We've got to be careful, though. They're real squirrely about Sucre." He and Scott followed their father back in the house.

Malcolm laughed as he unzipped the bag and rifled through the small baggies inside. "Heh. Let 'em wonder." He held up one small baggie and shook it. "No one ever figured out we put the ungrateful prick in power. They'll never know we took him down. But we will reap the benefits, boys."

He refused to let the disgust show on his face. The memory of a young Sucre at the table the night of the fire was as fresh in his mind as if it happened yesterday.

"Call everyone in, Scott," his father said as he returned the heroin to the black duffel. "It's time to talk distribution."

CHAPTER TEN

Amanda

Amanda itched to smooth her hands over the fabric of her black slacks, but her fingers were clutched around the copy of Joshua's birth certificate Mike had given her the day before. Her palms were damp; God, she hated how her body betrayed her anxiety. Maybe Kane wouldn't be able to tell.

Yeah right. The man had always been able to see right through her. Well, almost always.

She took a deep breath, trying to steady her pounding heart as she walked through the front door of the worksite.

Clipboard in hand, Xander's assistant, Robby, made a beeline straight for her. "Miss Griffin, I didn't realize you would be here today. Xander's not on site." His voice hardly wavered at all.

She steeled her expression, trying to mask her own nerves. "It's not a scheduled visit. I have some papers for Kane Hale. Where can I find him?"

The hammering around her came to a stop, and suddenly the eyes of every man in the room were on her. The big guy, Kane's friend Brick, one of the men who got shot, walked toward her. His eyes swept over her with the kind of judgment she saw from the nuns at her Catholic high school.

She returned his frank stare with a look fashioned to turn water into ice.

He seemed unimpressed. "Follow me."

Brick led her out back where Kane was cutting a two-by-four with an electric saw. He turned back and left her there without a word.

Kane glanced up as if sensing her presence. He turned off the machine and removed the glasses he'd had on to protect his eyes. "I wasn't sure you were going to come."

"You didn't give me much choice." Her eyes darted around the back porch as she grasped for a calm she couldn't quite reach. "I don't want to do this here. Can you step out for lunch?"

He grunted. "You're the boss." He took off his hard hat, then ran his hand over his beard, knocking off the tiny bits of wood settled there.

Leave it to Kane to make it sound like an insult. "I assume you don't want to share our personal history with the crew any more than I do." Though judging by the way Brick looked at her, he already had some idea. "I passed a Panera on the way here."

He rolled his eyes.

"Would you rather the Waffle House?" she huffed. "It doesn't matter where we go, Kane."

"Panera's fine," he growled. Giving her his back, he stalked around the side of the house. By the time

144

she made it back out front, he and his bike were gone.

I guess I'm meeting him there.

It was probably for the best they weren't riding together anyway. Kane would no doubt take up all the air in the car—and she absolutely was not riding on the back of his motorcycle.

It was a moot point anyway. The Panera was only a few miles away, and his bike was outside when she arrived. The packed lot and the fight for a parking spot only added to her growing tension. She tried to shake it off as she strode inside.

The Ice Queen mask wouldn't work for this, but maybe something like it. Something brisk, but honest. He deserved whatever honesty she could give. She simply needed to control her rioting emotions.

Kane waited at a corner booth, his jaw clenched and fingers drumming on the table. There were two drinks in front of him.

She took the opposite seat and slid Joshua's birth certificate toward his hand.

He picked it up and scanned it quickly, gripping the paper tightly enough to wrinkle the sides before he put it back down. "This could be doctored."

She reached into her satchel and dug out a packet of family photos. Christmas pictures showing Mike and Charlie, smiling next to Mom with her growing belly. Then Mom by herself in her last trimester. One of Charlie on his knees, kissing her stomach. There were about a dozen in all.

Kane flipped through them, dispassionately at first, his face slowly morphing into a sad acceptance. "You're not in any of these pictures."

"No. I was too busy feeling sorry for myself to visit her." She rubbed at the tension in her forehead. "Too wrapped up in my own misery to let myself be around anyone happy." She squeezed her eyes shut to block out his stunned expression. "I wasted so much time."

His hand touched hers on the table, and her eyes flew open. Just as quickly, his touch disappeared, but her skin tingled where the rough pads of his fingers had been.

She swallowed. "There was ice on the pavement. Crazy for February around here, but there it was. Charlie and Mom spun off the road and hit a tree." She reached for the numbness, the dead emptiness that kept her going when the hurt threatened to consume her. "They had to cut Josh out of her body. He was the only one who survived."

This time when Kane took her hand, he held it with both of his. It stole her breath.

She forced in a gulp of air and kept talking. "It made sense for Mike and Cindy to take him. They were getting married anyway, and I was such a fucking disaster, I could barely dress myself, much less take care of a baby." Her chest knotted with his hands around hers. So much for staying numb.

Such a small thing, his touch, but it shook her to the foundation.

With her other hand, she pushed forward her final piece of evidence. A laminated clipping of her mother's obituary. She couldn't remember who gave it to her, but she'd never had the heart to get rid of it. "It says right there, *survived by her three*

146

children, Michael, Amanda, and Joshua. I'm sure you could find another copy somewhere if you still don't believe me."

His slow blink and barely there nod projected patience. Comfort. It almost hurt more than the hate he'd radiated when she walked through the door. Hate was easier. In hate, there was no hope, and hope was the cruelest lie that ever existed.

"I believe you." With his gravelly voice and simple words, everyone else in the restaurant fell away. Kane was the center of the universe. His warm hands and the look on his face she hadn't seen in years. The look that said *I see you.*

You matter.

This is real.

It didn't make a difference how many years had passed or whether his looks had changed. Behind the long hair—beneath the beard and the tiny lines on his face he didn't have before—she recognized the man who set the bar for every poor bastard who came into her life or her bed after he left it. No one else had ever come close.

No one else ever would.

"I'm sorry I accused you." He squeezed her hand.

Her small laugh rang hollow as she pulled away. She couldn't think straight while he was touching her, and she needed to keep her wits. Unwrapping the straw next to the drink in front of her, she used it to stir the ice in the light brown liquid.

An Arnold Palmer. She hadn't had one in years. The iced tea-lemonade mix used to be her favorite.

"You don't owe me an apology, Kane. We both

JEN DAVIS

know it." She sipped at the sweet and tart drink, then forced her gaze back to his face. "I'm the one who's sorry. I'm sorry I was so awful you could believe me capable of keeping a child from you. I'm sorry I hurt you. And I'm sorry I couldn't tell you the truth then, and I still can't tell you now."

His eyes widened, and she knew instantly she'd said too much.

She shot to her feet. "You deserved better thirteen years ago, and you deserve better than how you're living now. It's not too late to have the life you wanted." Forcing herself to look away from those soulful brown eyes, she turned and approached the door.

She was almost through the crowd when his strangled voice carried to her ears. "The only life I ever wanted was one I could live with you."

Gritting her teeth, she fought the overwhelming urge to look back and kept moving out of the restaurant into the cold December sunlight. Nothing had changed. Her father's threat still hung over her like a scythe. Only now, the small flame of hope she'd been nursing inside her was a fire she wasn't sure she could ever put out.

***

Kane

Hours after his conversation with Mandy, Kane's head still reeled. It was crazy stupid to let his attention drift from the job in front of him, but his body still fucking hummed from the touch of her

148

skin and the sincerity of her words. It had been the first real exchange they'd had in more than a decade.

Cue Ball dug his heel into the top of Kane's foot.

The steel-toed boots protected him from most hazards, but Cue was a big man, and his weight was tough to ignore…which was probably the point.

He forced himself to focus on the exchange at hand. Cue Ball was holding court with two teenaged boys, one with light brown skin, the other slightly darker. Both wore T-shirts and jeans sagging halfway off their asses. They were recruits to help push the club's new products.

"Twenty bucks for a rock, boys. I'm giving you a dozen to start out with." Cue dropped a brown lunch bag into the hand of the taller teenager. He'd rolled down the top, creating a makeshift handle. "I know where you live." He leaned into the boy's face. "This is a trial run. Don't even think about trying to fuck me, got it?"

Kane had to give the kid credit. He didn't so much as flinch at Cue Ball's threat. "Yeah. I got you." Bag gripped in his hand, the teen led his friend back to the two bicycles leaning against the park bench.

The pink cast of dusk made the nearly empty field look a little less than the neglected lot it was. By day, it was easier to spot the mountain of cigarette butts next to the overflowing trash can or the rust creeping over the rickety see-saw. But among the warm colors of the diminishing light, the park looked almost inviting.

If only it were enough to let him forget the

reason they were here. It took everything he had not to drag his buddy out of here, to plead again for the club to reconsider. But the MC worked a certain way. After a vote, you were either with them or against them. At best, fighting the tide would mean a beating; at worst, excommunication for life.

"Well, look here, Cole. It seems we've got some race traitors on our hands."

Shit.

He cringed against the unmistakable drawl of David Bennett, VP of the Christian Soldiers MC. The group wasn't made of any real Christians or soldiers he was aware of. They were basically a bunch of white supremacist bullies who liked to pump themselves up by tearing everyone else down.

He wasn't in the mood for their particular brand of bullshit. "What the fuck are you doing here, Benny? Why don't you hit the mall? I hear JC Penney has some white sheets on sale."

The man's face tightened with the nickname Kane insisted on using. With his sharp features, blond hair and blue eyes, Bennett would have almost been pretty if he didn't have a perpetual snarl on his face. He was living proof someone could have the face of an angel and still be a cesspool of rot inside.

"One day you and I are going to have a reckoning over your smart mouth, Hale." Another blond-haired, blue-eyed goon stepped up behind him.

Kane rolled his eyes as Cue Ball took a position at his six. "I don't have time for this. Seriously. What are you doing here?"

Bennett flexed his jaw. "I heard the Skulls were taking over the wetback's drug operation out here."

Kane shrugged. Even if he hated what he was doing, he couldn't disrespect the club by making it public.

The other man lifted his own shoulder in return. "Doesn't matter to me if these thugs kill themselves with pharmaceuticals."

"But?"

"But you're working with a black supplier, employing black pushers. My men were ready to work this neighborhood with an Aryan supplier, putting cash in the hands of our own kind." Bennett's voice rose like a preacher on a pulpit.

He waved it off. "You know I don't care about all your racist shit. The only hands I care about putting cash in are my own. This is business, Benny, plain and simple."

"Don't be naïve. With Sucre gone, this was finally our chance to—"

"I don't give a good goddamn about your race war shit. Save your breath. This is about bankrolling my club. No more, no less."

Bennett took a step forward, and Cue growled. The Soldiers' VP froze, then purposely loosened his posture. He may have been trying to look unfazed, but he was failing spectacularly. "We have a very important man in our corner. You don't want to get on his bad side."

This time, Kane stepped forward. He was so close to Bennett's face, he could smell the stale cigarettes on his breath. "You don't want to be on *my* bad side, Benny. Why don't you take your

White Power bullshit and get the fuck out of my business? There are plenty of other places you can sell your product." He smiled. "Now get off of my lawn."

Bennett narrowed his eyes, but he took a step back. Then he turned and walked with his buddy back to the bikes they'd left at the curb.

Cue Ball ran a hand over his bald head. "You sure that was a good idea, brother? No real reason to make problems with the Soldiers."

What? "They came here to make problems with *us*. You think I should let David Bennett tell us how to do business?"

"I guess not," Cue mumbled. He took a breath, then shook off whatever was bothering him. "We'd better get going. Scott's got a surprise for us cooking over at the clubhouse."

He nodded. It was getting dark anyway. But something told him his brother's surprise was going to be about as fun as the meeting with Benny had been.

***

The prospect greeted Kane at the front door by handing him a surgical mask.

"What the hell is this?" He held it up between his fingers.

"Just put it on, KC." His mother beckoned him inside. "Don't want you breathing in any of the fumes." Mama V had her own mask secured tightly at the back of her teased blond head.

With a suspicious lift of his eyebrow, he did as

his mother instructed. "What's going on?"

The skin around her eyes crinkled, and she grabbed his arm, pulling him back toward the kitchen. "SP has everybody hard at work."

The kitchen table and counters were crowded with empty Coke bottles, coffee filters, duct tape, and a whole bunch of other shit. None of it registered until he caught sight of the tall stack of Sudafed in front of one of his brothers. Owen was punching the red pills out of the foil into a big plastic bowl.

"Are you kidding me right now?"

The mask couldn't hide Scott's wide grin. "What do you think, brother? We're really in business now."

"What do I think?" A pulse beat at his temple. "You set up a fucking *meth lab* in our clubhouse? What the fuck is wrong with you, man?"

Scott scowled. "Hey, what's your problem?"

He bit his tongue so hard he tasted blood. "In the chapel."

His brother followed him, pulling down his mask as they entered the private space. "You need to pull the stick out of your ass right now, K. Can't you let me have the win here?"

He whirled to face Scott, tugging his own mask down. "The win? This isn't about you getting credit for something. You set up a meth lab in our clubhouse!"

"It's not gonna make itself," his brother huffed. "Why is it you have to shit on every idea I have lately? We've been aces together for years, man. Best bros. Now, it's like we've gone back in time.

Like before you patched in. You thought you were so fucking special then, too good to do what the rest of us were doing. Fancy girl, fancy job, fancy college. Where did it get you? The exact same place as me. So maybe you should get over yourself."

His jaw dropped at the venom in his brother's voice. Scott had never been a fan of his plan to go white collar, but he'd never lashed out like this before. Except when it concerned Mandy, he was always pretty happy and affable. And yeah, they *were* best bros. He loved his brother, and Scott proved time and again over the years, there was nothing he wouldn't do for Kane.

He tried being reasonable. "This has nothing to do with me. It's common sense, Scott. A meth lab at the clubhouse puts us all in danger. First of all, those chemicals seep into the walls. I don't know about you, but I don't want to wear a mask in here forever. And we're assuming no one accidentally blows the place up first." He dropped into one of the chairs. Elbows on the table, he rubbed at his temples. "Even if we don't all get sick or die, all it takes is one fucking raid, and there is no explaining this shit away. We're all going to jail."

"Stop being such a pussy. We take risks all the time. I don't see you having a cow over the guns we run. Cops pull us over on one of those deliveries, we're looking at jail, too. None of our business is legitimate. We're a motorcycle club, not a Girl Scout troop." Scott leaned his back against the wall, one thumb in his jeans' pocket. "We're in the drug business, brother, whether you like it or not. Meth means cash. The shit is cheap and easy to make, and once we start selling it, we'll be making money hand over fist."

"This is a mistake, Scott." Why couldn't he see it?

"You've already made this argument and lost." Scott stuck a cigarette in his mouth but didn't light it. "We're doing this my way, little brother. You better get on board, because this train is leaving with or without you."

Scott put a hand on his shoulder and squeezed. The hardness drained from his face, leaving him with a hopeful expression. "I'd rather have you with me, man." Letting him go, Scott left the room.

He rubbed the same ache at his temple again. His brother wanted his approval. That much was obvious. How many times had he felt the same way? But this was a mistake, no matter how he looked at it.

What would Mandy think if she could see him now? Not only part of the MC. Not only running guns but pushing drugs. Hell, *cooking* the shit.

As much as it had killed him to watch her walk away from him at the restaurant, maybe it was better this way. At least now, he wouldn't know the shame, the look in her eyes, when she saw how far he'd fallen.

CHAPTER ELEVEN

Amanda

Amanda took a few minutes to collect herself before getting out of the car and walking the sidewalk to her father's front door. She didn't want to see him. The very idea of looking at his face made her stomach turn.

I can't have you upsetting the balance right now, he'd said.

She hadn't seen him since he ordered her to keep herself available for Nathan almost two weeks ago. She hadn't seen Nathan either, which was a blessing since the bodyguard her father had promised never materialized. Technically, she hadn't turned down any dates with the bastard because she hadn't taken any of his calls. Maybe he'd lose interest.

And maybe the earth will open up and swallow my car whole.

Not likely.

Nathan Shaw liked to win, and right now she was the prize.

She cursed her father for what felt like the thousandth time, though the hard truth was it wasn't only his fault. No one had forced her to accept his deal. No one had forced her to accept Nathan's attention. Or to leave Kane in his hospital bed years ago.

No. Those were her sins. The ones she stayed up at night thinking about. Why it was damn hard to look at herself in the mirror. Why she felt so fucking worthless sometimes, the next horrible thing someone asked of her didn't seem beneath her at all.

Enough feeling sorry for myself.

She needed the other twenty-five thousand her father had promised her, and she needed it now. Jared Berringer wasn't a man to rest on his laurels. She would be ready to start work the minute he made the call.

Which meant start-up costs had to be in place.

Steeling herself for whatever her father would throw at her next, she approached the front porch only to run into the groundskeeper, Raul, who was pressure washing the pavement.

He stopped the spray and tipped his hat. "You may want to go in through the back, ma'am. Don't want to ruin your nice shoes."

Though the advice came too late to keep her pumps completely dry, she turned, then rounded the house to enter through the French doors into the sunroom. There, she slipped her shoes off her feet and carried them into the house, in search of a hand towel to wipe off the patent leather.

The linen closet was only a few steps down the

hall.

What're a couple more minutes? It's not like Dad is expecting me anyway.

Frankly, she'd been rather surprised when she'd gone to his office, and his assistant had told her he was working from home for the day. Her father was never home during business hours on a Thursday, or any other weekday, come to think of it.

She padded in her bare feet toward the towels, trying to remember if her dad had ever worked from home in her life.

"—can't possibly stand for this."

She froze a few steps away from her father's office. The man's voice wasn't familiar, but it was a rare occasion to hear anyone talk to her dad in such a tone. Generally, he surrounded himself with smooth-talking politicians like himself, servants, or sycophants. This man sounded...angry.

"I know how you feel about the Skulls. It's a damn cautionary tale about getting on your bad side. Imagine our surprise you would allow this to happen."

The Skulls? Why was someone talking to her father about Kane's biker gang?

"To be frank, Mr. Bennett, I had no idea this was going on," her father said. "I pride myself on having my finger on the pulse of what's happening in this community. Though I was aware of Mr. de la Cruz's unexplained absence, I didn't realize someone had stepped in to fill the void so soon."

De la Cruz? The drug dealer?

"The darks are always gonna need their fix. It's a fact of life. But *we* should be the ones in charge of distribution; *we* should be the ones who profit from their weakness."

She ground her teeth at the man's racist rant.

"Why come to me? What do I get out of your success?" Her father gave words to the questions rioting in her head.

"Because nothing happens in this city without your blessing. If you don't want the Skulls taking over the drug line, you've got the connections to take them down. And here's the thing, Mr. Mayor. Taking them down is win-win for you. Not only do you get to stick it to the Hales, but you guarantee a stake in our business. One percent of our profits will go directly into your campaign fund. A penny of every dollar we'll make. You get *money* out of it...and satisfaction."

Silence greeted the man's offer. She let out a wavering breath. The man had underestimated her father. He wouldn't—

"Five percent. Direct deposit into the campaign fund."

"Done."

She braced her hand on the wall, her head swimming as her father wheeled and dealed in the next room.

"Give me a few days to get everything in place, and Mr. Bennett, don't call me; I'll call you. I'm sure you understand why discretion in this matter is vital."

She took two steps backward, then whirled and rushed back down the hall to the kitchen. Her thoughts spun out of control. Kane's club was dealing drugs? Was he? If her father had it out for him, it didn't really matter. He'd go down one way or another. Unless she warned him.

Even as her dad kept Kane out of jail all those years ago, in his own way, he'd stolen Kane's future. Their future. She'd be damned if she let him do any more damage.

Slipping her shoes back on, she rushed back around the house but froze when she caught a glimpse of Raul lugging the pressure washer back to his pick-up.

She couldn't leave without seeing her father. Someone would mention the fact she'd been here; she hadn't exactly been stealthy.

Her hand shook as she pulled her phone from her purse and pulled up her father's contact. He answered on the first ring.

"Now is not a good time, Amanda." He didn't even bother to say hello.

"I'm here at the house, Dad. Eddie said you'd gone home. Are you sick?" Her voice didn't shake once. "Raul's been working on the porch; I'm coming around back, okay?" Slowly, she started retracing her steps.

"No. There's no need. You and I can catch up later. Maybe have lunch tomorrow."

She paused. "It really can't wait. Dad, I need to talk to you about the money—"

"I'll wire it to your account before close of business," he said sharply. "Now if you'll excuse me, I'm really not feeling well."

He disconnected before she could say another word.

If he was sending the money, it was one less

thing to worry about, but she still needed to tell Kane what she'd heard. And she needed to do it fast.

***

Kane

Brick held up the closet door with hinges hovering over the holes in the frame while Kane knelt down and screwed them in place. Work on the house was moving much faster with a five-man crew. Brick's strength and construction know-how helped him do the work of two guys, and Cy's Army buddy was slowly getting up to speed.

He was glad to have the distraction of work. He was plagued by memories of holding Mandy's hand at the restaurant, the need in her eyes. He'd shake his thoughts away only to replace them with questions about how he could fix the club and save his brothers from disaster. No answers had presented themselves.

He grunted as he leaned into the drill. "Any word when Will's coming back to work?" If anyone would have the skinny, it would be Brick. His fiancé was Will's sister, after all.

Brick's deep voice carried over the electronic whir in his ears. "Probably the first of the new year. The doctors say he's on track, but the bullet collapsed his lung. He was a lot worse off than I was." Brick seemed to be no worse for wear after the shot he took to the shoulder. Meanwhile, the guy who pulled the trigger—one of Sucre's thugs—

was resting permanently, six feet under.

It was no loss. From what he understood, Tre Lowry had been every bit the stain on humanity his boss had been. With the bottom hinge secure, he stood to screw in the top. "Have you spent any time with the new guy?"

"Evan?" Brick shook his head. "Poor dude is really fucked up. Cy says an IED caused all those burns. Fucking brutal."

Brutal barely scratched the surface. Cy's friend had thick, ropey scars along the left side of his body. They covered his jawline and his neck as well as the top of his left hand. It was hard to tell where else the burns extended beneath his clothes.

He had never heard Evan speak. It wasn't clear if the guy *couldn't* talk or if he just chose not to. Neither would surprise him. Though to be fair, he hadn't worked with the man very much. Cy and Matt were showing him the ropes, which had to be interesting since none of the men were what anyone would call talkers.

"How's it coming, you guys?"

Speaking of talkers.

Robby grinned as he hugged his ever-present clipboard to his chest.

Brick gave his arm a gentle tap over the long-sleeved Oxford. "Almost finished with the doors. We only have one left. Master closet." He gestured at the remaining door, leaning against the wall.

Robby canted his head, his brown bangs falling into his eyes. "Xander says we need to be done here before the end of the month so we can get started on the new development. You think we're gonna make it?"

"No sweat." Brick lifted one shoulder. "All the bones are in place. Cabinet guys are coming tomorrow. Electricians and plumbers are putting in their fixtures at the beginning of next week. We'll be done by Christmas."

Robby bounced on the balls of his feet. "You'll be in your new house by then, right?"

"Yep. We close next week. Which reminds me, Olivia wanted me to invite all of you to the new place to have Christmas dinner with us. She—we—want—" He squeezed his eyes shut for a moment, then shook his head ruefully. "We want to celebrate with our family."

Kane warmed at Brick's reluctant admission. Celebrating Christmas with family would be a first for him too.

Robby was out-and-out beaming. "Of course, we'll be there, right Kane?"

"Sure, kid." He chuckled.

Brick shot Robby a sly look. "Why don't you go extend the invitation to Matt and the other guys?"

Robby's cheeks pinked, but he wasted no time bounding out the door in search of the object of his affection.

"You know Matt's going to figure it out someday, and when he rejects your boy, it's going to break his heart." Robby was really growing on him, and he found the idea of his heartbreak…unsettling.

Brick shrugged. "We can't help who we fall for, man. You know as well as I do."

"You can shove your fortune cookie wisdom

right up your ass." He grimaced at the knowing expression on Brick's face.

"What?" his friend asked innocently. "I can't help it if you can relate to the idea of carrying a torch for someone. Even when it's a bad idea." Brick rubbed at his jaw thoughtfully. "On a totally unrelated note, have you seen Amanda Griffin around lately?'

"Fuck you, brother." There was no heat in his curse, only grim acceptance. Brick saw right through his protests about Mandy, but it seemed everyone else did too. "Does everybody know?"

Taking a sip of the Gatorade he had pulled from the ice chest near the wall, Brick looked up at the ceiling, clearly weighing his words. He swallowed, then sighed. "Yeah. But nobody is judging you about it. We've all got soft spots that hurt when you poke 'em. She's yours. No shame there."

Kane's phone buzzed, saving him from having to find an answer.

"Speak of the devil," he murmured.

A text lit his screen.

I need to talk to you. It's important. Meet me at my apartment.
-A

No address, but then again, he knew exactly where she lived. He knew what kind of car she drove. What men she attended events with, splashed across the online society pages. Not that he ever Googled her.

He shoved his phone back in his pocket. "I've

got to go. You cool to finish up here?"

"Yeah. No problem." Brick grabbed his arm, then let it go. "You call me if you need anything."

He was out the door and on his bike before he realized he hadn't even answered his friend. Mandy called, he came running. She was his soft-spot all right.

His first love. His *only* love.

The only woman who made his heart race, his blood boil.

Even after all these years, he still treasured the memories of every kiss, every touch, and the promise of a future they never ended up having.

***

13 years ago

July

Kane flitted a nervous glance around the room he'd rented at the Hampton Inn. It was nicer than anywhere he'd ever slept before, and he'd skipped lunch every day for a month to save up the money to pay for it.

No doubt Mandy had slept in better places. Hell, her room at her dad's house was probably classier than this, but deep down he knew she wouldn't care. She'd never judged him for how much money he had or what he could spend on her. Still, he wanted to give her the best of everything. She deserved all the finest things, and one day, when he was a successful investment banker, he'd give them all to her.

Tonight, he'd have to settle for the king-sized bed he had covered in rose petals, soft music from a playlist on his iPod, and a bottle of white zinfandel. He didn't know anything about wine, but the lady at the store had told him it was good.

"Can I open my eyes now?" Mandy squeezed his hand, pulling him back into the moment.

He leaned down and brushed his lips over hers, breathing in the subtle smell of lavender. She hummed softly against him.

Taking a step back, he moved out of her line of sight. "Yes."

Her eyes flew open, and she took in the scene. She blinked rapidly.

Dread pooled in his stomach.

Had he read her wrong? Was it too soon?

Obviously, she had to have some idea where they were when he'd led her through the lobby and into the elevator, even with her eyes closed, but still, maybe his attempts at a romantic set-up were a bust. "We don't have to do anything you don't want to do, sweetheart. I would be happy to just spend the night with you in my arms." The sad thing was, he meant every word.

"Are you kidding? This is perfect. I love it." She bit her bottom lip. "Did you bring—"

"Condoms?" He grinned. "Two boxes."

Her eyebrows shot up. "My, aren't we ambitious? What happened to just spending the night with me in your arms?"

His smile dimmed. "Of course. I mean—"

Mandy's laugh was husky as she closed the

distance between them. "I'm teasing you." She kissed his throat, right above the neckline of his T-shirt, and he shivered beneath the soft press of her lips. "I want to make love with you." Her hands traveled up the outside of his arms. "I've been thinking about it for weeks."

With one kiss and a feather-light touch, she already had his dick standing at full attention. "Weeks?" he croaked.

"Mm-hmm." Her delicate hands slid over his shoulders, then her fingers moved down to trace his collarbone. "I want to see you." She pulled on his shirt. "Take this off."

Like a randy schoolboy, he couldn't move fast enough. He scrambled to pull his T-shirt over his head. His nipples pebbled in the chilled air-conditioned room.

Mandy's fingers moved straight to them, gliding over their peaks in small, circular movements. Her eyes flashed as she watched her hands glide down his torso, over the trail of hair beneath his navel, to the buckle of his belt.

"I want to see everything," she whispered. Her gaze flashed up to his.

Was she asking permission?

He gave it to her with a quick jerk of his head.

His Mandy didn't waste one second. She had his belt unbuckled and his fly open in a heartbeat. Tugging his pants down to his thighs, she freed his erection, and it strained to get closer to her.

She tilted her head as she surveyed his eager cock. "I'm not sure it's going to fit."

Mandy was always so self-confident, so poised

and perfect, it was easy to forget she was a virgin. No, not to forget her virginity, but to forget she might be nervous or unsure. God knew, if she ever was, she never showed it.

She stepped toward him, taking his shaft in her hands. "I've dreamed about it. What it would be like to feel you inside me." She put her lips against his ear. "I ordered a dildo online."

His dick jumped, and suddenly his mind was filled with the filthiest images imaginable of her pleasuring herself with his name on her lips.

"It's supposed to look like the real thing." Her tongue grazed his lobe; her breath was hot and damp. "But it's not like yours. You feel different in my hands." She squeezed him. "Show me how different you feel between my legs."

"You play dirty," he growled, then kicked off his shoes and tossed the rest of his clothing onto the floor. He palmed her between her legs and squeezed over the thick denim of her jeans.

She closed her eyes long enough to moan softly.

"You like it, huh?" He rubbed roughly over her pussy, and her breath shuddered. She looked like a fucking goddess with her eyes glazed and mouth slightly open in pleasure.

If he didn't get inside her soon, he was going to come right here in front of the mini-fridge and microwave.

He tore at the button of her jeans, and she scrambled to help him get her undressed. He needed her too much to have any finesse.

Thank God, she seemed every bit as hungry for him.

She lunged toward him, their mouths crashing together, tongues sliding over each other in frantic motion. They'd kissed dozens of times in the three months they'd been together, but this was different. This kiss consumed him.

His arms around her waist pulled her closer; the feel of her skin against his electrified him. It was everything, and still not enough. Fueled by adrenaline and need, he lifted her up, and she wrapped her legs around him. Their mouths still locked together, he carried her the short distance to the bed and lowered her body to the soft petals he'd scattered with care.

The last thing he wanted to do was to pull back, but he hadn't seen her yet. Not really. And goddamn, she was a revelation.

Her porcelain skin...her tight peach nipples...and the smooth, perfect surface of bare skin between her legs. His mouth watered.

"Kane," she whispered. "Please."

He wanted to do everything. Touch her everywhere. He didn't even know where to begin.

She rubbed her thighs together restlessly.

Never mind. He knew exactly where to begin.

"You're beautiful," he said hoarsely. Climbing onto the bed, he pulled those perfect, pale thighs apart and zeroed in straight to the place where he wanted to be the most.

She tried to bring her knees together, but he wouldn't be denied. He pulled them apart again and brought his mouth to the heart of her sex. The scent of her arousal intoxicated him. He flattened his tongue and swept it up between her glistening pink lips.

She squirmed beneath him, but he slid his arms under her thighs and clamped his hands over her hips to keep her still. And open to him.

He had to taste more of her. He licked over her slit again. And again. Each time, he drove his tongue deeper. Her taste consumed him as she grew wetter against his mouth. One of his hands released her hip to tease at her opening.

Mandy lifted her hips in a wordless plea, and he gave her what she wanted. He plunged his middle finger inside of her as his tongue swirled her clit.

She moaned, and it only pushed him harder. A second finger joined the first, and as he fucked her with his hand, she met every thrust with a swivel of her hips. He replaced his tongue with the flat of his thumb and let her ride out her own pleasure until he felt her walls pulsing beneath his hand.

Heart pounding, he grabbed one of the foil packets he'd stocked on the nightstand and ripped it open. He rolled on the condom and was inside her so fast, her pussy was still contracting around him. "Fuck," he gritted out. Nothing had ever felt so good.

He tried to move slowly. He really did, but she was so wet and hot, and her hands gripped his ass, urging him to drive into her faster. Harder.

When the orgasm finally crashed over him, an electric current of pleasure shot through his body. He went rigid. His toes fucking curled, and it was the most singularly perfect moment of his entire life.

Mandy released the hold she had on his cheeks,

and he rolled to his back, keeping her in the cage of his arms.

Only then did his actions catch up with him. He'd intended to take things slowly. To take her virginity gently and with care. He was the worst kind of asshole.

He ran his hand over her beautiful red hair. "Are you okay? Was I too rough?"

She sniffed.

Shit. Was she crying?

She sniffed again, and it turned into a giggle.

Wait. Was she—"Are you laughing?"

Her giggles gave way to full-on laughter.

He sat up. "Are you seriously laughing at me right now?"

"No." She stopped laughing, but a wide smile still lit her face as she faced him. "I'm laughing because I'm happy." Her soft, smooth hand caressed his cheek. "I'm laughing because this was perfect. *You* are perfect."

She leaned toward him, touching her forehead to his. "I'm happy, Kane. And I love you."

CHAPTER TWELVE

Kane

Mandy's condo was part of a five-story building on the very edge of downtown. The exterior was rust colored on the bottom floor, but the color yielded to a shade more like sand above the second level. At least half of the façade was glass, though.

Mandy always did like a sunny day. She probably kept the shades open all the time.

How many times had he looked at her to find her eyes closed, head tilted back, absorbing the sunlight? But those images were from another life. Another version of her, which had probably been dead for years, if it had ever really existed in the first place.

He shut down the memories of a fall afternoon at the corn maze where they'd intentionally gotten lost for hours. The Mandy with the bright eyes and open heart wasn't the one who had summoned him here.

The doorman shot him an appraising look, and Kane steeled himself for an argument. Even a child could see he didn't belong in a place like this.

"Mr. Hale?" the man asked smoothly, then opened the door without waiting for an answer.

He blinked, standing frozen for a moment before stepping over the threshold. The buttoned-up older man escorted him to the elevator and waved an electronic keycard over a sensor at the elevator. The doors parted immediately.

"Fourth floor," the doorman said solemnly. "Second door to your right, sir."

What the hell? Was he supposed to tip this guy? His experience with doormen was admittedly limited.

When the man gestured him into the lift with a blank expression on his face, he took it as an answer and stepped inside. As the doors closed in front of him, the shiny metal reflected his image back to him. Strands of his dark hair had escaped his low ponytail and fell into his face. His beard was getting long, hanging at least an inch or two below his chin; it was scraggly, in no way shaped, and it did nothing to mask the shiny scar bisecting his left cheek.

He diverted his eyes, knowing exactly what others would see. Shitkickers on his feet, jeans, and T-shirt covered by an unbuttoned heavy flannel, the sleeves rolled to his elbow to reveal a portion of the tattoos climbing both arms.

Mandy had obviously warned the doorman, or the poor old bastard would have probably had a heart attack when he approached the building. It was a reaction he was used to, at least among civilized folks.

A dainty chime sounded when he reached Mandy's floor. The doors opened soundlessly to reveal a relatively short hallway with hardwood floors. There were only three doors on either side. Smooth beige walls filled the space between them.

The pound of his pulse picked up as he covered the short distance to Mandy's space. Ignoring the small, gold knocker, he rapped his knuckles against the wood.

A hundred times he'd fantasized about being here, his imagination filling in the blanks of her life. After today, he'd never have to wonder what her private space was like. When he closed his eyes and his traitorous mind conjured her drifting to sleep on the sofa or the satisfied smile she made with the first sip of her morning coffee, he'd picture her in this place, in her real home. Not the hazy construct his mind had cobbled together.

His breathing stopped when she opened the door. There was no sign of the sharp business clothes she normally wore. No high heels or closed expression. Instead, she was the Mandy of his past. Soft T-shirt and jeans. Bare face. Bare feet.

She reached out, grabbed his hand, and pulled him inside.

From the corner of his eye, he noted an immaculate living space in shades of cream with a lot of glass, but his curiosity about her home paled with Mandy right in front of him.

The door swung shut behind him with a gentle snick, and before he knew it, he was sitting on the loveseat, Mandy only inches away. His hand was still in hers.

He was in Bizzaro World. "What am I doing here?" A hundred scenarios shuffled through his head. Had Mike taken a turn? Was something happening with the company? Did she—miss him?

Her eyes flicked away from his face to stare at their joined hands. She didn't let go. "You need to watch your back. Whatever your club is doing right now, it's made you a target."

The club? The Skulls had nothing to do with her; she'd made it clear a long time ago it was how she wanted it. He tugged his hand away and immediately wished he hadn't. "What do you know about my club?"

Her gaze lingered a moment on her empty hand, then clenched her fingers into a fist. Her green eyes sharpened when they locked with his. "I know you're turning into drug dealers." Her nose wrinkled.

Shame tickled his gut, as he knew it would, but he hardened himself against it. What business was it of hers? She had all the money she'd ever need. *She* never had to worry about making her rent. Her father was the mayor for fuck's sake.

The surge of righteous anger was almost enough for him to ignore he had wanted nothing to do with the plan to move in on Sucre's turf in the first place. "Your point?" he ground out.

If she noticed his ire, she didn't let on. "Do you know a guy named Bennett?"

He stilled. "*David* Bennett?"

She shrugged. "I don't know. I only heard his last name."

"Blond guy? Always has on a Christian Soldiers

cut?"

Mandy waved her hand dismissively. "I didn't see him. But listen, whoever this guy is, he's gunning for you."

There was no scenario he could imagine where David Bennett should be in Mandy's orbit.

"He is working with my father." She shuddered and reached for a half-filled wine glass on the glass coffee table in front of them. The burgundy liquid disappeared in two gulps. "I heard them talking at the house today."

Her knuckles turned white as she squeezed the stem of the glass. Gently, he pried it from her hand and set it on the table.

She took a deep breath. "He said a bunch of racist shit, but the bottom line is Bennett wants his club to take over for Sucre de la Cruz."

No surprise there, but…"What do his lowlife ambitions have to do with your father?"

Swiping the glass from the table, she stood and carried it to the adjoining open concept kitchen area where a wine bottle sat on a shiny dark countertop. She poured almost to the brim, then promptly drained half of it into her mouth. "Bennett offered my dad a percentage to help clear the way for him."

His stomach clenched. "Your father said yes."

Mandy pursed her lips. "I don't know why I'm surprised, but yeah. He didn't say what he was planning, but whatever it is will happen in the next few days." Draining the rest of her glass, she left it on the counter and returned to her spot on the loveseat. "I guess I'm not helping very much."

He hated the tightness around her eyes, the strain

in her voice. His protective instincts now in the driver's seat, he pushed his concerns about her father's threat to the back of his mind. "You are. At least I know we need to be on guard."

"I'm sorry," she murmured, rubbing at her right temple. "My family has brought you nothing but grief."

Even though her words were pretty damn close to the truth, he couldn't let them stand unchallenged. "It wasn't all bad." The memories rose, flooding him with images of her flushed cheeks as she rode him and her lips swollen from his kisses. Her laughter still echoed in his ears; the silky softness of her bare skin tingled on his fingertips. No matter how many years passed, it was all still there, right beneath the surface.

Her tongue darted out, wetting her bottom lip. There was nothing hard in her expression, only a softness he hadn't seen in years. It was the same look she'd given him when he used to tell her about how he'd grown up. None of the earth-shattering stuff. Just the uncelebrated birthdays or the TV dinners he had to cook himself. Things like that. He'd tried to tell her it wasn't so bad. He liked frozen nuggets fine. But it was never fine with her. She'd tell him how she loved him and how he deserved better, and somehow, she was the one who hurt over things he chalked up to reality.

It always ended with him kissing her, trying to replace her sadness with something else. Showing her he was happy and whole in her arms. Watching the sorrow in her eyes give way to pleasure untangled knots inside him he'd never realized were there.

He wanted to do it now. He needed to.

Honestly, he'd never stopped. She'd been the only force in the world capable of keeping them apart. Anything else was a lie he told himself so he could live with her decision.

Without even thinking, he reached out and tucked a lock of red hair behind her ear. Her eyes widened, but she didn't pull back.

He palmed the back of her head right where it met her neck and pulled her toward him at the same time he leaned toward her. Making his movements slow and deliberate, he gave her every opportunity to stop him. Her absolute stillness told him everything he needed to know. He kept his eyes locked with hers until the moment their lips touched, then his lids squeezed shut, and his other senses took over.

Traces of wine teased him as his mouth moved over hers, and he breathed in her familiar scent, the lavender from her favorite soap. The one from Before. It was like coming home.

His left hand glided up her arm, and she shuddered beneath him. Then she wrested control of the kiss, taking it deeper. The sharp bite of the zinfandel bloomed stronger as he slid his tongue against hers.

Crushing Mandy against him, his heart sang with the rightness of having her in his arms again. It was as if the past thirteen years had never happened. All those times he'd tried to convince himself it hadn't been as good as he remembered, there had been a *reason* he hadn't been able to let go.

Nothing had changed in all these years.

She was everything. The sun in the sky. The air he breathed.

Her arms were around his neck, and she moaned softly against him. Every cell in his body screamed to feel her skin-to-skin—to strip her bare and plunge his aching hard-on into her wet warmth.

It could be like it was. She could be mine again. We could go back and get it right this time.

Only, he had no idea where it had gone wrong before.

Digging deep for every drop of self-control he had, he broke the kiss and rested his forehead against hers. "You're killing me, Mandy."

She choked back a small sob, sending him on instant alert. He pulled back to see her face, which she immediately buried in her hands.

"What's wrong?" His heart raced. "Did I—"

Her hands dropped to her lap, revealing green eyes shining a little too bright. "You didn't do anything wrong. I—nobody's called me that in a really long time."

He doubted it was the name so much as the possibility she was drowning as much as he was right now, though he could be wrong. She'd never stopped being Mandy in his mind, but he couldn't remember the last time he said it to her face.

A lock of hair fell over her left eye, and he itched to reach out and smooth it back again. He stifled the urge, rubbing at his beard instead. The culprit behind the now scraped, tender skin around her mouth, a telltale redness left in its wake. She'd always hated beards. He had a sudden, overwhelming urge to shave.

What the hell was wrong with him? Nothing had changed. She was still the woman who broke his heart, and he still had no idea why. He took a deep breath. "I was going to buy you a ring. The day it happened. The day you left."

She swallowed, then wrapped her arms around herself.

"Scott offered me a ride to the mall, but he took me to the apartment building instead. It was a set-up, my brother and Sucre changing the balance of power." He scoffed. "I see it now, but back then, I had no idea. I put myself in front of a knife to save Scott. I almost died. Then you damn-near finished the job when you left me broken in my hospital bed."

"I'm sorry." She curled into herself, getting smaller before his eyes.

He didn't like it. His Mandy was tough as nails. She could look a tiger in the eye without blinking. "Don't be sorry," he said gruffly. "Tell me what happened. I deserve the truth."

"You do." She straightened.

Finally. He was getting an answer to the question haunting him for more than a decade.

A beat of silence. "I did it to save you."

He stopped breathing.

To save him? Of all the possible explanations he'd considered over the years, that had never been one of them.

"Someone threatened to have you arrested for killing those people in the fire. It was a dirty cop; he blackmailed my father, knowing about the connection between you and me."

He heard the words she was saying, but they didn't make sense. "I didn't kill anyone. I didn't even know about the fire until after you left me."

Releasing her death grip on her arms, she sagged against the back of the loveseat. "I never thought you did it. But seeing you there was a win-win for the cop. Either he got the glory of making a major arrest, or he could take early retirement with my father's money."

"What reason could I have for setting a fire? It takes more than one cop's word to put someone away." He pushed off the seat and started pacing the floor. None of this made sense.

Her gaze tracked him as he walked from one side of the room to the other. "My father said it benefited your family. Something about the drug trade. I didn't know it then, but later, I figured out it was the night Sucre de la Cruz came into power. What I don't understand is what it had to do with the Skulls."

He put one foot in front of the other. Moving helped him think. "It never made sense to me either." Why they'd helped Sucre take over. He'd asked his brother—even his father once—but they'd only say he was better off leaving it alone. It was need-to-know information, and he didn't need to know it. Who cares if it ruined his fucking life? Of course, now it was as plain as the nose on his face.

Money.

There was no level they wouldn't sink to for money. For fuck's sake, look at what they were doing right now.

Whether the fire was intentional or not, he'd probably never know.

"I never thought you were a part of any of it," she said quietly. "Doubting you never came into the equation." She climbed to her feet and moved toward him, blocking his path. Her fingertips ghosted over his cheek, touching him, but not. "I couldn't take the risk your life would be over."

He clutched her hand, holding it firmly against his face. "But that's exactly what happened. My life—was over."

Her eyes searched his, and he let her see the truth in his words.

"I would have wanted to deal with bogus charges a hundred times over before facing a future without you." He released her hand. "You didn't give me the choice."

"Because I knew." Her voice cracked. "I knew if I told you, you would have said to ignore it. You would have put yourself in front of a moving train to keep us together. I loved you too much to let you do it. No matter what it cost me." She whispered, "They could have locked you up for the rest of your life."

He tried to make sense of the distant look in her eyes. There was grief there, the kind he knew all too intimately. It may have dulled over time, but it never truly went away.

Good God.

She'd never wanted to leave him.

His heart stuttered. His chest literally hurt. There were a thousand things he wanted to say, but his mouth couldn't form the words. Hell, his brain couldn't even line them up into coherent thoughts.

There was only *want. Need. Mine.*

Who needed words? It was just time wasted when he could be kissing her.

Maybe something gave away his intention in his eyes because she moved at the same time he did. They met in a clash of teeth and tongue. The softness of their kiss on the sofa was gone, replaced with desperate greed impossible to satisfy.

He wanted to consume her or burn her alive with the same kind of fire scorching his soul. Growling, he tangled his hand in her hair, holding her to him.

But Mandy made no move to get away. Instead, she gripped his shirt so fiercely her knuckles dug into his back.

His body was as tight as a bowstring ready to pop. With two steps, he had her crowded against the wall. He released her hair to lift her up, and she wrapped her legs around him, pushing her core against the almost painful ridge of his erection.

Only some denim and probably a tiny scrap of lace separated him from her pussy. He groaned, now obsessed with the idea of seeing what kind of panties she wore. Would it be a thong? Black? Pink? Would it be soaked with her want?

Did she need this as much as he did?

He pulled back. The answer would be in her eyes.

Sure enough, her gaze mirrored the hunger driving his every move. Her mouth was slightly open, and her chest rose and fell quickly as she panted for breath. The skin around her lips, darkened further from the scrape of his beard.

Yes, her body wanted his. But did she want more? Gone was the man he'd been when he'd dreamed of making her his wife. Could she want *this* Kane? Or were they both chasing a dream better left dead in the past?

The default chime of a cell phone sounded nearby, but she made no move to answer it.

As he released his grip on her thighs, she slid down the front of his body until her feet hit the floor. The need to touch every part of her consumed him. Starting with her hair. He'd always loved her beautiful hair. He ran his hands over it gently, sliding over the thick locks to her shoulders. He feathered his thumbs over her collarbone before continuing his path down her arms.

The phone rang again, and he fought the urge to grab it from the table and toss it against the wall. He kept his focus on the prize in front of him.

Where was he? Oh yes. Now to her hips. Her tiny waist.

The phone rang again. And again. And it suffocated the fire in her eyes.

"Ignore it," he gritted.

She shook her head and tugged his hands away from her body. "I can't. I know who it is. And this is something I need to put right." She kissed his knuckles before she let him go and moved away to silence the phone.

He wanted to argue or to demand an explanation but he did neither. His stomach was in knots; too much rattled around in his head.

Mandy slipped on the pristine sneakers on the floor next to the door and grabbed a thick navy cardigan from the table where she had her purse and keys. "We'll talk again soon, okay?" Her eyes searched his, and he nodded without thinking. Her smile wasn't quite right when she stepped backward out of the door, leaving him alone in her condo, but what did he know? Nothing could have made *him* walk away from a chance to make love to her again.

What the hell could be more important than what was happening here?

CHAPTER THIRTEEN

Amanda

Amanda's pulse pounded in her ears as she slid behind the wheel of her red Prius. Kane Hale had just kissed her into oblivion.

In the years since they split, she'd tried so hard to convince herself his mouth hadn't been as amazing as she remembered. He'd been her first love. Of course, she'd built him up in her mind.

But after tonight, she'd never be able to lie to herself again. If anything, time and distance had dulled the memory of how fucking phenomenal it was. He kissed her like she was the sun and the moon. His hands were like firebrands on her body. No man had ever turned her on so much, and none had ever made her feel, well, anything. Certainly not the overwhelming rush of hope and fear, need and abandon Kane inspired.

She would have made love to him tonight without a moment's hesitation. Hell, she was tempted to turn around, even now, and finish what they'd started, but if she didn't deal with Nathan, it would only come back to bite her in the ass later.

The insistent ringing on her phone told her it was him before she even needed to check the display. No one else would act like they were so entitled to an immediate response.

She glanced at the phone as she pulled to the exit of her parking garage. The screen was filled with texts.

Nathan: Pick up.

Nathan: Where are you?

Nathan: Why aren't you answering the phone?

Nathan: You push me too far.

Swiping through several more without even reading them, she cleared his messages and sent one in return.

Amanda: I'm on my way to your place.

Barely a second passed before his response.

Nathan: Good.

Shivering, she turned up the heater. The fire in her veins Kane's arms had ignited turned to ice with the prospect of facing Nathan tonight, but at least after this, it would all be over. The four weeks she'd promised her father weren't nearly finished, but he'd changed the terms of their deal once. Now it was her turn. It's not like he could take the money back now. He'd completed the wire transfer less than an hour ago.

She hovered on the cusp of starting over with Kane. He deserved honesty. God knew, keeping secrets from him had only led to heartbreak. She would not have the shadow of her ties to Nathan jeopardize her chance at happiness.

If she wanted a clean slate, she needed to break up with him now and for good.

Idling in front of Nathan's building, tendrils of doubt crept in. Maybe she should have met him in a public place. He'd never lay a finger on her in front of an audience. It was too late to change the plan now, but she wouldn't be a sitting duck. Leaning to the side, she unlatched the glove compartment and slipped the contents into her purse.

With a deep breath, she surrendered her car to the valet and forged on into the elegant lobby. Each step towards the elevator felt like walking through molasses, but she forced one foot in front of the other. The fingers on her left hand gripped her purse, while she lifted the right to knock.

Nathan swung the door open before her knuckles met the wood. His normally perfect blond hair was slightly askew, one gelled lock falling over his forehead. His mouth twisted, and the dim light from the single lamp in the corner cast shadows across his face. As he tugged her into the room, the unmistakable whiskey scent of Chivas Regal came off him in waves.

"Do you have any idea how many times I have

called you over the past few days?" he snarled.

At least fifty. "I'm sorry, Nathan." She willed herself to sound contrite, but his grip on her arm didn't ease. "I've been working on a deal for Cooper, and it's kept me very busy."

"I don't give a damn about your silly little company. You have an obligation to me, Amanda. Ignoring me is very disrespectful." Even in the low light, his eyes gleamed with malice.

Rip off the Band-Aid. "You're right. You deserve someone who can give you the time and attention you deserve." She cleared her throat. "Right now, I don't think I can."

Nathan released her arm with a dark chuckle and gave her his back. He moved to the kitchen and flipped on the light to refill his highball glass. "You don't think you can," he echoed, knocking back his drink, then pouring another. He murmured something unintelligible as he refilled the glass.

She stepped closer. "I appreciate the time we've spent together, but I think we'd be better off as friends."

He was smirking when he turned back to respond, but in seconds, his eyes bulged, and his cheeks mottled. The thick crystal glass cracked as he slammed it on the countertop and amber liquid pooled around it. "Friends?" he thundered. "As if I would lower myself to be friends with a two-bit whore like you."

She took an involuntary step back, expecting him to advance.

Instead, he bellowed, "Lights. Full." His smart-home features followed his command, triggering the can lights in the ceiling. He dropped his voice. "Who is he?"

She shook her head. There was no way he could know about Kane.

Nathan slammed his hand on the counter next to his abandoned glass. "You barely let me touch you. All your pretty words about waiting for the right time, and you were out fucking some guy tonight. Don't you dare deny it. The evidence is all over your goddamn face."

Her fingers flew to her lips.

"I should've realized you'd like it rough, baby. Maybe I should grow a beard and see what I can do to your delicate skin. Or maybe I'll take it out on your ass. See how much your sidepiece wants you after I'm done with you tonight." With a sweep of his arm, he sent the glass crashing to the floor. He unbuckled his belt as he moved toward her.

He stopped when she pulled the Colt out of her purse and pointed it at his chest.

"No." The steadiness of her own voice shocked her. "You won't touch my ass or any other part of me. Not tonight. Not ever again."

Nathan narrowed his eyes. "You expect me to believe you would shoot me?"

"You expect me to let you abuse me?" She scoffed. "I was a fool to take it for as long as I did. I promise you, it's over. Don't call me. Don't text me. And for damn sure, don't touch me. Or I will do whatever is necessary to protect myself."

"You're going to regret this," he hissed.

"Not as much as I regret ever taking your shit to begin with." She edged backward toward the exit and kept the gun trained on Nathan as she used her other hand to open the door.

Then she was free.

***

Amanda eyed her brother.

Mike Cooper excelled at celebrating good news. Generally, because he loved any excuse for a celebration and predictably partied with beer, fried food, or both.

His medications had ruled out any alcohol for weeks now, but he could still put away French fries like nobody's business. One after another, he shoved the ketchup-laden potatoes into his mouth, barely taking a moment to chew.

"Stop staring at me, and eat your own damn food," he grumbled, but he didn't seem terribly bothered. He got to pick the restaurant, and Zaxby's topped the list of his favorites.

Conversations overlapped across the room. A variety of people enjoying their lunch breaks filled the seats, from the corporate-type guy next to them in a suit and tie, to the table full of utility workers in their Georgia Power Company uniforms. Fried chicken, it seemed, was the great equalizer.

She raised her hands in surrender. "Forgive me, Oh Great One. I couldn't help but watch you suck down those fries. Somebody had to be ready in case you needed the Heimlich."

He snorted and kept eating. The return of his appetite had to mean something good for his recovery, as did his willingness to come out and celebrate their official groundbreaking at the new site.

"So," Mike drawled, smearing his chicken through the mountain of ketchup he'd mixed with the Zaxby sauce, "I don't suppose you know if Kane is going to be at the new development today."

She shook her head. Even though she knew it was far-fetched, part of her had hoped to find him waiting when she returned to her condo last night. The first thing she did when she woke was call Robby Jordan, the foreman's assistant, to find out who was on the crew sheet. Kane had been assigned to the nearly finished project a few miles away.

"I, uh, did see him last night. Kane, I mean. He came over to my place." Her cheeks burned as she sipped her Arnold Palmer. For the life of her, she couldn't remember why she'd ever stopped drinking these.

Wonder of wonders, Mike looked up from his food. His jaw was slack. "You said Kane was at *your condo*?"

She hummed against her straw. "I took your advice. I told him the truth."

He spun his hand in front of him, urging her to say more.

"It's complicated." She sighed. "Or maybe I made it complicated. I wanted to protect him. I still do. His stupid fucking biker gang is about to ruin his life all over again. You know they're getting into drugs now?"

Mike blinked slowly. "Too much information and not enough." Shaking his head, he took a sip of his soda.

"We kissed."

Her brother choked on his drink, and Dr. Pepper sprayed out of his nose onto the remnants of his meal.

With a shudder, she pushed her napkins toward him, but he was already wiping his face with the back of his arm.

"Forget the napkins. Tell me everything, and don't skip a single detail, or Cindy will never forgive me."

She didn't doubt it. Cindy had always been a romantic. "Some guy approached my dad, pretty much offering him money if he helped get the Skulls out of the running to deal drugs in some neighborhood where he wants to do it."

Mike nodded. "And your dad took the deal."

"No one seems surprised." Was she the only one? "Anyway, they've got something planned to take Kane's crew down. Of course, I had to warn him."

"Of course." Mike batted his eyelashes at her.

She didn't take the bait. "He came over, and we got to talking. I told him why I left, and I think he understood because then he was kissing me. God, Mike, it was like I was alive for the first time in years. He—"

"No." Mike covered his ears with his hands. "I'm still your brother. I don't need those kinds of details. Save the dirty bits for my wife. You can expect the full inquisition tonight."

"Nothing too dirty," she said primly. "Nathan called and interrupted us. I left to end things with him. He didn't take it well."

Nodding, Mike rummaged around in the food still in front of him before making a face and pushing it away. "So now what?"

"The million-dollar question, isn't it?" She gathered the trash from the table and tossed it in the can.

They made the ride to the new development quickly and without much conversation, which gave her time to relive Kane's kisses over and over again. When they got out of the car, she stood behind Mike's wheelchair, ready to push.

He reached up and touched the back of her hand. "You're going to figure this out. I don't know if the man Kane is now is still right for you, but I do know you have unfinished business together. I'm glad you've finally stopped running from it. I love you, sis, and I will be there for you any way I can."

She made a noise acknowledging his words as she patted down the strands of hair the chilly breeze threatened to pull from her simple twist. Time to be professional. Her Ice Queen mask in place, she pushed her brother toward the crew assembled at Lot 258. Not too many guys yet, since the work hadn't started. Only Xander, the foreman, his assistant Robby, and three other guys. The clean-cut African American guy with a polo she recognized as Matt York. The guy with the burns on his neck was the latest recruit, Evan something. And next to him was his Ranger buddy, Cyrus Amir. The man was of Middle Eastern descent, and more than a little good looking, with sharp cheekbones and wavy dark hair longer than she'd ever seen it, which was to say it was no longer in the buzzcut he used to sport.

Robby, Matt, and Cyrus all eyed her with—not hostility, but maybe suspicion or wariness. Obviously, the guys were aware of some of the dynamics between her and Kane. But she was still the boss, and some lines they couldn't cross, even for their friend.

The corners of Xander's eyes crinkled when he saw Mike. "Michael Cooper. What an unexpected surprise." He crossed the short distance from the trailer on the side of the property to shake Mike's hand.

"I wouldn't miss the chance to be here for the kickoff of the new project, or to see you, old friend." Mike had worked with Xander since before Charlie died. It was one of the reasons Kane was assigned to Xander's crew: minimum interaction with Amanda. It made total sense for everyone here to look to him as their boss. She was just the bitch who dumped their buddy a hundred years ago.

She stepped back to let everyone catch up with Mike and for him to meet Evan. They still had another five minutes before Jared Berringer's scheduled arrival to give his official blessing on the start of the project.

"I know you're the boss." She startled at Robby's voice behind her, then she turned to face him. His big brown eyes looked troubled.

She tilted her head, waiting for him to continue.

He furrowed his brow. "I love my job, and I know I'm taking a risk by saying this, but Kane is my friend." He cleared his throat. "I scheduled him at the other house today because I knew you would be here. It, um, upsets him to see you."

This guy had some unexpected fortitude. It took some epic balls to have a conversation like this with her. She raised her eyebrow.

His cheeks pinkened. "What I'm trying to say— what I was wondering—are you, could you maybe give me a heads up when you're coming? Then, I could assign him to something else." Robby couldn't be more than twenty-two or twenty-three years old. With his shuffling feet and his bangs falling into his eyes, he could have passed for a teenager.

She should have resented his nerve, but she couldn't help but be a little impressed. The guy was obviously apprehensive as hell, but Charlie always said, *It isn't courage if you're not afraid.* "What do you think Kane would say if he knew you were talking to me like this?"

Robby blew the hair out of his eyes, giving her an unobstructed view of his defiant glare. No fear now. "I don't care. He needs somebody to look out for him."

She smiled despite herself. "Yes, he does."

Robby blinked rapidly as she patted him on the shoulder. It wasn't clear whether he noticed she never gave him the promise he asked for. There was no chance for him to object either way.

Jared had arrived. He shook hands with Mike and followed suit with Xander and all the guys in the crew. When she approached, he greeted her with a warm smile. "Miss Griffin, so good to see you." He gave her hand a firm squeeze. "I have a photographer here to take some PR photos for our website."

The woman snapped a few shots. Everyone exchanged pleasantries about the partnership, then Jared left as quickly as he'd arrived. The job here today was done.

As she waited for Mike to finish his goodbyes with Xander, she felt a prickle of unease on the back of her neck. Was someone watching her from the copse of trees across the street?

She spun around, trying to catch whoever it was in the act, but she saw nothing. Even after berating herself for her obvious paranoia, she couldn't stop herself from looking over her shoulder one more time as she got in the car.

Nothing.

Shivering, despite the warmth from her wool peacoat, she cranked the engine and threw the car into gear the moment Mike settled beside her. Paranoid or not, she was ready to get out of here, even if an inquisition from her sister-in-law waited at her next stop.

CHAPTER FOURTEEN

Kane

The meth operation in the clubhouse had progressed even further since the last time Kane had been here. The pool table now served as a work surface for two of his brothers. With his bald head and towering height, no one could mistake Cue Ball for anyone else, despite the surgical mask covering his face. A blender whirred in front of him, powder swishing around inside. A garbage can overflowed with boxes of cold pills on the floor beside him.

Frank appeared to be mixing some of the powder from a plastic bowl with…was that fertilizer? Three partially filled soda bottles were lined up on the table beside him.

He moved deeper into the house where his mom hunched over the kitchen counter, doing some kind of surgery on Double-A batteries. A few more two-liter bottles bubbled on the table where Scott presided with several containers of Lye.

The room smelled like cat piss.

"We've got to get all of this shit out of here."

Scott looked up but didn't move from his position.

"I'm serious. Where's Malcolm?"

His mother answered. "Out in the backyard, I think. Didn't think it would be safe to smoke in here."

With a roll of his eyes, he ventured out into the cold. Sure enough, his father stood in the carport, smoking next to a portable heater. The coils burned orange in the small box.

"We've got to clean up the mess inside the house."

"Oh?" his father mocked. "Do we?"

"I'm serious." He moved closer, so he could speak softly. "Someone is trying to set us up. I'll bet you anything we're gonna have a raid here. The idea is to put us out of business, so the Soldiers can get a foothold."

Malcolm stood up straighter. There were few people in the world he liked less than David Bennett or the club president, Billy Meers. "Where did you hear this?"

He'd been dreading the question. His father had made no secret of his disapproval when Mandy had been part of his life. He'd only met her once, but like Scott, he loved to call her Princess Bitch and said Kane was better off once they split. Any intel from her would be dismissed out of hand. But his father would need some source to take his warning seriously.

So he lied. "My friend Brick. The guy who hired us for the Sucre hit. He, uh, said he heard it from a reliable source. I trust him. If he says it's going down, it will."

His father scratched at his beard, considering his words. "Meers is behind this?"

"Bennett. I don't know if Cue told you, but he gave us some shit out at the park the other day too. Thinks they're entitled to dealing, part of their white crusade or whatever."

Malcolm took a deep pull from his cigarette, then blew out a cloud of smoke. "When is this supposed to happen?"

"Within the week." He dug his hands deep into the pockets of his jacket, his fingerless gloves doing little to provide warmth. "We need to clean up now. Find somewhere to store our product and our cash. The guns too. The cops know who we are, so our regular places are out."

Gritting his teeth, his father tossed the butt of his cigarette on the ground and smashed it under his boot. "What do you suggest?"

To get out of the drug business.

They should have never gone into it in the first place. The truth would do nothing to help his cause, though. It would only start the same argument over again. "A self-storage place could work. Get one of the prospects or the girls to rent one in their name. Something no one can trace back to us. And we need to do it fast, or we're going to end up in jail."

Building an argument around keeping his freedom was a language his father understood. Malcolm served a six-month stint on a gun charge once. He'd said a dozen times since then, he'd never go back. "Fine. Let's get it done."

He followed his dad back into the kitchen, where Malcolm barked orders for everyone to start cleaning up. Scott scowled, then shot Kane a look that could melt asphalt. "You responsible for this?" He stomped around the table, vengeance burning in his eyes. "You can't fucking admit I was right about this. Do you have any idea how much money this could mean for us? And you want to throw it all away on some Boy Scout notion about drugs being bad?"

His brother lunged forward, but Malcolm grabbed him by the back of his shirt. "Cut it out, Scott."

Scott froze in his father's grasp.

"We got a tip we're gonna be the target of a raid. We need to get moving and clear out right now."

"But—"

Malcolm swatted the back of his head. "But nothing. We'll find out soon enough if the tip was legit. Either the cops show up here and prove him right, or they don't." The part about what it would mean if the cops *didn't* come remained unsaid.

Mama V pulled down her mask. "It'll take two or three hours to finish up with the batches we've got working now."

"Use up anything we can't transport as is." Malcolm glanced around. "Where are the rest of the boys?"

"We've got the last steps going in the chapel. Pete, Scratch, Randy, and Joe are in there. Cue is working with Frank and one of the prospects up front. Everyone else is at their day job." Scott's evil eye still trained on Kane. "Ain't you supposed to be at yours?"

Any other day he would be, but he cut out early to warn his family.

His father saved him from any more conversation with Scott. "It's actually a good thing you're here. I got a call from Ace McClinton. He wants a meeting."

Scott tried to run his fingers through his tangled hair, but the knots were too strong. A brush every now and then would go a long way. He let out a frustrated breath, then planted on a serene smile. "I'll go. Since Kane wants to clean house so bad, he can stay here and pack up."

Malcolm gave a sharp shake of his head. "He wants to meet with your brother. The man was real clear about it. Besides, Kane is the one with a head for business. He can finally use the shit he learned in night school to help the club instead of just walking around thinking he's smarter than everyone."

There might have been a trace of a compliment somewhere in there, deep down. Very deep down.

Scott's hands fisted, his knuckles turning white. He didn't argue with Malcolm, though. He swallowed whatever words he wanted to say and stalked off toward the chapel.

Mama V scuttled behind him. "SP, baby, you all right?"

Her clucking would only make it worse.

Malcolm's gaze followed them out of the room before it swung back to Kane. "What the hell are you still standing around for, boy? Go make us some money."

***

At least he didn't have to go back to the damn apartment complex. Kane held no misconceptions he wouldn't have to return there at some point, but anytime he could avoid the burned-out reminder of his past, he considered it a small victory.

He arrived at the café five minutes before the meet time with Ace. It gave him the chance to brave the line which curved almost all the way to the glass door. Who knew so many people spent their Friday night in a coffee shop?

The middle-aged mom in front of him gave Kane a wide berth. She wrinkled her forehead a little as she propelled her two kids in front of her, almost into the generous backside of the woman ahead. The boys squirmed to carve out a little more room, but their mother hemmed them in with her body.

He didn't blame her; he probably looked like a nightmare. His ponytail reached the middle of his back these days and he'd wrapped a black bandana around the top of his head. No doubt his eyes were bloodshot since his churning brain refused to give him any peace last night. His beard had grown long and ragged. Top it all off with the scar across his face, and Ms. Middle Class probably saw a demon incarnate standing next to her and her kiddies. At least his long sleeves covered his tattoos.

He was used to reactions like hers. For the first time in a long time, though, it bothered him.

The line moved quickly, despite its length, and one of the kids was brave enough to wave at him as his mother ushered him out of the door. He'd just sat down with two lattes when Ace took the seat across the small table.

The guy had dressed a little more casually for this meeting than their last one, but his slacks and dark cashmere sweater still contrasted sharply with Kane's flannel shirt and jeans. Ace tilted his head toward the two coffee cups. "Thirsty?"

He pushed one of the large mugs toward the club's supplier. "I got one for you, but if you don't like lattes," he lifted his shoulder, "I won't let it go to waste." He plucked two packets of sugar from the black plastic square at the center of the table, tore them open, and dumped the contents into his cup. As he stirred, the rich fragrance of the espresso made his mouth water.

Ace chuckled and lifted a blue packet for himself. "I like lattes fine." He sweetened his drink, then sighed in appreciation with his first sip. With his face relaxed and a smile playing on his lips, he looked like an everyday guy chilling out with a cup of joe. He could be someone's neighbor or banker or realtor. Not the guy piping a shit-ton of heroin into the community.

But Kane was the guy the moms shielded their kids from. He swallowed down his indignation with a gulp of his coffee.

Setting his drink on the table, Ace gave him an assessing look. "You are one surprise after another, Mr. Hale. No one has ever asked to meet me at a cafe before." He glanced around the crowded room, his eyes catching briefly on the dry erase board declaring:

EVERYTHING IS BETTER WITH CHOCOLATE. TRY A MOCHA TODAY.

"It's a nice change of pace."

No way did he want to go back to their last meeting place. For sure, he wouldn't invite this guy anywhere near his own life, which left somewhere public. Someone might have recognized them at a bar or somewhere close to the neighborhood where they sold their product. He used to visit this little café when he was in college. No trace of the club life anywhere for miles.

But Ace didn't want to meet to talk about any of those things, so he drank his coffee and waited.

When he offered no small talk, the soft look on Ace's face sharpened. "All business, eh? I wanted to touch base with you on how things are going for the, uh, candy sales for the…church."

Kane let out a small snort. "The candy sales," he echoed. "They're going well. The H—Halloween type stuff isn't moving as fast as the crack—erjack boxes." This shit took ridiculous to a new level. "I'd say we've probably sold half of what you gave us."

"Half?" Ace blinked. "Quite impressive. You move faster than I expected."

"Pretty basic supply and demand. No one's been filling the void and people are *hungry*. We've changed the pricing system and expanded the distribution from the earlier operation…folded in some of the college bars. College kids love candy, too." The club's pretty boy, Frank, now sported a clean-shaven face and had a costume from American Eagle to wear when he hit the college bar circuit. He was bringing in cash, hand over fist.

Ace's eyes twinkled. "Yes, they do, Mr. Hale. Kudos to you for considering it. I like the way you think outside of the box."

Whatever. Becoming a successful drug dealer had never been high on his to-do list. "We're also making some of our own stuff, and it's moving pretty well. The ingredients are cheap. Not a lot of time in the kitchen, but it's keeping everyone busy enough."

"You don't like it."

He didn't bother to lie. "No. It's profitable, but it's messy. The whole thing is messy, but cooking brings it to a whole different level. I can see why you don't fool with it." He drained the last of his latte. "It's not up to me, though."

Ace was silent for a moment, then spoke quietly. "What if it was?"

The man had said, himself, he was a businessman. The old-school variety, it seemed, with his own kind of code of honor. And he clearly saw something in Kane he found intriguing.

Dangerous as he was, something about Ace made him feel like he could speak freely. Maybe that was part of his skillset.

Walk into my parlor said the spider to the fly.

"If it was up to *me*, we wouldn't be doing any of this. We're tempting fate, and it's going to come back and bite us in the ass. You seem like you let your guys speak their minds. My family isn't like your crew. Dissent isn't an option. And even if it were, my father would be the boss, not me."

Ace spoke slowly. "You could come work for

me."

He barked out a laugh. "No offense, man, but the last thing I want is to fall down deeper in this rabbit hole."

Thankfully, Ace didn't seem ruffled by his honesty. He lifted his hand, palm up. "Get out, then. I barely even know you, and I can see you'd rather go straight, so do it. I can always find a new distributor." He shrugged like it was no big deal. "Take it from someone who knows firsthand. Your life is what you make it. If you don't like it, make it into something else."

"It's not so simple." Of course, he wanted to get out. Hell, he'd never really wanted in, but after everything went down with Mandy, the club felt like the only safe place. Stupid, but his head and his heart didn't always see eye to eye. The club had never been and would never be safe, but he did have family there, and they'd held him together when he thought he would shatter into a thousand tiny pieces.

"It *is* simple. You're the one making it complicated." Maybe the man could have been a motivational speaker in another life. Ace pursed his lips and leaned forward. "I'm not trying to tell you how to live your life, because, hey, I'm not exactly on the PTA, man. But I am a little older and maybe a little bit wiser, so let me say this. It's not gonna get better. The situation you're in? It's not going to change unless you change it. Bottom line, either you modify your organization or you modify your circumstance. You can't be a passive participant in your own life, Mr. Hale, not if you want it to turn out a particular way. If you simply follow the current, you can't be surprised if it doesn't take you where you want to go."

He was right. Course, he was right. Still, what Ace suggested was no small thing. Either you're in the club or you're out, and if he chose to get out, it meant leaving his entire family behind. There would be no welcome for him as an outsider, not even from his mom. He'd be starting over, completely alone, and the idea terrified him.

I wouldn't have to be completely alone.

Mandy's face flashed in his mind, then Brick's and Robby's. He had people in his life who cared about him.

Ace's advice gave him a lot to process, and he wouldn't come up with an answer at a coffee shop, three feet away from one of the biggest drug distributors in the state.

Thankfully, Ace didn't wait for a response. He stood and paused with his hand on the back of Kane's chair. "Think about what I said. In the meantime, it sounds like your boys have a solid system in place. You know how to get back in touch when you're ready for your next box of chocolate." He lifted his hand in a brief salute. "Thanks for the coffee, son."

Son.

He almost laughed at the word, but in truth, he didn't find it funny so much as a little bit sad. Sure, Ace ran a criminal syndicate or whatever, but the guy actually seemed to be looking out for him. In one conversation, the man had given him better advice than his own father probably had in his entire life. Malcolm wasn't the kind of guy who would ever win father of the year, but it seemed more obvious now than it had for a long time the man was only interested in looking out for Number One. His wife, his sons…hell, even his club…he considered them all tools to advance his own interests.

He knew it well enough when he was younger. How could he have let himself forget?

But knowing his father's flaws didn't make him prepared to walk away from the club. He wouldn't only be leaving his dad. He'd be cutting off his connection to Cue Ball, Scott, and his mother. Just like Uncle Wes had.

For what?

Unbidden, an image of Joshua Cooper danced through his head and with it, the fragile thread of hope he could have a family of his own. Josh wasn't his, but the dream of a family didn't have to die. He didn't have to be alone; he could make a new future.

His phone buzzed.

He didn't have to decide right now. But he wasn't getting any younger. If he was going to start a new life, he'd have to do it soon.

CHAPTER FIFTEEN

Amanda

The summons from her father came faster than Amanda had hoped. Not even forty-eight hours had passed since her break-up with Nathan. Apparently, her desire for a longer reprieve was unrealistic.

The hairs on the back of her arms rose as she left her condo late Saturday morning. For the second time in as many days, she felt like someone was watching her, but she focused on the dread pooling in her stomach over the idea of facing her dad.

He'd never handled disappointment well. When she'd decided to join Charlie's company, for instance, he went on a tirade spanning more than an hour, covering everything from her lack of loyalty to him to the disregard for her future and the waste of her education. Honestly, he still wasn't over it. The man put up a classy, Old Southern front, but he had a temper hotter than Tabasco sauce.

The ride over stretched interminably yet ended instantaneously. She wanted to get it all over with, but facing the music was going to suck beyond imagination. Part of her had fought the summons, but the man was her father, and years of conditioning had taught her not to ignore him.

She'd even dressed in an armor of sorts: dark blue jeans, with calf-hugging brown boots, and a dark green sweater. It felt like crushed velvet, warm and soft and casual, and her dad would probably hate it for all of the same reasons she loved it.

Steeling herself, she sought him out in the study. He sat rigidly at his desk, red pen poised over a stack of papers. His face tightened when she stood on the opposite side of the heavy wooden surface, but he didn't look up. "You reneged on our deal." His voice cut like pure ice.

She could do ice too. In fact, that particular mask gave her an extra shot of courage. "It depends on how you look at it." Folding her arms, she ran her hands over the comforting softness of her sleeves. "I kept up my end of the original agreement perfectly."

His gaze shot up to her. Forget ice, now he was all heat. "So, you never intended to give me those four weeks?"

The answering fire inside her came as something of a surprise. "I intended to give you six months, which is exactly what I did. Six months of laughing at his shitty jokes. Six months of tolerating his abuse and making myself small." The heat burned hotter. "Now I'm done. He'll never belittle me again. Never hit me. Never kick me. And *never* hurt me."

Her father tossed his pen onto the table with an

exasperated huff. "No need to be crass, Amanda, or so dramatic."

"Dramatic? Would you like to hear about the time he pushed me for disagreeing with him? Or when he threatened to sodomize me to teach me my place? It happened only a couple of weeks ago, Dad, and a few days later you tried to extort me into keeping him in my life." She clasped her hands together to stop the shaking. But fear no longer fueled her, rage did.

Her father didn't so much as flinch at her words. His expression stayed infuriatingly neutral. "Enough."

"Really? Because you summoned me here to talk about it. You want to talk about the time he kicked me in the ribs? Or hey, I can show you the marks he left on my arm two days ago."

He rose to his feet. "We're done here." He looked at her like a piece of gum stuck to his shoe. "I expect you won't be returning the money."

The money? After everything she'd just told him? Fuck him. "You expect right." It wasn't about the money; it was about him. About her bowing and scraping to him, trying again to fill his bottomless well of need—for attention, adulation, obedience. A fool's errand, and she was done being a fool. She'd figure out some other way to keep Kane safe from his threats.

"Do you have any idea how much this is going to cost me?" he hissed.

She turned on her heel and paused at the office door, looking back at him over her shoulder. "I know exactly what it cost you. It cost you your daughter."

He didn't say another word as she resumed her path out of the room and out of his life.

***

Kane

The I-95 route to Jacksonville took a little longer thanks to the detour along Highway 17, but the view made up for the delay. Cue Ball said all road trips were the same, but something about being close to the water on his bike made hours on the road go by in half the time.

Though he'd never really minded making gun runs for the club, getting away from all the drug garbage, even if for only a day, came as a downright relief. He and Frank left right after dawn to make it for the lunchtime meeting with Sergei. Frank drove the SUV, and Kane escorted him on his Harley. They could have ridden together, but Kane was in no mood to hear about who the man fucked last night. He struggled more and more to fake any enthusiasm about his friends' sexual conquests or even to jump in on singing the praises of the club. It seemed like those were the only things anyone wanted to talk about anymore.

Had it ever been any different?

He let his memory stretch as his body relaxed into the rhythm of the open road. When he had tried to exorcize Mandy from his life, his brothers provided an endless string of distractions to keep him from going crazy. If he got too sad, someone—

usually Scott—would drive him to the strip club down the street from the clubhouse and slap a Bud in his hand.

At the time, the club provided security for Bottoms Up, so they never had to pay a cover. Most of the guys would've said the free admission was payment enough, but the job also brought in a few extra bucks.

Those first few years after the break-up blurred into a loop of lap dances, benders, blowjobs, and even a few three-ways. They were bitter and broken years, where he intentionally scraped the bottom of the society barrel as a big fuck you to the woman who would have been devastated to see him sunk so low. After a while, it simply became the reality of his life.

He stopped shaving or cutting his hair. He used the money he'd saved for Mandy's ring as a down payment on his bike. And visited the tattoo parlor more times than anyone else in his club.

Only his first tattoo had any real meaning, Mandy's name inked large and proud across his back, spanning shoulder to shoulder. He'd lied and told the other guys he got it before the break-up, but she would've hated him marking his skin with her name or anything else. No, he'd gotten the tat right after she left him. He'd told himself it was so he would never forget how completely she fucked him over, a reminder to never fall for another woman again. Another lie. She'd branded herself on his fucking soul; the tat only made it visible to the world.

The next one came a year later. He got another

every few months, all with the same themes: skulls in honor of the club and an array of female demons and angels. After all, he considered women both heaven and hell, so it made sense.

Now, he bore little resemblance to the clean-cut guy who went to night school and picnicked with his girlfriend under the stars. Mandy's willingness to let him kiss her the other night was a fucking miracle. And not only because of the way he looked. He gave up the dream of winning her back years ago, but he'd convinced himself she'd never loved him…she left because she didn't care.

Could he believe her explanation now?

Yes. Maybe that made him a fucking idiot, but he didn't doubt her for a second. Her abrupt change of heart about their relationship had never made sense. He would've bet his life she'd loved him every bit as much as he'd loved her, and her version of events gave him a lifeline. It said he hadn't misjudged her; she did love him—so much she gave him up to protect him.

The gray waves churned in the corner of his stinging eyes as he considered her father's bullshit extortion story. It had a thousand holes in it, but the important thing was, he believed *she believed* it. She didn't just break his heart, she broke her own.

How was he supposed to feel about that? His gut tangled in knots. He wanted to shake her for her naivety and for carrying the weight of it all on her shoulders. He would have never allowed a threat to tear them apart, but then again, she probably knew that from the beginning. She didn't give him a choice.

She thought she was saving him, but even if all Beau's shit about the cop was real, hell yeah, he would have gladly done some time, knowing she was waiting on the other side. It would have been better than the endless emptiness he got instead.

He could examine it a thousand times, ask himself *what if.* He could rage about it, mourn over it, question it. Truthfully, though, the moment he could tell himself it wasn't her fault, he'd grabbed onto it with both hands. He'd grabbed on to *her.*

Mandy was the only thing he truly ever wanted in his life, and if he could find a way to have her now, his tattered soul still yearned for it. The question was whether she could ever want the man he had become. Dirty and used and jaded.

Arriving at his destination gave him a much-needed break from his thoughts. Sergei stood outside the warehouse, his thick arms folded over his black wool coat, his white-blond hair slicked back from his face.

Kane climbed from his bike, his legs like Jell-O after the long ride. Ignoring the sign of weakness, he approached his contact and shook his hand. He only wanted a nice, easy exchange. "Hope you weren't waiting too long." He couldn't read the Russian's impassive face.

"No. You are right on time."

Even after five years of working with the man, he still enjoyed listening to the unusual cadence of his accent. Unfortunately, Sergei was a man of few words. He led Kane and Frank, who had pulled up right behind him, into the warehouse where twenty-five AR-15s waited inside a parked black van.

Frank walked straight to the guns to examine them.

Sergei firmed his jaw, then turned to Kane. "Rumors are circulating about your club dipping into the drug trade."

Shit.

"I won't waste my time or yours asking if it's true. But I will say this, my people expect our business to be the focus of *your* business. The drug trade is perilous. When you put yourself at risk, you put us at risk. We have no interest in being at risk. Let me be clear. If the rumors are true—if you are endangering our operation—stop it now." His voice echoed in the warehouse, cold and vaguely menacing. "We can overlook a misunderstanding, but our position is known now, and we expect you to behave accordingly. Is there any part of this you don't understand?"

Sergei had never said that many words to him in every conversation they'd had combined. And Kane couldn't miss the message. He couldn't blame the icy winds for putting a chill in his bones. "I understand."

Sergei nodded. "Good. Take it back to your father."

Frank returned. "Everything's in order. Let's load it up." Together, they crated the guns in the false bottoms of boxes filled with bags of coffee, then loaded them into the back of the SUV.

He pulled an envelope full of cash from his back pocket and handed it to their Russian contact.

Sergei tucked it into the inside breast pocket of his coat, then walked away without another word.

Frank chuckled. "A man of few words. If only

they made women who can be as quiet."

He forced a smile. "Let's get back on the road, brother. We need to get the merchandise back to A-T-L."

Oblivious to his churning stomach, Frank got behind the wheel and cranked up the old Bronco's engine. They road side-by-side, headed back to the interstate.

The Skulls had been in partnership with Sergei's syndicate for the past five years. They'd never had an ounce of trouble, but they'd never made trouble either. The Russians only ever demanded two things: discretion and fidelity. Sergei had been crystal clear. Working with Ace violated the terms.

But would Malcolm take the warning seriously? Probably not. Unfortunately, his father was a narcissist and a stubborn one to boot. He'd end up dead or in jail before he bent to the wishes of another man, if he even believed the warning at all.

You could walk away from the club and be done with the whole thing. The traitorous voice in the back of his head definitely had a point. It would also go a long way in getting his life back on track, but on track to where? Back to school? He never got his degree. Back to Mandy? What kind of man would he be to turn his back on his brothers for a woman who dumped him a decade ago? But she wasn't just some woman, was she? She was everything.

Round and round he went, arguing with himself. Five hours later, he'd gotten no closer to an answer, at least about his future with the club.

He thought about the way Scott had refused to

let him wallow in his misery the first year after Mandy pushed him away. His brother took him everywhere he went, so he'd never feel alone. They went to hard rock concerts together, bowling alleys, bars. Scott taught him the basics of bike mechanics over the course of dozens of beers. Stayed up with him all night when he needed it, watching *American Pie* and telling bad jokes.

He thought about Cue Ball and the dozens of lap dances he'd paid for. Frank and his sage advice about how to hustle college kids on a pool table.

Then he thought about Uncle Wes, whose face he only sort of remembered. He could no longer recall the sound of his voice, what kind of food he liked, or what he did to earn a living.

Hell, he could have a passel of first cousins out there for all he knew. He'd probably *never* know because that's what patching out meant. Wes was cut off, now and forever.

One thing he did know: he had to tell his brothers about Sergei's warning.

Frank followed him inside the clubhouse, leaving the guns in the Bronco for now. They'd move them to the storage place where they stashed the meth later.

The inside of the house still stunk to high heaven, the chemical aroma so thick, it made his eyes water. He found his father and Cue Ball out back, smoking in the carport, the small space heater glowing orange next to the folding chairs where they sat.

He shoved his hands into the pockets of his jacket. His fingers were numb from his hours on the

219

road. "I have a message from Sergei. You're not going to like it." He filled in his father on the conversation at the warehouse.

"Fuck that commie-bastard." Classic Malcolm. "He doesn't get to tell me how to run my club."

Technically, it wasn't supposed to be Malcolm's club. Yes, he was president, but they decided everything by a majority vote. Still, his father founded the club, and his proprietary vein ran deep.

"I think we need to put it in front of the table," Kane warned. "The Russians have been our partners for a long time. It's a mistake to dismiss what he said without even talking about it."

His father tossed his cigarette butt on the ground. "We did talk about it. Just now." He stood, and Cue Ball followed suit. "Now, let's get the merchandise to the storage place. Don't want to have a bunch of weaponry around if a raid ever comes about."

The dismissal couldn't have been clearer, which made his blood boil. Malcolm shouldered past his son, forgoing the shortcut through the house, to walk around the outside.

Cue Ball stopped beside him. "You coming with? Scott and me, we're going out for a drink tonight. We can head out after the drop-off."

His phone buzzed in his pocket. He shook his head. "Nah, man. Maybe I'll catch up with you later." He waited until his friend rounded the house before he checked his display.

Amanda: Can I see you tonight?

Mandy.

For all of his introspection, for all of his soul-searching, he didn't need to think at all before he typed out a response.

Kane: One hour. Your place.

He needed the time to get presentable. His apartment was a quick ride; he made it home in minutes. It took a bit longer in the shower to clean off the evidence of the road.

Once he was clean, he wrapped a towel around his waist and stopped at the sink to brush his teeth. Afterward, he forced himself to look in the mirror. He'd avoided it for so long, he could barely remember the last time he studied his reflection.

Damn, he looked like shit. Why any woman would want to get near him was a mystery he couldn't begin to unravel. He used to be a good-looking guy, but the scar gave him a rough edge he could never erase. The hair and the beard, on the other hand, those things he could do something about.

But how much? She'd know it was for her. She'd have to.

He couldn't erase everything he'd become in the last thirteen years. But he could do something. He pulled out the drawer beneath the sink and dug around inside before his hand landed on the thick-handled scissors inside.

With a deep breath, he lifted them up and began to cut.

CHAPTER SIXTEEN

Amanda

The setting sun cast an orange glow through the sliding glass door as the minutes ticked closer to Kane's arrival. Amanda had wanted to call him the moment she'd walked out of her father's house, but she forced herself to think long and hard about it first.

What was she doing with him? Was she trying to get back what they'd lost? Sure, those stolen moments in his arms had moved the earth beneath her feet, but did they have any chance of something more? He was in a biker gang, for God's sake.

His hair was longer than hers, tattoos covered his arms and who knows what else, but it was way more than the physical. Kane was different and in ways she still probably knew nothing about. He'd sworn he would never be part of club life. The drugs, the free sex, the misogyny and complete disregard for the rules of law or society.

She was no prude, but she could never share her

man with another woman, certainly not several other women. She couldn't live with constant fear for his safety or his freedom. With a man she really loved, she wanted everything he could give: every birthday, every Christmas, every kiss, every dream, every fucking fantasy.

For all she knew, Kane could have a dozen kids out there with as many different women. He could be getting a blowjob from some random stranger right now without even thinking twice because the club considered it normal. She'd seen it firsthand when they'd been dating. Kane hadn't lived that way, but his father did...his brother too.

Scott was such a douchebag. He used to call her Your Highness or Princess Bitch, though she'd never done anything but try to be nice to him. She hoped he got a nasty STD from one of his club girls. Thinking of a dozen ways Scott's dick could fall off kept her mind from circling around the hard questions about her and Kane.

Then a knock sounded at her door. She'd told Mickey, her doorman, Kane had a permanent pass to come up to her floor. God knew what he thought going from Nathan's high-class appearance to Kane's scruffy biker look. He'd have no idea Nathan's three-piece suit actually hid a monster underneath, while Kane's fuck-you exterior housed a heart of gold.

She smoothed her hands over her hair before turning the knob to open the door. Her greeting died in her throat when she saw him.

Trimming his beard shouldn't have made so much of a difference, but he took her breath away.

Yes, his hair was still long, but it was pulled back into a tame, low ponytail. The long sleeves of his black T-shirt covered his tattoos. He looked more like the Kane she remembered than she would have thought possible. Different, but the same.

"Wow," she breathed, and his brown eyes twinkled.

"I'll take *wow* over hello any day." He tilted his head. "Are you going to invite me in?"

Her cheeks flamed as she stepped aside. "Cocky doesn't suit you," she said primly.

"I'd say it suits fine." He winked.

He fucking winked at her.

She closed the door, unable to stifle her smile. When she turned back to him, though, she was paralyzed by how awkward this all was. What she really wanted to do was throw herself in his arms, breathe in his scent, feel him all around her…inside of her. Sex wasn't the answer, though, at least not yet. "Would you like a drink?"

He walked over to the bookshelf where she had a framed picture of her and Mike from around the time she and Kane had been together. He picked it up for a closer look. "Yeah. A drink sounds good."

"I, uh, I'm not sure what you like anymore." Why did it hurt so much to admit?

Kane looked up from the picture. "I'm still me, Mandy."

For some reason, his quiet words punched her in the gut. Everything had changed, but he claimed he was still the same. It was what she'd wanted, but it only seemed to drive home all the years she missed. Time she could have had with him but bargained away to her dad.

Tears clouded her vision. She turned away, but they spilled down her cheeks before she could hide them. What the hell was wrong with her? She couldn't even remember the last time she cried.

He stepped behind her and rested his hands on her shoulders. "You don't have to hide."

"I don't even know why I'm crying." A lie. She cried because everything in her needed what he said to be true at the same time she feared it couldn't be.

He tsked as he turned her into his chest. His body was bigger than it used to be, but she would have recognized the feel of his embrace anywhere. "I think we have a lot to figure out about each other." He kissed the top of her head. "I'll take a beer. Bud if you have it."

She took in one more deep inhale of his clean scent before she let go to get the drinks. When she returned from the kitchen, Kane stood at the bookshelf again, looking at the same photo.

"This is how I remember you." He accepted the beer and used the front of his shirt to protect his hand as he twisted off the cap. It gave her a brief glimpse of rock-hard abs sprinkled with dark hair; he had more of it now than before. If he realized how he affected her, he didn't show it. His gaze drifted back to the photo, and his face softened. "This was the best time in my life."

She sipped her zinfandel, despite the temptation to guzzle it down. "It was the best time in mine too." Another sip. Ah, fuck it. She finished the glass and drifted back to the kitchen to grab the bottle.

Now he relaxed on the love seat, and she sat

beside him, her heart racing as if she'd just run a marathon. "Are you seeing anyone right now?"

He shook his head slowly, sending a thrill through her heart. "You?"

"I was." Shame kept her from sharing the whole story. "I broke it off."

"Because of me?" He searched her eyes.

"Partly, but mostly because of me. I didn't love him. It wasn't a relationship built on feelings. I was his arm candy. He was...a means to an end. It had already gone on too long." Nathan was the last thing she wanted to think about.

He took a pull from his beer as he considered her words. "There was someone for me, not too long ago, but she—it wasn't anything real. None of them have been anything real, but I have to tell you, I haven't exactly been a saint since we were together."

Oh look, something she wanted to think about even less than Nathan. "It's been thirteen years." She refilled her glass. "I never expected you to live like a monk."

"Mandy—"

She held up her hand. "Stop. I know you're trying to be honest, and I appreciate it, but I don't want to hear what you're about to say." The vague idea of all the women who'd shared his bed over the years hurt bad enough. She wasn't sure if she could stand listening to the particulars. "We've both been with other people. But here's the bottom line for me, no bullshit. I have never loved any man in my life except for you. There was no one before and no one since who has come anywhere close. No one I

226

wanted a future with. No one I wanted a family with. It was only you. Only ever you." The confession left her stripped bare. She reached for the wine bottle, but he stopped her hand with his.

"And for me, it was only ever you, Mandy." The truth swirled in the chocolate depths of his eyes.

She swallowed. "You keep calling me Mandy. I'm not her anymore. I'm not even sure I remember how to be that girl. The kind of girl who believes in wishes and fairy-tale endings. I can't go back and unlearn the lessons these years have taught me. I'm not sure I would if I could. I do miss her, though. Your Mandy. I was happier when I was her."

Kane scooted closer, his thigh brushing against hers, and framed her face with his rough hands. "You could be happy again."

Her eyes closed as she leaned into his touch. It would be so easy to block out the world, to simply be here in this moment...with him. But all the questions and doubts would still be here afterward. If this was going to happen, they had to learn each other all over again, not just the ghosts living in their memories, but the real-deal people they were now.

She forced her lids open and focused on his soft gaze. She could drown in those eyes.

What was she going to say?

Her resolve vanished as he leaned forward and brushed his lips over hers. The beer lingered on his breath, and her tongue quested into his mouth for deeper contact. The crisp flavor tingled over her taste buds, but as he deepened the kiss, she only tasted desire.

She couldn't breathe. She couldn't think. She needed to get closer.

Kane didn't make her wait. Sliding his arm around her waist, he tugged her toward him, and she went willingly to his lap, her legs straddling either side of his.

Now the kiss was a full body experience. The beard still scratched some, but in her hunger, it barely registered. Her hands clutched his broad shoulders as she molded herself against him. Everything about him was bigger than before. His chest, his powerful thighs, even—

He groaned as she ground against the hardness between her legs. The arms he had around her waist dropped abruptly, and his hands gripped her hips. Now, he urged her on. Setting the rhythm.

It had been years since she'd been with him this way, but her body had forgotten nothing, and apparently neither had his, because they writhed and arched against each other in a breathless harmony.

Kane broke the kiss and trailed his lips down the column of her neck, and she tilted back her head to give him better access. His grip on her hips eased as he slid his hand beneath her shirt, climbing her ribcage on a path to her aching breasts.

With a curse, she tugged the simple V-neck over her head and tossed it on the floor.

His eyes widened, but he didn't miss a beat, unfastening the bra and pulling it away from her body. "Offer them to me," he growled, and she was all too happy to comply. No sooner had she cupped her breasts, he had one nipple in his mouth.

The sharp pull shot straight to her pussy. She

groaned and swiveled her hips harder. Faster. The need for him climbed, the summit just out of reach.

As his teeth played over her sensitive flesh, his fingers tugged gently on her other nipple. He pinched and pulled, sucked, and licked. A moan climbed from the back of her throat as the whole world centered on his mouth, his hands, and the cock straining against his jeans.

"Come for me," he demanded, his breath hot against her wet skin.

She ground harder against him, the pressure just right on her aching clit, as he pinched both nipples hard enough for a prickle of pain to ratchet up the pleasure. Then she was flying, his name a cry on her lips.

The orgasm shook her to her foundations. Her movement stopped as the waves rushed through her. But it wasn't only her body reaching its plateau; it was like every emotion she'd ever had, built into one big peak exploding inside her. She wanted to laugh and cry and scream. But more than anything she wanted—she needed—to get even closer.

Pressing her chest to his, she buried her face in his neck, fighting the fresh wave of tears threatening to embarrass her again. Crying once tonight had already been one time too many. His arms held her with exactly the right amount of strength, and though his erection was still nestled between her legs, he did nothing to push for more.

She allowed herself the luxury of peace in his arms until she could pull herself together. Then she pulled back and kissed him gently. "Let me take care of you," she whispered. It was a testament to the fire between them Kane could make her come without even taking off her pants.

He ran his hand over her hair, the way he always used to. "You're so beautiful like this. Your eyes are like fucking emeralds right now." His thumb brushed over her bottom lip. "Your mouth looks thoroughly kissed." His soft gaze turned proprietary. "I did that. I want to keep doing it."

Her mouth curled into a smile. "Kissing me?"

"Making you mine." The way he said it rang with truth. "I don't know how we're going to make this work. I don't know what we've got to change or how we're going to have to bend, but I am not letting you go this time. Do you understand?" A fierce look came over his face. "We're going to figure this out, Mandy, and you're going to be mine forever."

Her brain issued a hundred denials. What if they were too different now? What if he couldn't love the woman she'd become? What if he'd turned into his brother…or his father?

The doubt must have shown because he shook her gently. "Don't. Don't talk yourself out of it before we even try."

She'd forgotten what it was like to be with a man who knew how to read her. Was she talking herself out of it? "I'm not."

"But?" he prompted.

"But where do we start? We already know this," she gestured in the small space between them, "isn't a problem. You can just look at me and get me wet."

His eyes darkened, and she shoved against his

shoulder.

"Stop. This is my point. We still want each other, but so many other things have changed. Like how much I hurt you." She hesitated. "Like the fact you joined the MC."

The heat left his eyes. "I know."

"So where do we start?"

He was quiet for a moment. Then a smile broke out across his face, transforming him from handsome to knock-down, drag-out gorgeous. "The same place anyone starts. At the beginning."

CHAPTER SEVENTEEN

Kane

The excitement from the college football fans translated as a dull roar in Kane's ears. Turner Field was almost unrecognizable in some ways since Georgia State converted it into their stadium, but the vibe from the charged sports fans was universal.

Mandy stood spellbound as they overlooked the field, which was now Panthers football territory through and through. "I haven't been here in years," she breathed.

She looked so young in her jeans and sweater; she wore no make-up, and her cheeks had turned red from the cold. Her breaths came out in cloudy puffs of smoke.

He gripped her icy fingers. "You want a hot chocolate?" Without waiting for an answer, he tugged her to the line for concessions.

She didn't pull away, but her eyes narrowed.

"You never used to like college football." The woman had a memory like an elephant.

"It's not like I hated it," he hedged. "I never had time to get into it."

"A newly acquired taste, is it?" Her voice sounded all innocent, but her smile was sly.

He tucked her hair behind her ear. "I think I could learn to love it."

Now he'd bet the red in her cheeks had nothing to do with the cold. He smiled at her discomfiture as they moved to the front of the line, and he bought their drinks.

She blew into her cup before taking a tentative sip. "Where are our seats?"

Checking the tickets, he led her to their spot in the twenty-fifth row. Not exactly close to the field, but not in the nosebleed section either.

"They're still blue," she mused with a small smile as they found their seats.

They didn't have much time for talk as the teams took the field. Georgia State faced Tennessee, and the din from the crowd made conversation impossible. The energy spread like electricity through a live wire.

Mandy had told him more than once she loved football. She'd even come close to coaxing him to a Falcons game right before they broke up. Seeing the pleasure light her eyes made him wish he'd given in sooner.

Minutes into the game, she was on her feet. The quarterback had thrown a successful long pass, and the wide receiver was on the run at the thirty-yard line. "Go, go, go!" she yelled.

A Tennessee player tackled him at the twenty-five.

She swore as she plopped back into her seat, and he smirked until she delivered a sharp elbow to his arm. "Get your head out of your ass, Hale. Participation is not optional."

The next time when she jumped to her feet, he followed suit, and by halftime, he'd screamed his voice almost raw. By the end of the game, he felt so charged up, he no longer even noticed the sting.

She looped her arm through his as they wove through the crowd to get to her car. She'd let him drive to their surprise destination, but now she slid into the driver's seat. "I'm starving. Want to grab a bite?"

He nodded. He didn't want the day to end, but he had less than two hours before his meeting at the clubhouse. Despite his father's dismissal, he refused to let Sergei's warning go unheard by the rest of his brothers.

But now wasn't the time to think about his problems. He was going to enjoy every second with Mandy he could. The night before had been a fucking revelation. Watching her come apart in his arms had been even better than he remembered. Maybe because he appreciated it more this time around.

She'd looked like a fucking goddess with all her pale, perfect skin and peach nipples. They'd practically begged for his mouth. And fuck if he wasn't getting hard again even thinking about it.

He had no doubt she wanted him every bit as much as he wanted her, but she wasn't ready to trust him yet. Hell, he couldn't blame her. She'd seen club life back in the day, and her impressions were spot on. By his brothers' way of thinking, he could fuck anything that moved, and she'd have no right to complain. Not one of them believed in monogamy, and he hadn't tried it once in the past thirteen years.

It didn't mean he couldn't go back. He'd cut off his left nut to go back. The only way to prove it, though, was to show her, so he would. He would show her she was his sun, and his world would revolve around her once again.

"Burgers okay?" Her question interrupted his thoughts.

He looked around, surprised she'd pulled into the parking lot at Applebee's while his brain went on sabbatical.

A small group already stood waiting for a table near the hostess area, so they grabbed the last two seats at the bar.

"Let me guess." He held his fingers to his temples. "You want a Cowboy Burger with the barbeque sauce on the side." It was the only thing she'd ever ordered when they came here together.

She stuck out her tongue. "Show off."

The bartender brought them their sodas, then sent back their order.

Mandy tore the paper off her straw. "Today was amazing." She had a guarded smile, but it looked sincere. She rested her right hand next to his on the bar, the side of her pinkie brushing against his. "It was like before, but different."

He linked his pinkie with hers. "Sort of like us."

She chewed on her lip. "Should we tackle the big stuff first or build up to it?"

The club. She had to be talking about the club. He lifted his shoulder. "Ask me anything you want."

Her mouth opened, then closed again. The only sound came from the other people at the bar. Just when he was convinced she wouldn't say anything, she spoke. "You always said you hated it." Her gaze rested on their hands. "I would have bet my life your feelings were never going to change. I—I did this, didn't I? I pushed you into this life when I walked away."

He wanted to deny it. What kind of pussy did it make him if he couldn't even stick to his own principles because his girlfriend broke up with him? It didn't change the truth, though. "You didn't make me patch in, Mandy, but yeah. Obviously, it was my way of dealing with what happened between us. The guys in the club were there for me when I was low, and I guess part of me felt like I was giving you a big *fuck you* for leaving. But they loved me. They still do. And I love them. They're my family."

She tugged her hand away, and he felt the loss immediately. "Has anything changed? In what they do? How they treat women?"

If anything, things had gotten worse. Not with the women thing, which had already been pretty fucking bad. The illegal shit, though, was at an all-time high.

The food came, taking their attention away from the conversation. He bit into his ribs and watched Mandy pick at her fries. "I thought you were starving."

She frowned. "You didn't answer me."

Why would he think he could ignore the elephant in the room? "No," he said softly. She was only talking about one part anyway. "It hasn't changed."

She dragged a fry around in the pool of ketchup. "How can you still be you and be one of them?"

He hated how unsure she sounded. With a sigh, he wiped his hands on the napkin, then turned to face her fully. "I've done shit I'm not proud of. If I'm being honest, I'm still doing shit I'm not proud of. I think maybe I forgot who I was for a little while, or maybe I thought I couldn't be a good guy without you. Which is weak, and I'm not proud of it."

She didn't look up from her food.

"I'm trying to figure out how everything fits together for me right now. I can't just walk away from them because I've found you again."

No longer even pretending to eat, she folded her hands in her lap. "Of course not," she murmured.

"But there are no other women. I swear it on my life."

Now she looked up.

He couldn't tell if she was angry or upset. "I haven't so much as looked at another woman since you and I started talking again. I promise I wouldn't betray you."

She nodded, but the sparkle in her eyes had dulled. Calling over the bartender, she asked for a to-go box. As she scooped her food inside, she spoke quietly, "It's getting late. I'm tired. Do you mind if we head out?"

"Sure." He'd lost his appetite too. Dropping two twenties on the table, he followed her back to the car, and she drove the short distance to her condo, where he'd left his bike.

She parked right next to the Harley. Once they got out, she gave him a soft kiss on the cheek. "Thanks for the game. I had a good time."

He slid his hand over her arm. "Don't give up on us. We can work all of this out."

She revealed no joy in her smile, but she said the words he needed to hear. "I won't." She stepped back. "I'll talk to you soon, okay?" Without waiting for an answer, she turned and walked away.

***

Two police cars were driving away from the clubhouse as Kane pulled up. Cue Ball's big bald head shone like a beacon in the backseat of one cruiser, but he couldn't tell who was in the back of the other.

Killing his motor, he covered the distance to the front door in a few long strides. He stumbled back a step once he got a good look inside.

Someone had trashed the clubhouse. Garbage cans rested on their sides, their contents scattered across the floor. All the shelves hung askew from the rickety entertainment center; the TV was cracked, broken DVDs all around it. The sofa cushions were strewn about the room, their stuffing hemorrhaging from newly acquired slashes across their centers.

Mama V sat at the kitchen table, her head in one

238

hand, a cigarette in the other. It was the first time he had ever seen anyone smoke in the clubhouse since he was a child. She acknowledged him without looking up. "I guess you were right about the raid."

He searched for a piece of furniture to sit beside his mom, but she seemed to have the only chair left unbroken and intact. He leaned against the counter to her right instead. "What happened?"

She took a drag from her cigarette and tapped the ashes directly on the floor. "They got here a couple of hours ago. SP, Cue, and the prospect were shooting pool. Your brother started spouting off when they showed their warrant. They dragged him out of here faster than you can say your name." Another puff. "Then, the cops started tearing shit up."

Cue Ball was too smart to cause trouble if he'd already seen Scott in cuffs, which meant…"They found something."

She sniffed and gave a reluctant nod. "Your brother had some meth stashed in the chapel."

Kane gaped. "I don't understand. We knew they were coming. We agreed to get everything out of here."

"It wasn't much. They'll get charged with possession, probably not enough for an intent to distribute, but maybe. He said he was going to deliver it to someone after your meeting tonight." She stood and walked to the back door, then flicked the cigarette butt into the yard.

Dammit, Scott. Why couldn't his brother listen to reason? Now someone had to go bail the guys out of jail, for fuck's sake. But at least they didn't get busted with a full-blown meth lab running in the house. The club stayed safe, at least for now. "Where's Malcolm?"

Mama V shrugged weakly. "I don't know. I tried calling him a dozen times, but you know your father."

He sure did. Malcolm did what he wanted, when he wanted, and the needs of his old lady were never high on his list. "I'm gonna try the bar really quick." Traveling the two blocks to the Watering Hole wouldn't waste too much time, even if his father wasn't there.

His mom grabbed a bottle of vodka from the freezer and unscrewed the cap without acknowledging his words. She wasn't allowed at the Watering Hole. Malcolm found his extra entertainment there.

He felt like an asshole for even mentioning the place, but the damage was already done. He jumped on his Harley and made a beeline for his destination.

About a dozen bikes glinted in a line outside the run-down façade, about par for a Sunday evening. He spotted his father's right away and pulled up beside it. The strains from an old Metallica song carried through the red wooden door at the entrance.

He stomped through the loose gravel up the three groaning wood steps and forged inside. His eyes burned as he tried to focus through the fog of cigarette smoke, but he fought the urge to squeeze them shut as he executed a slow sweep of the room.

A Coors hanging light illuminated the pool table in a hazy glow. He recognized both of the old guys playing as riders from his dad's generation. He gave a respectful nod as he passed them by.

A dartboard overlooked two banged-up tables to the right. Two women in skin-tight jeans held court with a couple of guys who were "teaching them" how to toss. It was an old dance where everyone knew damn good and well the lessons were only an excuse to put their hands on each other. Dollars to donuts, all four of them would be gone and getting freaky before the hour was up.

The bartender affectionately dubbed "Hangman" waved him over before he finished his circuit of the dark room. "Can I get you a Bud, boy?" Hangman had to be pushing sixty-five, so the nickname gave no insult.

He shook his head. "Looking for my pops. It's urgent."

Hangman raised an eyebrow and scratched his head with his index finger. The movement dislodged a gray strand or two from his ponytail and sent it hanging into his face. He blew it away as he leaned forward on the bar. "He's back in the storeroom." His voice climbed as Kane stalked off. "But I wouldn't go back there right now."

Whatever. Everyone knew what the storage room was used for here, and it wasn't to store booze. Besides, it's not like his father made a secret of his extra-curricular activities.

No, Malcolm getting busy in the back didn't surprise him. The surprise came from who he was getting busy with. "Is there anyone in my family you haven't fucked?"

Charlene looked up from the crate where

Malcolm had her bent over. Her elbows were propped beneath her, and her tits bounced perilously close to the rough wood. "Why?" she purred. "You jealous?"

Malcolm didn't even have the decency to stop drilling her. "Get the fuck out, son. I'm busy here."

It would serve everyone right if he did exactly what his father demanded. Let Scott pay the price for his own arrogance with a night in jail. Let his father come home to a trashed house and what was probably police surveillance. But walking away would also leave Cue Ball and the prospect hanging out to dry, to say nothing of his mom's sorry state.

No, walking away wasn't an option. He fixed his gaze somewhere over his father's right shoulder. "It's a family emergency." The words were code for club emergency, as in *drop whatever you're doing and deal with this first.*

His father muttered a foul curse, and a moment later, Kane heard him zip up.

"Aren't we going to finish, baby?" Charlene whined.

"Some other time," Malcolm growled.

Sure his father was on his heels, he turned away from his ex and got the fuck out of dodge.

CHAPTER EIGHTEEN

Amanda

For the umpteenth time, Amanda glanced at her rearview mirror, searching for the cause of her disquiet. She spotted nothing but normal traffic on the interstate, but really, what did she expect? A vague paranoia had followed her for days, and it didn't take a rocket scientist to figure out why.

She'd pissed off two very powerful men in a short period of time. Neither was the type to simply let things slide, so yeah, the other shoe would likely drop soon.

But there was nothing she could do to mitigate any unknown plans Nathan or her father were making. She needed to keep her eyes on the prize. Focus on the new development.

And Kane.

She swiftly rejected the plaintive voice in the back her head begging for a fix to her love life. That way lay dragons.

It had been only thirty minutes since her very productive meeting with Jared Berringer, and he'd essentially given her carte blanche in organizing the build schedule. He'd also promised her input on the marketing campaign starting after the holidays. She had a flash drive in her coat pocket with about a dozen pitches he gave her to review.

Cooper Construction stood poised on the precipice of a huge leap forward. She only had to play her cards right. Start out on the right foot. Consult her team and rely on their expertise. She'd called Xander and two of her other foremen for a meeting right away. They knew better than anyone what expectations were reasonable and what their men could accomplish.

An hour after her phone calls, she pulled up beside Xander's truck outside his trailer at the new site. The heels she'd selected for her meeting with Jared looked great with her pantsuit but were clearly a terrible choice for the newly turned dirt. She had to walk on her tiptoes as she approached the short rise of stairs.

Three members of Kane's team worked nearby on the frame for the concrete slab the crews would pour in a few days.

Xander waited inside the trailer, along with her two other senior foremen, Carl and Gene. The men sprang from their chairs as she stepped into the trailer's warmth.

"It's good to see you all. Please, sit." These guys could give some lessons to her shareholders. It was nice to be greeted with manners for a change.

Carl gave up the chair opposite Xander at the desk and moved to sit beside Gene on the frayed loveseat along the far wall.

She shot him a grateful smile and took the vacated seat. "I know you all are very busy, so I will get right to the point. Berringer is giving us the green light to write our own ticket."

Xander ran his hand through black wavy hair shot with strands of gray. "What exactly does he mean?"

She'd give her eye teeth to kick off her shoes right now. "He means our build schedule is up to us. Or really, up to the three of you."

Xander didn't smile, but his tense features relaxed a fraction. "You want us to formulate a rollout schedule."

"Exactly." Her left pinkie toe throbbed, but she refused to let it sap her focus. "I know winter is a slow season for contracts and sales, but with five months of lead time, we need to start building the spec houses for May sales. As far as how many of those projects your teams can successfully juggle, I need to defer to you."

It took about an hour to hammer out a tentative plan. When they were done, Gene and Carl wasted no time getting back to their crews. Xander stood to see them off. "If you'll excuse me, Miss Griffin, I need to step out to pick up some lumber. No need to lock up when you're done. My guys outside will keep an eye on things here."

Her toe now screamed for attention, but she kept her nod placid. "Thank you. I just need to make a quick call, if you don't mind."

He lingered briefly at the door. "Take your time." He may have said something else, but all she could think about was him closing the door so she could take off her goddamn shoes.

When she finally removed the instruments of her torture, she wanted to cry in relief. Her right baby toe was an angry red and swollen to twice its normal size. The left foot was uncomfortable, but no more than normal when she wore these shoes. An inspection of her footwear revealed a tear in the right shoe's lining, right where her toe had been jammed.

One mystery solved. At this point, she had to figure out how she was going to get back to her car. With her damn shoe finally off, she couldn't imagine forcing it back on. The other option was walking back through the dirt in her bare feet. Very professional.

She was so busy considering her feet, she didn't hear anyone climb the stairs to the trailer or even the knob turning to open the door. It's how she didn't know Nathan was there until he spoke her name.

"Amanda."

She jumped.

Dammit.

Way to give him the upper hand. "What are you doing here?" She stood in her bare feet. No way would she have him hover over her any more than their height difference already allowed.

His smile betrayed his simmering cruelty. "I wanted a closer look at where you're slumming it."

She eyed the door, but he stood squarely in the

path of her only way out. "You have no business here." Her voice betrayed none of the terror she felt being cornered by him.

"You are my business as long as I say you are." He advanced, and she took a step back. It wasn't fast enough. His backhand threw her back against the wall.

She braced for another hit as he cocked back his fist, but a strong, dark hand wrapped around his bicep and yanked him back.

"Get your filthy hands off me," Nathan sputtered. "Do you have any idea who I am?"

"A piece of shit as far as I can tell." She didn't recognize the voice, and she couldn't see the face of her savior.

Nathan strained against the man's grip. "Who the hell do you think you are? Go back to your own country."

"This *is* my country. And I'll tell you exactly who I am. I'm Staff Sergeant Cyrus Amir, Army Ranger. The man who's going to kick your privileged, entitled ass if you don't step away from the lady."

Cyrus? Yes, he was one of the guys Xander had working outside.

Nathan laughed low in his throat. "Lady? The only woman I see here is a whore."

She didn't have to see the punch Cyrus threw. She heard the hard crack of his fist against Nathan's face. And she couldn't miss the way Nathan's head snapped back with the force of the blow.

He didn't fight back at Cyrus, though. He charged at her, wrapping his hands around her neck, cutting off her oxygen before she could gasp for air. "Is this the one? The man who scratched up your pretty face with his beard? The one you were *fucking* when you were supposed to be mine?" His eyes bulged, and a vein pulsed on his Botox-riddled forehead.

As her vision darkened, she glimpsed several hands pulling at Nathan's arms and shoulders. Or maybe she was seeing double. Triple? The world was spinning. The trailer—Nathan—everything was getting further away.

Until his iron grip released, and her lungs filled with air. Her knees buckled, and she dropped to the floor in front of the loveseat, gasping like a fish on land. The sounds of violence echoed around her, but her brain struggled to make sense of what was happening only a few feet away.

Nathan lay flat on his back, a man straddling his chest, pounding his face like his fists were mallets. Blood splattered warm onto her skin. She heard yelling, but it was as if her ears were stuffed with cotton.

It wasn't Cyrus pummeling Nathan. It was a white guy with burns on his neck and the side of his face. Cyrus was trying to pull him off, him and a big man. What was his name? He was Kane's friend. The one who got shot.

She was still trying to remember his name when the world went dark.

***

Kane

Kane almost ignored his phone when it buzzed in his back pocket. Only the haunted look in his mother's eyes at the kitchen table the day before made him reconsider.

What if the cops had come back? What if they found the storage unit with the drugs and the guns?

He tugged it out and glanced at the screen, expecting to see the photo Mama V had attached to her contact.

"Brick?" He could count on one hand the number of times his friend had called him. "Everything okay?"

"You need to get over to the new site. Fast." Though Brick pitched his voice low, it nearly vibrated with intensity. "It's your girl. Some guy messed her up really bad."

He may have said more, but those were the last words Kane registered. If he were thinking clearly, he might have asked questions or tried to find out exactly what had happened. He didn't need to clarify his friend was talking about Mandy. There was no other girl, and they both knew it.

The normal drive time to the new development lasted about five or six minutes. The Harley got him there in three, weaving in and out of the cars on the road, even taking him over a couple of sidewalks.

He drove straight up to the steps outside the trailer, where he noticed right away the door hung open, but two men blocked it. He shouldered his way past them.

Mandy lay on the floor, her back propped against

the wall next to the desk. Her left cheekbone was red with the telltale swelling he'd seen on his mother's face too many times to count. Her blouse was ripped at the sleeve, and she winced as her fingers slid back and forth over her neck. From the unfocused look in her eyes, it was obvious she didn't register his presence.

White hot rage nearly froze him in place, but the need to touch her, to comfort her rose to the surface. He knelt beside her, resting his hand on her shoulder.

She lashed out, leading with her fists and following through with the weight of her slight body. Her knuckles skimmed over his chest, but she kept fighting, either unconcerned or unaware her strikes weren't landing.

He slipped his hands around her wrists, holding them immobile, and the wild look in her eyes twisted his gut.

"Let me go," she rasped, struggling against his grip.

"Mandy." He said it gently, the way his mom had said his name when he'd woken up in the hospital. "It's Kane. Baby, look at me."

Her body stilled, and her gaze shot around the room. From the corner of his eye, he could see no sign of Brick, but Cy and Evan still crowded around the door. She would hate having witnesses to something like this. "Can you give us some space, guys?" He had a feeling they could help him fill in the blanks, but his first priority was taking care of his woman.

The door clicked shut behind him, and Mandy's

shoulders slumped forward. She made a small cry as he pulled her into his arms. "Shh. You're okay now. Everything is going to be okay." He kissed the top of her head and rocked her gently.

She didn't make another sound, but her uneven breaths and shaking shoulders spoke volumes. Someone had hurt her beyond words, and he would not rest until the perpetrator paid the price in blood and fucking tears. But Mandy came first.

Five minutes may have passed—or maybe fifty—but it felt like an eternity before Mandy's breathing evened out, and she relaxed against him. "I want to go home," she whispered.

He helped her to her feet, which he realized were bare. "Do you have any shoes?" When her face started to crumple again, he didn't hesitate. He swept her into his arms and carried her to the door, swiping her purse from the desk along the way.

Cyrus and Evan were keeping vigil at the foot of the stairs, and Evan nodded gravely, jaw clenched, as they passed by. Cyrus rushed ahead to Mandy's car and opened the passenger door so Kane could release her inside.

Kane closed the door as she wrapped her arms around her legs and buried her face into her raised knees. He turned to Cyrus. "Who did this?"

Cy shook his head in frustration. "I didn't get his name, but he was definitely Old Money, and he definitely had a history with your lady." He stepped closer and lowered his voice. "I think he might have thought she and I—" He cleared his throat. "He asked if I was the one who scratched up her face with my beard. If she was sleeping with me while

251

they were still together."

Mother fucker. His jaw clenched. "Was this before or after he put his hands on her?"

"I knew something was up when he went storming into the trailer. He looked like he was ready to burn the place down, you know?" Cyrus cracked his knuckles as he spoke. "I followed him, but he was a little ahead of me. He'd already hit her once by the time I got inside."

"And then?"

Cy's hands balled into fists. "When he called her a whore, I let him go long enough to clock him in the face. I didn't count on him going for her throat afterward. I had to call Evan and Brick to help me pull him off her."

His instincts tugged him in separate directions. The drive to find this guy and kill him was a fire in his veins. But the need to protect Mandy, to comfort her, and help soothe whatever pieces of her the attack left broken, jagged, and raw…that duty was paramount. He would keep her safe, full stop.

"Where is this guy now?" More importantly, was Mandy still in danger?

"We were going to hold him for the cops, but your girl wouldn't let us. She was afraid he'd manage to turn it back around on one of us—get me or Evan thrown in jail." He scoffed. "The day I'm afraid of a prick like him will be the day I need to trade in my nuts for a handbag. But she was kind of freaking out, so Brick took him out of here. Evan really cleaned his clock. Don't know if the guy will be eating any solid foods for a while, much less coming back around here to make more trouble."

Seemed like he owed the new guy big time. "Thanks for everything. I'm going to get her home." He flashed Cyrus a look, meant to convey the depth of his gratitude, then rounded the back of Mandy's car to approach the driver's seat.

He was going to kill her ex, but first, she needed him to take care of her.

When he climbed behind the wheel, she hadn't moved from her curled-up position on the passenger seat. "Hold on, sweetheart. I'm talking you home."

She finally lifted her head. "Not mine." Her voice was like sandpaper. "Yours."

She wanted to go to his place? The idea hadn't even occurred to him, though it probably should have. Her ex had no idea who he was, much less where to find them. He simply never invited women over; something about the idea of a person he may never want to see again imprinting herself on his personal space. It wasn't the case with Mandy, though, was it? She was already imprinted on every part of his heart, body, and soul.

"You got it. Buckle up. We'll be there before you know it."

CHAPTER NINETEEN

Amanda

Amanda wasn't sure what she expected Kane's apartment to look like. Something cheap or messy, maybe? Dirty clothes on the floor or empty beer bottles on the coffee table. Not the clean, comfortable space he led her into.

She focused on her surroundings, forbidding her thoughts from reliving the events in Xander's trailer.

All Kane's furniture matched. The plush brown sofa against the wall clearly came from the same set as the overstuffed chair near the sliding glass door. The same unblemished walnut used on the coffee table made up the two end tables and the small entertainment center supporting the TV.

A landscape print hung, framed, on the pristine cream-colored wall. The beige carpet felt soft beneath the pads of her sore feet.

A prickle of shame climbed inside her. Why wouldn't he have a nice place?

Because he's in a nasty-ass biker gang, a sharp voice hissed in the back of her head.

Kane was more than just the club, though, wasn't he?

The way his brother and his father talked about women—the way they put their fucking club above their family, their jobs, basically everything—it turned her stomach. But the club meant something different to him.

After all, he'd never treated her like trash. Hell, even when he had every reason to hate her, he'd worried about how she was doing after Mike's crash. Even when he was hurt, even when he thought she kept him from his own child, he gave her a chance to explain. He listened. He was reasonable.

Now he took care of her. He wasn't going all caveman, beating his chest, trying to track down Nathan, though she had no doubt he wanted to. No, instead he opened his arms and his home to make her feel safe. And it worked. At this moment, she wasn't the least bit worried about her ex. Maybe he'd seek retribution for this, but not here and not now.

Kane stepped in close behind her and put his hand on her shoulder. "What can I do? What do you need?"

She turned into his arms. His warmth seeped into her bones. "I want to lie down," she murmured. Her throat protested with the effort to speak.

Lacing his fingers with hers, he led her into his

bedroom. His bed nearly took up the entire room.

How many women has he brought here?

She blinked away the mental images assaulting her brain.

"I'm, uh, going to go get changed." Kane stood next to a tall dresser, clothes in hand. "Help yourself to anything in the top drawer if you want to get more comfortable." He disappeared into the adjoining bathroom and shut the door.

Part of her wanted to dig through every one of his drawers, look under his bed and inside the closet. She wanted proof he wasn't too good to be true, proof she wasn't a fool to trust him, but trust didn't come from proof. So, she opened only the drawer he offered and pulled out a gray t-shirt and a pair of black boxers. Quickly, she stripped down to her panties and donned his clothes. They smelled like him.

So do his sheets, she noted as she climbed in his bed. Did he still prefer sleeping on the left side? Unsure, she situated herself in the middle. It was still early evening, but her body was wrecked.

Minutes later, Kane returned, wearing some sweatpants cut off at the knee and a thick white-T. The black and red ink of the tattoos on his arms contrasted sharply against the fabric. She couldn't take her eyes off them as he climbed into her right and leaned back against the pillows on the headboard.

Her fingers traced over the various devils and angels in the design. Each one was slightly different from the next, but they were all women, either with wings or a pitchfork and horns. The other arm featured a collage of skulls. "Tell me about them," she whispered.

He scooted down so she could rest her head on his chest. "The tats?" His chest shook a little as he chuckled. "I wish I had some deep meaning behind them I could share, but I don't. They aren't based on any real people or anything. The angels and the devils, I guess, they—women can be either. Or both. Or neither. Obviously, my feelings about the opposite sex are complicated."

He paused. "No, actually. My feelings about *you* have been complicated. I didn't really have feelings about any of the others. They were just...there. Shitty of me, I know, but I never lied to them. I never pretended there could be any kind of future for us. I was too dead inside, you know? I was always looking for something to make me feel alive."

His palm smoothed over her hair. "I got the first devil a year after we broke up. I got a new one every year. Every October twenty-fifth for twelve years after, some remembered the good times, some didn't."

"They're all about me?" she croaked.

"No. Well, not really. More about how I felt about relationships and women at first. Later, I guess, it got to be a tradition. And the skulls, they're obviously about the club. I got those whenever I got the urge to go back under the needle. Like what I was saying before, I was looking for ways to feel alive. The sting did it. So did my brothers."

She itched to stop him there. She didn't want to talk about the club or hear about it. What if it was

257

the one thing ultimately destined to keep them apart? Once they put all their cards on the table, this fantasy of a happy ever after between them would be ruined. Maybe she needed a boot in the ass, though, a swift kick of reality.

Kane kept talking, oblivious to her internal battle. "I know we're both tiptoeing around the club thing, and I guess I'm a bastard for bringing it up now, but we need to face reality. Okay?"

She squeezed her eyes closed and nodded against his hard chest.

"My feelings about the club are complicated. All the shit I hated about the culture before, I still hate. The thing is, I'm probably a big fucking hypocrite because I haven't treated women a whole lot better since I patched in, but it's different with you. I have never and will never treat you the way the club treats the old ladies."

He pulled back to look at her face. "If it was only about my dad, I would walk away without ever looking back, but some of the other guys, like Cue Ball and Frank, they're what family is supposed to be. They're more than friends to me; they're my brothers, Mandy. They picked me up every time I fell down. Scott too. They would lay down their lives for me. What kind of brother—what kind of person—would I be if I pushed them aside the minute you came back into my life?"

She didn't even try to answer. A thousand words wouldn't have been enough to hash it all out, and it hurt like hell to try to say any at all. She shook her head and touched her throat with a frown.

"I know." He hugged her to him again. "The sad

thing is, even if you could talk, I don't have all the answers. There are days I want out, and it doesn't even have anything to do with you. Sometimes, I just want to get away from all the stupid fucking choices they're making, because I can see they're headed for a disaster, and they won't listen. I keep thinking I can save them, but every time I try, it's like I'm beating my head against the wall."

Two truths shone like beacons in her head. One, Kane wanted out of the club, and two, the only way their relationship could survive was if he made the decision to leave on his own. The way he was talking, it might actually happen. She tipped her head to kiss the spot on his chest above his heart, then burrowed into his warmth.

"Let's get some sleep." He flipped the switch above his nightstand, casting the room in darkness.

There would be plenty of time to talk tomorrow. She relaxed into his arms, and for the first time she allowed herself a glimmer of hope. Maybe this time they'd get the happy ending they were long overdue.

***

Amanda woke up with a radiating heat against her back and a rock-hard dick nestled against her ass. She squirmed against the iron grip locking her in a man's arms. Tattooed arms. Kane.

He groaned, his breath hot on her neck, and his hand moved to cup her breast. The touch sent a zing of awareness between her legs.

How many times had they made love this way?

Him pushing in slowly from behind, his fingers plucking her nipples or strumming her clit. There were nights she dreamed of it, waking with his name on her lips and her own hand beneath her panties.

The reality was so much better, even without the penetration she was already craving. But it didn't have to stop here. She covered his hand with hers and dragged it down to where she wanted to feel him most.

Kane didn't disappoint. His fingers slid beneath the silky fabric of her panties, over her mound, to the slick slit beneath. His middle finger parted her folds. "Fuck. You're so wet."

She tilted her hips toward his hand. "It's what you do to me." She moaned as he slid his finger inside her. "It's what you've always done to me."

The pressure against her ass intensified with his answering thrust. "Feel what you do to me."

She pumped her hips forward and back, riding his hand and rubbing on his impressive cock. "I'd rather feel it inside me."

In a heartbeat, his hand was gone, and he was tugging off his clothes. When his dick pressed against her moments later, only the thin silk of her panties separated them.

Looping her thumbs in the elastic, she slid the drenched material down her legs. His heated flesh was already sliding between her lips, teasing her with his thickness, and it took every drop of resolve she had to whisper, "Condom," rather than impaling herself on his arousal.

A knock sounded at the front door.

Kane slid his tongue along her pulse. "Ignore it." His fingers toyed with her from the front, as he continued to torment her with the promise of fulfillment from behind.

Another knock.

She groaned in frustration.

"Shh," he murmured. "They'll go away. Just—"

They both froze with the sound of the deadbolt turning.

"Kane. Why aren't you answering the door, brother?"

No. Anyone but Scott.

Kane grabbed the comforter and yanked it up to cover their bodies seconds before his dickhead brother sauntered in the room. "You sleeping off a bender or—*holy shit*—you brought home a piece of ass last night?" The laughter died in his throat as his eyes met hers. The smile on his face twisted into something ugly. "Not just any piece of ass. *The* piece of ass." He tipped an imaginary hat. "Your Highness."

"You can let yourself out the same way you came in," Kane growled.

"And miss the opportunity to catch up on old times?" He shook his head. "No way." He parked himself on the foot of the bed. "So, have you managed to pull the stick out of your ass sometime in the past decade, or is it trapped up there forever?"

A vicious kick from Kane knocked him off the mattress, but he popped right back onto his feet with a dark chuckle. "C'mon now, little brother, you know I speak the truth. Getting ditched by Princess Bitch here was the best thing that ever happened to

261

you. But maybe her tight ass is good for something you never told me about."

Kane sprang from the bed and lunged at his brother. "Get the fuck out of here before I forget we're family, Scott."

"Wouldn't be the first time, with *her* in the picture." Despite his big talk, Scott backed out of the room, ducking Kane's swing.

Both men completely ignored the fact Kane was stark naked. She could not. His physique was damn near perfect. Broad shoulders and sculpted arms framed a strong back that tapered down to his waist in a vee. The muscles in his ass flexed as he walked, and his legs had a thickness they didn't carry years ago.

She barely even noticed the tattoos anymore, though the relatively empty expanse of skin on his back was a bit of a surprise. There was only…

For a moment her heart stopped. Then it started racing.

MANDY was written in thick, bold print across the expanse of his back. Each letter looked to be the size of her palm, and the word stretched over his shoulder blades.

Distantly, she heard raised voices echo from the next room. Kane was pissed; Scott sounded like he was mocking him. But she couldn't focus on their words.

How long had he had it?

Why? Why would he do such a thing?

Even as she asked herself the questions, she knew the answers.

He loved her. He'd always loved her. Even when

she broke his heart. Even now. She knew it like she knew her own name. Like she knew the sun would rise every morning and set every night. Kane Hale was as constant as the northern star. And she was so very ashamed she'd ever doubted him.

The club was not who he was, and even if it took time for him to figure it out, she knew it now. She'd wait.

When he returned to the room, the full-frontal view wiped out all ability to think. There were no tattoos on his torso, only muscular pecs and washboard abs, both dusted with dark hair. His dick hung heavy between his legs, all signs of arousal gone, but still impressive.

His gruff voice snapped her attention up to his face. "I'm so fucking sorry. He should have never spoken to you like that." His eyes darkened. "Or seen you like this."

Crap. She was naked too. At least the blanket covered most of her. "It's not your fault. You couldn't have known what would happen."

He grunted as he bent over to grab his underwear off the floor. "There's no excuse."

Why was he getting dressed?

"I have to go." He buttoned his jeans, then sat beside her on the bed and took her hand. "God knows I'd rather stay here with you."

So, do it.

He sighed. "But there's club business I need to give my attention." His scowl softened the longer he stared at her face. "You look so right, here in my bed. You belong here. With me."

Damn right she did.

"Stay as long as you want." He let go of her hand, then dropped a silver key into her palm. "Scott can't let himself in anymore; I want you to have this. Be here any time. All the time. We're going to figure this all out, Mandy, as long as we do it together."

The image of her name on his back flashed through her mind, and her fingers curled around the metal in her palm. "We'll figure it out," she whispered.

He gave her a small smile, then stood and covered his beautiful chest with a T-shirt. "My brother is waiting outside. I'll call you, okay?" His gaze raked over her one more time, and he strode out of the room. Moments later, she heard the door close behind him.

This wasn't going to be easy. Nathan was going to be an issue. Scott. The club. Her father.

But they would figure out how to deal with it all. Together, they would find a way to put all their demons behind them.

CHAPTER TWENTY

Kane

Scott had an obnoxious smirk on his face when Kane walked out of the apartment. Like he took pleasure in forcing him out of bed with his girl.

Where was the guy who gave up two months of Saturdays to help him rebuild his engine last spring?

"You're an asshole." The idea he had to ride bitch behind his brother only made his irritation burn brighter, which was quite a feat, considering how pissed he felt walking away from a naked Mandy.

They'd been so close to making love this morning. He'd had no doubt she'd wanted him. Her body had been so wet and welcoming. She'd looked at him the same way she did the first time they were together.

She was right fucking there, and Scott had to ruin it.

He growled as he climbed on the bike behind his brother, and the bastard had the nerve to laugh.

"Stop whining, man. It's only pussy; it's not like you can't hit it later." Scott fired up the engine and pulled out onto the street. The wind and the purr of the motor made talking impossible on the way to the clubhouse, but once they arrived, Kane had plenty to say.

"You enjoyed being a blowhard back there. You've never liked Mandy. You made it clear back in the day. You probably cheered in the hospital waiting room when she dumped me." He shoved at his brother's shoulder as he climbed off. His adrenaline still needed an outlet after the shit her ex pulled at the work site.

"Aw, fuck you. You always put that gash before your family. Who put your sorry ass back together when she dropped you like yesterday's garbage? Me." Scott stalked toward him on the sidewalk. "Hell no, I don't like her. She's a rich, entitled cunt who thinks she is better than everyone else. Everyone, including you."

He cocked back his fist, ready to pound Scott's mouth shut, but his arm was caught in an iron grip.

"I don't know what's going on here," Cue Ball rumbled, "but y'all need to stop. We've got work to do."

That's right. Malcolm had insisted on a club meeting, but Scott hadn't said why. He relaxed in his friend's grip. "I'm fine. Let's go."

The rest of the crew already sat around the table when they walked into the chapel.

"So glad you could join us," Malcolm muttered. "Now, let's call this meeting to order." The low rumble of chatter died. "My son and I have been

266

talking about the intersection of our two current business ventures and how one could impact the other."

Thank God. Malcolm was finally taking his warning seriously.

"We've been running guns for the Russians for a while now, and though business there isn't what it used to be, it's a relationship I feel we should maintain. I've been thinking over the best way to do it, and Scott had an idea."

Scott? Aw, fuck.

"We should offer to keep selling our guns to Ace and his crew."

Kane shook his head mutely. This was exactly what they shouldn't do. Unfortunately, no one cared what he thought. He cursed himself for not taking the time to talk to each and every brother ahead of the vote, try to convince them one on one. At least this time, his vote would be heard. "I vote nay."

A dozen heads swiveled sharply in his direction.

"Why not, brother?" Cue Ball tilted his head. "Sounds like a win-win."

"Because Sergei doesn't want us in the drug business." He turned to Frank. "He made it very clear during our last run."

"You think so, Frank?" Scratch asked, stroking his long goatee.

Frank shrugged uncomfortably. "I didn't really hear much of what he said. I was checking out the guns when he talked to Kane."

His face heated. "You questioning my word, Scratch? Since when have I ever lied to you?"

Now it was the older man's turn to look

uncomfortable. He shifted in his seat. "No, I'm not questioning your word. I'm only wondering if you really understood him right."

Bullshit. "I understood him fine."

Scott smiled and opened his arms wide. "Even if it's true, Sergei is a businessman. When we sell his merchandise and give him the money, he's not going to care where it comes from. Profit is a great motivator."

"You're wrong." Wrong and pigheaded. "I vote nay."

"It's a yay for me." Malcolm's voice was ice-cold.

"And a yay for me," Scott echoed.

The other guys shifted in their seats, clearly torn in their allegiance.

"I vote nay," Cue Ball said quietly.

"Nay," echoed Frank.

Scratch cleared his throat. "The word of my president is enough for me. Yay." Every other man followed suit.

"The yays have it." Malcolm grinned. "Kane, reach out to Ace. Extend the offer."

"No."

Everyone froze. No one told Malcolm no; moreover, no one worked against a club vote. This was no small transgression. He had just given the middle finger to a very sacred code.

Scott banged his fist on the table. "You're back with your ex-bitch for five minutes, and you're already turning your back on your brothers. Where's your fucking loyalty?"

His fingernails dug into the wood. "This *is*

loyalty. I love my brothers. I'm not going to be the reason a single one of them ends up dead."

Scratch scowled. "You were outvoted, son. You've got no right to make decisions for the rest of us."

"I won't do it." Damn the consequences. He was no fool…there *would* be consequences. "I'll be out back. Y'all do what you have to do."

He walked to the carport, trying to ignore the sinking feeling in his stomach. This was a clear violation of club rules, and he'd have to pay the piper. The wait wasn't long.

Scratch barreled out the door, fists clenched at his side. Kane dug his hands in his pockets and tensed his muscles against his friend's punch to the gut. The guy fucking pummeled him, cursing after each hit until the next guy stepped in to take his place. Pete was up after him. Then Joe.

Every member of the club had the right to take a pound of flesh, but it seemed Scott was the last one in line. Kane expected him to smile when he threw his first punch, but his brother didn't look happy at all. In fact, with each hit, his face grew more somber. He stopped at three, though he could have easily claimed more. Kane slid to the ground.

"Why can't you be on my side?" Scott murmured. "I love you, man." Shaking his head, he walked away.

Kane curled up, letting the warmth from the space heater wash over him. Everything hurt, but honestly, he'd expected worse.

What really threw him was the look of betrayal on his brother's face a minute ago. No one could make him mad the way Scott could. For fuck's sake, he'd been ready to deck the guy less than an hour ago. Still, he had no doubt his brother loved him. But Scott wanted a blind kind of devotion he couldn't give. Loving someone didn't mean you agreed on everything.

For Scott, though, love meant loyalty and unflinching faith. At the end of the day, he knew it was the root of his dislike for Mandy. Scott was jealous. It was one thing to share his brother with the club, but with a woman? No way.

It hadn't been an issue for a long time.

He closed his eyes for what could have been a few seconds, a few minutes, or an hour before a deep voice prompted him to open them again.

"A ballsy move in there, brother." Cue Ball's big black shit-kickers took up his entire field of vision. "You're lucky you're still in one piece."

He took the man's proffered hand and allowed himself to be pulled to his feet. The world spun momentarily around him. "I was only trying to protect the club."

His friend ran a hand over his bald head. "I understand, but it's not how things work here, and you know it." Cue sighed. "You look like shit. Let's go get you cleaned up."

He staggered toward the house, his mind moving faster than his bruised body. Tonight made it very clear his club would not see reason. If they kept blindly following his brother, it would be a disaster for everyone.

He knew what he had to do.

***

Amanda

The ride back to her condo gave Amanda plenty of opportunity for reflection. Her thoughts mostly centered on the almost-sex she had this morning and the view of Kane in all his naked glory afterward.

He could be hers again. He might be already.

She was still reliving it all when she pulled into her garage and found her father leaning against the trunk of his BMW, arms folded and crossed over his chest.

He stood up straight. "Where have you been?"

She sighed. "None of your business, Dad." Walking past him, she headed toward her building.

He followed a half-step behind but didn't speak again until they were inside her condo. "I saw Nathan this morning. He looks like he was hit by a truck."

"Good." She eyed the bathroom door. A shower sounded like heaven. Her feet had to be disgusting after walking around barefoot all morning.

His eyes widened. "Good? Are you stupid? He's out for blood. Yours and mine, thanks to your knight in shining armor."

She wasn't sure how she still managed to be surprised by her father's lack of interest in her well-being. "Sorry I wasn't thinking about your run for governor while he was trying to choke me to death, Dad. I've always been selfish when it comes to breathing and everything." With another longing look toward the shower, she then turned her attention to the kitchen. She hadn't eaten in twenty-four hours.

"Always so dramatic. Nathan was not trying to kill you."

With a dull laugh, Amanda unwound the scarf of Kane's she'd donned in the car. The evidence of Nathan's attack was an unmistakable palate of purple and black bruises around her neck. "Dramatic?" she deadpanned. "Get out, Dad."

He froze for a fraction of a second, staring at her battered skin. Then, he continued his rant. "He says you were unfaithful to him while you were together. You couldn't just keep your legs closed for a few months?" He paced the room. "He said you were slumming with one of the men on your crew." He stopped, realization dawning in his eyes. "Kane Hale."

She pulled a loaf of bread from the top of the refrigerator and started assembling a roast beef sandwich. No chance she was going to hash out her relationship with her father for the umpteenth time.

She got as far as spreading the mayo when her dad stepped into her space. "What is it about a piece of garbage like him you get so enthralled over? Tell me. There are hundreds of white-trash, blue-collar fortune hunters out there. Why this one? And for God's sake, why now?"

She tossed the butter knife in the sink and lifted her chin. "Fortune hunter? You really think so? Kane doesn't give a good goddamn about your money. He never has."

"Of course not. He only wants you for you." Her father's voice dripped with derision. "Why else would he latch onto a woman he has absolutely nothing in common with?"

"Nice to know you think my connections are the only reason a man could want me." She piled the deli meat onto the bread and took a savage bite.

"I'm sure your loose morals didn't hurt either," he sneered.

She forced herself to swallow before she choked. "I am a grown woman. Who I sleep with is none of your concern. I don't ask where you stick your dick, Dad, and frankly, I don't want to know."

"I wish I had the same luxury. Unfortunately, your actions reflect directly on me, and I will not have you regressing back into a relationship with a thug you should have outgrown a decade ago." His eyes blazed fury. "Kane Hale will rue the day he tried to enter your life again, you hear me? I am going to absolutely annihilate him. There will be nothing left of his life to put back together when I'm done."

"Dad." She dropped her sandwich back to the napkin on the counter and followed him as he strode to the door.

"No." He looked at her over his shoulder as he turned the knob. "I've given you every opportunity to make something of your life. An education. An introduction to the right kind of people."

"The right kind? You mean the rich kind. The kind who could help you with your aspirations. It never mattered if they were snobs or bigots or bullies. It never mattered if they talked down to me or got too handsy behind one of the potted plants." Her voice climbed. "Because it was never about me.

273

It was always about how it could benefit you. It's probably the only reason you have me in your life at all. To use as a tool for your gain."

"How dare you? If anyone is a user in this relationship, it's you, darling." He drawled the endearment with malice. "You made no secret you preferred your mother and Charlie's family to this one. Their home was the only place you wanted to be. The only thing I was ever good for was my money."

"That's not—"

"Not true?" He laughed. "Whose money solved your little criminal's legal problems all those years ago? Who bailed out your precious Charlie's pathetic company? Dear old Dad. The same one who used you as a commodity. The same one who doesn't care whether you live or die. How do you reconcile the knowledge with your image of me, I wonder?" This time when he turned the doorknob, he pulled the door open and stepped out. "I meant what I said. Hale's life as he knows it is over. He thinks he knows what it means to suffer. His suffering has only just begun."

CHAPTER TWENTY-ONE

Amanda

Amanda couldn't force herself to finish her sandwich after her father left; the taste had turned to sawdust in her mouth. She texted Kane, then finally trudged to the shower.

The hot water was a balm on the tense muscles of her shoulders. Resting her palms against the wall, she lowered her head, allowing the spray to beat over her back.

Her confrontation with her dad had left her shaken. She had no doubt he'd meant every word he'd said. The part where he questioned her loyalty was par for the course. He'd always been paranoid she loved Charlie more than him.

What really worried her were his threats against Kane. He already had something in motion after his meeting with the Skulls' rival biker guy. Now, who knows what he would do? He had the money and influence to do almost anything. His only limit was his imagination.

She turned to relax on the built-in bench, then massaged the soap over her feet. The time in the water had already made inroads into the dirt, but rubbing her thumbs over the pad of one foot, then another, comforted her. By the time she finally felt clean, her fingers had started to prune.

A quick check of her phone showed no response from Kane when she got out. So, she slipped into her favorite pair of flannel pajama pants and an oversized T-shirt before tumbling into bed for a nap. She didn't wake until a knock sounded at the door.

Her chest tightened as her first thought flew to Nathan. Then, she remembered she'd told Mickey to take him off her white-list. Her father sure as hell wasn't coming back. Only one possibility remained. "Kane."

When she threw open the door, the tight feeling in her chest came back with a vengeance. Yes, it was him, but it looked like her father had already made good on his promise.

He sported a black left eye and a shadowed right cheek. He stooped over a little and clutched his ribs as he shuffled in.

She slid under his arm and allowed him to use her for support as he lurched slowly to the sofa. "What happened?" she breathed. "Did you get jumped?"

He ran his hand through his unbound hair. "In a manner of speaking. The guys in the club did this."

She gasped. "Not because of me?"

"No. It had nothing to do with you." He patted her leg lightly. "It was club business."

Oh no. This was not a road they were going down. "Club business," she repeated carefully. "So basically, what you're saying is...it's none of *my* business."

His lips thinned.

"I mean, it's okay to spend the night in your bed. Hell, I can even let myself in your apartment. But I can't know why you can barely walk, because it's *club business,* and I'm only—what's it called—an old lady." She shook her head ruefully. "As if I could forget how much respect the title affords."

Her face flamed with anger. After everything she'd been through in the past twenty-four hours, she felt like someone had pulled her guts out and stomped all over them. All she wanted, all she needed, was to get back inside the little bubble she and Kane had created at his apartment. Only, she knew her wish was unrealistic.

He rubbed his eyes. "It's not like that."

She took a deep breath, forcing her raging emotions into check. "Okay." Deep breath in. Deep breath out. "Tell me what happened."

His mouth opened, then closed again, indecision dancing across his features.

This was it. The moment of truth. The moment where she would know how tight the club had him in its grip.

A minute passed. Two. Her chest squeezed painfully, and she sank deeper into the cushions of the sofa and closed her eyes. "Just go." Despite her nap, she was so tired. Maybe she could sleep right here. Sleep until all of this went away.

She was so sure he wasn't going to answer. When he did, his voice made her jump. "My brother and my father are leading the club into making a major mistake."

Her eyes flew open.

Kane had his head in his hands. "They're going to get someone killed." He looked up, seeking her eyes. "I defied them. I refused an order after the club voted." He gestured to his face. "This was my punishment."

Gasping, she sprang forward, examining his injuries with new eyes. "Your own friends did this to you...because you *disagreed* with them?"

He nodded. "I know how it sounds, but it *is* club business, and I'm not supposed to talk about it. I also know I don't really belong there. Not because of the beat-down, but I don't know. I thought maybe I could make a difference, turn the club into something better or at least keep it from getting worse, but I was living a fantasy. I can't save anyone who doesn't want to save themselves."

Carefully, she wrapped her arm around his shoulders. "Oh, Kane, I'm sorry." She really was. Not because he realized he didn't belong in a motorcycle gang, but because it hurt him to admit it. She was sorry, too, if it meant he had to mourn his friends.

"I'm going to talk to the guys about patching out. It's going to suck. I'll probably lose them all. No way around it." He sounded so desolate.

She wanted so much to find the right words, but she knew how unforgiving their code was. He'd told her himself, years before. "You won't lose me," she said gently, and his muscles locked beneath her hands. "You'll never lose me again, Kane. I'm yours, as long as you want me."

He held his body rigid for a moment, his eyes blinking rapidly. "Are you sure?" He cleared his throat. "Because I'm not sure my heart can survive breaking again, baby. The last time damn near killed me."

"You *won't lose me*. We need to be honest with each other, though. I ruined things before by thinking I was protecting you. It was the wrong call. We could have faced it together. We'll do better this time. We'll learn from my mistake."

In the somber silence, his stomach let out a growl so loud she could have heard it in the next room. The tips of his ears turned red, and he chuckled self-consciously. "Sorry. Guess I haven't eaten in a while."

The reminder about food made her own stomach answer the call with a growl of its own. "How about I make us some dinner?"

He lifted his eyebrows. "You're offering to cook? The woman who put a boiled egg in the microwave and made it explode?"

"A lot of time has passed since then," she said primly. "Plus, I took some cooking classes a few years back. You may be surprised to discover what I can do in the kitchen these days."

"To the contrary." His face relaxed into a genuine smile. "I'm not surprised by anything you're able to accomplish. You have it in you to take over the world someday."

"I don't need the whole world. Only you, Mike, and the company." She stood and offered him her hand. "Let's start with conquering the kitchen."

He allowed her to lead him to the sink where they both washed their hands. "Okay, Iron Chef, what do we have on the menu?"

She opened the refrigerator door and surveyed the contents. "I've got some leftover grilled chicken." Stepping over to the pantry, she stooped down to examine one of the lower shelves, then triumphantly pulled out a can of artichoke hearts. "Oh, yeah, I know just the thing. If we work together, it can be ready in ten minutes."

With her goal in sight, she piled ingredients onto the counter: green onions, mushrooms, olive oil, and feta. Then, she turned on a pot of water to boil. "Cutting board is in the drawer in front of you, Hale. Those green onions aren't going to chop themselves."

With a small salute, he got to work, chopping the vegetables, while she melted some butter in a pan. Soon, the kitchen filled with the savory scent of sautéed mushrooms.

Kane hummed a song she didn't recognize while he opened the can of artichoke hearts. The whole thing felt so simple and domestic, like this was their kitchen, and they'd cooked together a million times. Like they had done it before, and it was a given they would do it again. And again. And again.

But would they really? With her father and Nathan and the club all wanting to tear them apart?

He looked up and caught her watching him, but he didn't call her on it. "You want these in the pan with the other stuff?"

The knot of emotion building in her chest kept her from answering aloud, but her smile and nod were enough. He stepped in beside her at the range and dumped in the drained contents. His nearness was almost a physical caress.

She leaned into him, and he kissed the top of her head. Oh yeah, she could get used to this. "Grab the chicken," she murmured. "We need to add some too." Pouring some angel hair into the now bubbling water, she tried to quiet her swelling feelings for the man currently taking up all the air in the room. Though she failed miserably, it wasn't in her to regret it. The way she felt about Kane was like sunshine warming her from the inside out.

Within five minutes, they'd drained the pasta and tossed it with the chicken, vegetables, and a dressing of olive oil, lemon, and Greek seasoning. He eyed the feta cheese as she carried it to the table. He always used to call it *the stinky stuff.*

"Don't worry." She rolled her eyes. "I'll keep it on the side."

They ate in companionable silence the first few minutes, their mutual hunger keeping their attention on the food in front of them. It wasn't until her plate was clean, Amanda took a sip of her wine and leaned back into the chair.

"Dinner was amazing," Kane announced as he wiped his face with a napkin. "Whoever gave you cooking lessons deserves some kind of medal."

She balled up her own napkin and tossed it at his head. It flew past his ear as he evaded the projectile. "I like cooking. The class was originally only something to pass the time, but it ended up being more than just another distraction. I needed a lot of those at first."

"I get it." He tried the wine and wrinkled his nose before returning his glass to the table. "My distractions were a little less...constructive...but I did the same thing."

"You know what I miss?"

"The amazing sex?"

She searched for another napkin to throw but came up empty. "Dancing with you." One of her favorite memories was Charlie's Fourth of July party, where they ended the night dancing under the stars to an old Journey song.

"A problem we can easily fix." He got up and bowed slightly. "May I have this dance?"

Amanda bit her lip. She had the entire album on her phone. With a few swipes of her finger, the opening strains of "Lights" drifted from her small, mounted speakers.

His eyes closed briefly as he took in the music. "You remembered."

She took his hand. "I'll never forget."

Stepping into his arms felt like going back in time. She was reliving one of her best memories, but now it was even better. It meant more because this time she knew to savor it. Even if they only had this night, she would treasure every second. Resting her head on his chest, she breathed in his familiar scent. She reveled in the feel of his strong arms around her.

They didn't do much more than sway; they never had, but it was a thousand times more satisfying than the perfect waltz her father's connections loved to show off at their fancy Christmas parties. When he started singing into her hair, she wanted to melt into a puddle on the floor.

As the song ended and another ballad began, she lifted her head.

His eyes were fathomless. "I want to dance with you for the rest of my life."

When he leaned down to capture her lips, it was so much more than a mere kiss. It was a reassurance, a promise, a claiming.

What started as a gentle brush of his mouth intensified in seconds. His tongue slid in her mouth, and she answered with all the longing and passion she'd suppressed for years. It was perfect, yet she was greedy for more. Nothing would be enough. Forever with this man would not be enough.

She broke the kiss only long enough to lead him to her bedroom. Immediately, she went to work on his clothes, pulling his shirt over his head. This time, she allowed herself the luxury of touching his beautiful skin. Her fingertips ran up his arms, over his wide shoulders, and down over his chest to his puckering nipples.

He held himself still while she explored him, his body pulled taut as a bowstring.

She could see in his face, the exact moment he let himself go, his gaze reflecting hunger and heat.

He had her shirt off in seconds as she worked her pajama pants to the floor. In two strides, he backed her up to her bed and climbed on top of her, blanketing her body with his.

The weight of him felt different, heavier, but she

would have known the feel of him anywhere. The way he kissed her neck, the way he worshipped her collarbone as he worked his way down to her breast. He'd refined his technique a little, but it was still classic Kane.

Her hands moved over him with urgent desperation. She needed his pants off, his thick cock driving into her body. The foreplay was sweet torture.

Lifting his hips, he gave her access to the button of his jeans, and once his fly was open, he tugged them down and kicked them off before returning to his ministrations.

He licked and sucked at one nipple while rolling and twisting the other between his fingers. His dick pushed insistently against the thin barrier of her panties.

She groaned and lifted her hips to meet his thrusts. The pressure and the friction only drove her need higher. "Kane, please."

His head dipped lower, giving her a clear picture where he was going. *Yes.* Finally, she would feel him where her need pulsed so desperately. But when his face was just inches from her panties, he didn't take them off as she'd hoped.

Instead, she felt his hot breath over the silky, damp material. Her body quaked as he slid his finger around the elastic, directly inside her. Her muscles clenched around him, grateful for the invasion, but still needy for more.

That's when he fastened his mouth over her clit. He sucked at her straight through her panties, and her body almost came off the bed. It was amazing;

it was masterful; it was pure fucking torture. "Stop teasing me," she cried.

He looked up, his dark eyes hooded. "You always liked my mouth on you before."

"Later," she pleaded, reaching blindly for her nightstand. When her hand found the foil packet she was looking for, she held it out to him. "I want all of you. Don't make us wait any more."

With a growl, he ripped the side of her panties, revealing her to him completely. "Just one taste," he gritted, before delving back between her legs. His tongue swept a path over her core up to her now-aching clit. Then he pulled the condom from her hand and covered himself with practiced ease.

Before she could dwell on how many times he'd done the same with countless other women, he plunged inside her with one stroke. As wet and wanting as she was, her body offered no resistance. She cried out with the rightness of it.

For a moment, Kane's eyes went hooded. He stopped moving entirely, his dick seated fully inside of her. "You're perfect," he whispered. Then his body let loose.

His hips pistoned, and he drove inside her with an almost frenzied pace. It was unmeasured, unrefined, and his lack of control only drove her higher. His hands touched her everywhere, as if he was starving, and she was a feast. But the best part, along with his recklessness and needfulness, came reverence and worship. He never stopped telling her how beautiful she was, how good she felt, how his dreams were coming true.

The last exaltation drove her to the edge. His

weren't the only dreams coming true. Kane was here, in her bed, and though he hadn't said the words, he loved her. She knew it in her bones. With the gift of the knowledge in her heart, and his thumb working in tandem with his dick between her legs, her body crested in a shattering release.

His orgasm followed a heartbeat behind with a roar of her name. He didn't pull out when he was done but levered the top half of his body onto his elbows and gazed into her eyes. His stare never wavered as his heavy breaths slowed into their natural rhythm. Finally, he rolled to his back, pulling her into his arms.

There was no need to talk for a while. She lay in the comfort of his embrace, listening to his heart beat in his chest. She never wanted to move.

He spoke first. "I told myself it wasn't as good as I remembered." He shifted slightly so he could pet her hair. "I convinced myself I'd built you up in my head so much, no one else could ever compete. I mean, if it was really perfect with you, how could I—what chance did I have to ever be happy again?"

His words could have come from her own mouth. For years, she'd tried to lie to herself too. "It's so good because we were always supposed to be together. Anyone else, in my life at least, was only a placeholder. For a while, I pretended they were you. Eventually, it just hurt more, so I tried to pretend you never existed." She kissed his warm skin beneath her cheek. "Which was an even bigger failure. In the end, I was going through the motions, but really I'd just given up."

"Is that what you were doing with the guy who

hurt you? Going through the motions?" He kept his voice tightly controlled.

She didn't want to talk about Nathan, but she had promised him honesty barely a couple of hours ago, and she'd meant what she said. "Nathan was a business arrangement with my father." Wow, it sounded even worse when she said it out loud. "I asked my father for a loan to help out with the company. He offered me the money free and clear if I would be Nathan's armpiece for six months."

"Why?"

She sighed. "Because he's politically connected, and my father wants to be governor. Because my father wanted to get an opening into Nathan's good graces. Because I needed the money, and I didn't care if it made me a whore. Like I said, I'd given up, at least on finding someone I could love. And with Nathan, there was really no chance I'd develop any feelings. It almost made it easier for him to be such a dick; I never felt guilty for the fact I didn't love him. Who could love someone like him?"

From the corner of her eye, she watched him ball his fist and let it go. "Did he hurt you? When you were together?"

She shifted. "A little. Sometimes. Which is why I told my father I didn't want anything more to do with him. My six months was up at Thanksgiving. But my dad tried to change the deal; he made me promise to give him four more weeks or he'd withhold the money. I said yes, but I never saw Nathan again until the night I broke up with him. The night you came here and kissed me."

"He was the person on the phone."

It wasn't a question, but she answered him anyway. "Yes. I went there to end things for good, and he saw the beard-burns on my face. It went downhill from there."

Kane sat up, pulling her with him. "He hurt you that night? Because of me?"

"He wanted to. But I knew it might happen, so I brought a gun." She couldn't hold his gaze, dropping her eyes to her lap. "I think he's been stalking me ever since. I'm hoping the beat-down he got from Evan Ryan takes him down a notch or two."

"Not good enough." His eyes burned with fury. "I want to rip his fucking head off."

She shook her head. "He'll be waiting for it. You'll only end up in jail, and I refuse to lose you again, especially because of him. I'm going to clean up my own mess and do it the legal way. I'm going to file a restraining order."

His fingers found her chin and tilted her face back up. "This is not your fault."

It was sweet of him to say so. "I don't know if I agree with you. I opened the door. Nobody forced me. I'm ashamed I let him into my life, but I can't blame anyone but myself."

"Blame *him*. Only a bottom-feeding pussy puts his hands on a woman in anger."

"Oh, I do, but what I meant—"

"And your father—"

"My father is a businessman," she said firmly, "and I'm just another one of his assets. Or at least I was. He's as pissed as Nathan is right now." Oh, shit. How could she have forgotten her father's threat? "It's the reason I texted you earlier. My dad is gunning for you. He says he's going to ruin you." Her words started running together as her fear for him returned. "You've got to be careful. He's furious we're together again."

He smiled.

What the hell?

"Then it really is like old times."

She swatted his arm. "Not funny. My father is a powerful man. He was already working with the white supremacist freak I told you about. Now it's personal."

Kane blinked lazily and pulled her back to him. "Scarier men than Beau Griffin have tried to take me down. Let him try. With you at my side, I'm fucking invincible."

CHAPTER TWENTY-TWO

Kane

Kane couldn't remember the last time he'd been so excited about Christmas. He didn't have just one, but two invitations to celebrate this year. Neither was with his own family, of course. Nothing had changed about the way the club ignored the holiday.

He'd meant it when he told Mandy he planned to patch out, but selfishly, he wanted to wait until after Christmas. They wouldn't be sentimental about it, but he would. He didn't want to face the holiday knowing he was dead to them. Plus, if he was there to oversee one last exchange with Ace, they'd have at least something to work with before they lost their drug connection. Because he had no doubt, without him, Ace and his products were history.

So, he kept his head down; he went to work every day and the clubhouse every night to see his mom. As much as she loved him, she'd choose the club when the dust settled. Her devotion to his father lived above all things, and Malcolm would never forgive his defection.

Mandy didn't offer a word of complaint. After all the time they'd spent apart, he knew how much she craved his company. God knew, he felt the same way. But she also knew how serious it was to walk away from his brothers. In less than a week, he'd be all hers.

He worried for her safety, though. She'd filed the restraining order she'd told him about, but her ex, Nathan, was a loose cannon. A quick call to Mike filled her brother in on everything. His old friend hired private security on the spot, and at least two guys had quietly trailed her ever since.

He didn't cut himself off from her entirely. In addition to texts and a few private pictures on social media, he'd surprised her with a quick visit and a few amazing kisses at her place Monday after work and more of the same in her parking garage Wednesday morning. He was tempted to crawl in her bed after he finished his club business every night, but after dealing with drugs and guns day in and day out, he felt too tired and dirty to face her.

Now his last deal with Ace was done. It was Christmas Eve, likely the last night he'd ever spend with his brother. Like all the others, Scott would shun him when he turned in his cut. For all the stupid shit the man said and did lately, he was family, and they had a lifetime of history. Kane loved him, and his heart hurt as he let himself into the clubhouse.

Scott was shooting pool by himself at the table.

"Got any room for me over there?"

His brother's face lit at the offer, and he gathered the balls together to start a new game. Whatever disagreements they had over the drugs or with Mandy, Scott clearly welcomed the opportunity to hang together. "Wanna break?" He offered Kane his stick.

"Nah. You've always been better at it than me."

Scott preened a little before taking his shot. The balls scattered, and the one-ball sank in the corner pocket. "Solids," his brother announced and proceeded to drop two more balls before missing his third shot.

Kane tanked his shot on purpose to make his brother grin.

"Ha, ha. Out of practice, baby bro. Watch and learn. The master is at work." Afterward, Scott ran the table, his smile growing progressively bigger with every ball he put in the pocket. Once he sunk the eight-ball, he let out a whoop and spun around on his heel. "Come out with me tonight, K. We'll grab a beer at The Watering Hole." He wrinkled his nose. "Unless Princess Bitch has you on too tight a leash."

He let the dig on Mandy slide. "Sure, brother. First round's on me."

It wasn't surprising to see the crowd gathered at the bar. If anything, he was shocked his father wasn't there picking up a piece of Christmas ass. Thank heaven for small favors.

He bought his brother a beer, which turned into two and eventually three. They shot pool again, played a round of darts. He even paid to play

Scott's favorite song on the jukebox, so they could sing along together. What he wanted to do was explain why he was patching out, to tell him he loved him. To beg him to understand. He knew Scott too well, though, to even try. Instead, he bought yet another round of drinks; he sang more songs, and he laughed at Scott's lame-ass jokes. Then he let his brother use him as a sounding board for his ideas about a new tattoo.

"I was thinking a scorpion, man." Grabbing a pen from Hangman, Scott sketched a design on the top of his hand. "Maybe we could get a matching set this year. Something special for my blood-brother."

He doubted Scott would feel the same in a couple of days, but he nodded anyway. "Yeah, man. Sounds great."

At closing time, he had to force himself to leave. When he dropped Scott back at the clubhouse, he walked him to the door and pulled him into a tight hug. "I love you, brother."

Scott took it in stride, returning the embrace with a drunken smile. "I love you too, man. Thanks for tonight. Most fun I've had in ages."

He rubbed his chest as his brother let himself in the house. Scott didn't know this was the last night they'd spend together, but the knowledge burned a hole in Kane's heart. With one last hug, he'd just told his brother goodbye.

***

Having lunch with Brick and his fiancé provided

a welcome distraction from the cloud hanging over Kane's head. The potluck meal gave him a chance not only to break bread with his only real friend outside of the club but some of the other guys from the construction site too.

Before they ate, he quietly thanked the man again for his help with Mandy's ex. They'd talked about it once already this week, but it bore repeating. He owed Brick, Cyrus, and Evan more than he could ever repay.

Brick waved his words away. "You've done plenty for me. I wouldn't even be here without you. Wouldn't have my girl, this house. You don't owe me shit. It was my pleasure dragging his sorry ass off the property. I only regret Evan got a crack at him and I didn't."

He told no one about his plans to leave the club after the holiday; instead, he absorbed the laughter and the love in the room like a sponge. As fun as it was, though, it was only the warm-up for an afternoon at the Cooper house.

Mandy was already there, working on the food with Cindy. When he'd told her about his invitation from Brick, about the growing friendship they had, she'd insisted he go there first. His arrival at the Coopers' was supposed to be a surprise; he hoped everyone would consider it a good one.

Why was he so nervous? He'd known these people for years. He was only there a couple of weeks ago.

But I wasn't back with Mandy then.

Would they be happy to see the man he'd become as a permanent fixture in their family? He'd find out soon enough.

He took a deep breath and knocked on the door. It swung open before he even let it out. Then Mandy fell into his arms, and nothing mattered but the smell of her hair and the way she whispered his name.

"Who is it?" Cindy's voice drifted out from the living room. "Amanda?" She exhaled sharply. "Oh my God, Mike. It's Kane. Is he…are you…*are you guys together?*"

The joy in her voice put to rest any concerns he had about his welcome. When Mandy finally let him go, Cindy practically elbowed her aside to give him a hug of her own. "We've been waiting a long time to have you back here, my friend. I hope you're sure about this because you're stuck with us now."

He hugged her back with the same warmth she bestowed on him. Her grip was strong and after all these years, she still smelled like coconuts.

"All of you need to get your asses in the house and shut the door," Mike grumbled. "I'm freezing my nuts off."

Flanked by the women, he followed Mike's voice into the warmth of the house. Mandy's brother looked transformed from a few weeks earlier. Though he was still in the wheelchair, the casts were off his legs, and he'd put on at least ten pounds. His little girl had her arms locked around his neck. "Looking good, old friend."

Mike set his daughter on the floor, and she toddled away on pudgy feet. "I'm living right. It looks like I'll finally be able to get back to work in a couple of weeks. I'm sure my better half is ready to get me out of the house. If she has to spend much more time with me in close quarters, I may not make it out alive."

Cindy tapped the back of his head playfully. "If I wanted you dead, I wouldn't have wasted so much time nursing you back to health."

"Hey, Mom, are we going to eat or what?" Joshua tilted his upper body into the space of the doorframe to the kitchen. "I'm starving."

Mandy's hand nestled tightly in his, Kane walked with the family into the kitchen. He hadn't eaten too much at Brick's place, knowing he'd be sharing dinner here. Once the smell of Cindy's pot roast took over his senses, he knew he'd made the right choice.

"Mana, up. Mana, up." Mike's little girl was tugging on Mandy's jeans and quickly got scooped into her aunt's arms.

His woman looked right at home holding a toddler. Maybe they could talk about having one of their own.

His heartbeat picked up.

It could really happen. All those dreams he thought had died were waking up from hibernation.

The meal was delicious, and the family was everything he remembered from before. Everything but Charlie and Elizabeth Cooper. Still, their picture hung on the wall over the table, giving him the feeling the couple watched over them from wherever they were now.

It might have been perfect if Joshua would have stopped staring at him every once in a while. He crooked his eyebrow at the boy from across the table. "Do I have spinach in my teeth, or what?" He glanced down at his T-shirt. "Food on my clothes? Twigs in my hair?"

Joshua smirked. "You thought I was your kid, didn't you?"

Cindy slapped her forehead, then ran her hand over her face. "Joshua Charles Cooper, do you have no filter at all?"

The boy had a lot of nerve. Kane decided he liked it. Shooting back his own crooked smile, he feigned a shudder. "Thank God, I was wrong."

A moment of silence passed before Mandy let out an inelegant snort, and the entire table erupted in laughter. A roll flew across the table and bounced off Kane's head, leaving Mike doubled over in mirth.

It was the kind of Christmas he had always dreamed about.

He was still smiling when the phone buzzed in his pocket.

Malcolm: 911. Family emergency.

The one call he couldn't ignore. Family emergency meant shit was hitting the fan. The club needed him. This one last time, he would go.

"Thank you, guys, for including me in your Christmas dinner, but I need to get home." He kept his eyes on Mandy as he tilted his head toward the door. "Will you walk me out, babe?"

She raised her eyebrows but did as he asked. "Everything okay?"

He shook his head. "Something's wrong. I need to find out what. But after this, I'm out." Grabbing his jacket from the hook on the wall near the front door, he pulled a small box from an inside pocket. "Hold on to this. You can open it when I come back to you tonight."

Her face lit up, then her lower lip shot out as she shook the box gently. "No. You can't make me wait. You're just mean."

Leaning forward, he took a quick bite of her bottom lip. "As if I could ever tell you no. Fine, open it, but then I really do have to go."

Grinning widely, she ripped off the paper and peered inside the box. A breath escaped her as she pulled out the delicate silver chain. Attached were two entwined hearts. One was silver, engraved with the words *I Love You*; the other was white gold, marked with the word *Forever.* "I love it." Her voice cracked a little at the end. "Will you put it on me?" She lifted her hair and presented him with the back of her neck.

His big fingers were clumsy handling the tiny clasp, but after two or three tries, he managed to get it fastened. "All done." He kissed her neck. "Tonight, you can wear it for me and nothing else."

When she turned back toward him, her eyes already sparked with heat. "You can count on it."

Images of Mandy waiting for him in her bed kept him warm on the icy drive back to the clubhouse. It also kept him from speculating much about whatever crisis had inspired the text calling him home.

It never even occurred to him the plaintive wail

of sirens could be headed to the same destination he was. At least, he didn't realize it, until he turned the corner onto the clubhouse street and an array of red and blue flashing lights nearly blinded him.

At least six police cars lit up the night from their haphazard parking spots around the house. Two ambulances were on the lawn, backed up to the walkway outside the front door.

Mama V knelt in the grass, sobbing, her face tilted up to the sky. His father, shell-shocked, sat cross-legged on the ground beside her. His expression remained blank, even as Kane approached. But when his mom caught sight of him, she let out a keening cry and wrapped her arms around his legs.

He squatted to her eye level. "What's happening? Mama, what's going on?"

"My baby. My baby," she cried. It barely even sounded like his mom, her voice broken and raspy.

He wasn't getting any answers here. Pulling out of her grip, he moved toward the open front door to the house. He barely made it two steps before a gurney blocked his path. Two EMTs were rushing someone out of the house. He recognized Cue's bald head instantly. One of the medics called out his vitals.

All at once, his eyes took in the broken windows. The bullet holes scattered across the front of the house. The blood on his mother's clothes.

The EMTs quickly rolled the gurney around him, spiriting Cue Ball to the ambulance and revealing a second crew not far behind. The team in the back moved slower. A sheet covered the body on their gurney.

"Hey," he called out. "Who is that?" An officer appeared out of nowhere and grabbed his arm. "Let me *go*. I need to see who it is."

"I'm sorry, sir," the cop said firmly. "You're going to need to step back and let the men work."

"You don't understand." Panic rose. "This is my family." The second gurney rolled past. "You have to tell me. Who—" He swallowed his next words as the wheels bounced off the sidewalk into the grass, and a man's hand slid out from beneath the white sheet speckled with blood.

Twenty-four hours later, the scorpion drawing was still there.

He sunk to the ground, only a few feet away from the spot where his mother still wept.

His brother was dead. And he wouldn't rest until somebody fucking paid for it.

CHAPTER TWENTY-THREE

Amanda

Amanda ran her fingers along the outline of one of the hearts on her pendant. Wearing the necklace, she couldn't tell whether it was the one engraved *I Love You* or *Forever*. It didn't matter. Either one alone was enough to make her heart fill to bursting.

She didn't bother to hide the wide grin on her face when she returned to the table from walking Kane out. Knowing the entire family was watching, she plucked the spoon out of Mike's bowl and stuffed a bite of butter pecan ice cream in her mouth. Bliss.

"What the hell, woman?" Her brother tried to swipe the spoon back. "Get your own."

"Oh, give her a break, hon." Cindy shot her a wink. "She's got a reason to celebrate."

"Yeah, well, she doesn't need my ice cream to do it," he grumbled.

Joshua waved his hand in the air. "If anyone cares about my opinion, I like the guy. He fits right in with us…kind of weird…definitely a smart-ass."

Mike swiped the back of his head. "Watch your language," he warned, but there was no evidence of any real anger. He lifted the toddler in his lap and handed her over. "Go get your sister ready for bed, and we'll pretend like this never happened."

He waited until Joshua swept Aliyah in his gangly arms and carried her out before he spoke again. "You know I always considered Kane like a member of this family."

He wasn't exaggerating. Even though he never gave her a hard time about it, she knew Mike had suffered when Kane left their inner circle.

"Tonight was awesome," he continued. "In some ways, it was like he never left. I've got to ask, though. Are you sure about this?" He looked up at the ceiling before meeting her eyes. "A lot of time has passed. He's been running with his dad's gang. Those guys are involved in some serious shit. Last I heard, they were running guns. Not to mention, those look like some leftover bruises on his face."

She didn't know the details about their criminal activities, but she didn't doubt Mike's word. Kane didn't like to talk about how the club made its money, even when they dated the first time around, but with what she'd learned about their movement into the drug trade, nothing would surprise her. "He's patching out."

"He told you he was leaving the club?" Mike couldn't have sounded more dubious.

It annoyed her. "Actually, yes. He did. Days ago

and again tonight. He's got an emergency to take care of, then he is coming back to me."

Cindy scraped the remnants of food off the remaining plates onto an empty platter. "I hope it's true. If it is, great, but what about the years he's been part of the crew? Even if he walked into his father's club with his hands clean, you think they are now? And for God's sake," she lowered her voice to a whisper, "I hope you make him get tested before you get freaky. Who knows where he's been dipping his wick?"

Mike groaned. "Do not talk about my sister having sex, Cin."

"Why not?" Cindy stopped cleaning long enough to shoot him a dirty look. "Amanda is full-grown, and she deserves to get laid every bit as much as you do. I just don't want her to end up with a raging case of the clap."

"I'm not getting the clap." That's why God invented condoms. "Look, I appreciate you both looking out for me, but as you said, I'm a big girl. All I need from you guys is your love and support. And if it's not too much trouble, maybe you can be happy for me. I haven't felt like this in a long time."

Mike stirred the soupy remains of his dessert. "We are happy for you, and really, I want Kane back. I always thought we would end up raising our kids together and being the cool dads our kids want at parties."

"No one wants you at parties, Dad." Joshua's taunt came in loud and clear from the next room.

"Keep it up, and I'll say no to the PlayStation game you asked to download." Mike shook his head and muttered, "Smartass."

The idea of a little boy with Kane's dark hair and big heart was what her dreams were made of. Even when the possibility of a future with him had been less than zero, all her fantasy children had his smile. "I'd love for my kids to grow up with yours."

"All I'm asking is if you're sure all of this is what Kane wants too. The kind of happy ever after domestic family thing we're talking about doesn't jive with the Skulls; we both know it. And if what you say is true—if he's dropping out—you've got to be ready for it to rock his world. The club has been practically everything to him for his entire adult life. I'm only saying it might be hard." He cleared his throat. "I'm going to go load the dishwasher now."

Cindy placed the stack of dishes she'd collected onto his lap and waited until he wheeled away before she spoke. "He means well."

She didn't doubt it for a second. Mike had never done anything but support her, from her choice in career, to her love life, to her relationship with her father. Her brother was her biggest cheerleader and her best friend. "I know. I'm not sure what he's asking me, though. Do I know the club is shady? *Yeah.* Do I know it's a big deal for him to patch out? *Again...yeah.* But it was his choice. It's what he wants. I'm what he wants."

"I think you're right." Cindy stood, opening her arms for a hug she was more than happy to provide. Her sister-in-law's embrace felt familiar and fortifying. "If anyone can find the magic again after a thirteen-year break, it's the two of you. I never stopped hoping you'd find your way back to each other." Cindy kissed her cheek. "Now get your ass out of here. I have a feeling he'll be calling any minute."

The lady didn't have to say it twice. She couldn't wait to get home, to have her man back in her bed.

Just as Cindy predicted, the phone buzzed moments after she walked in her front door, but her heart sank when she saw the text.

Kane: Can't make it tonight.

No tender words. No explanation.

Her mind went straight to her brother's warnings. Had she read Kane wrong? Had he changed his mind already?

She grasped the pendant at her neck, the cool metal a comforting weight in her hand. *I Love You. Forever.* She was being paranoid. Kane wouldn't change his mind; he was in it for the long haul, leaving his old life behind, if not tonight, then tomorrow.

No reason to worry. She'd tell herself as many times as it took until she could make herself believe it.

***

Kane

Kane shoved his phone into the inside pocket of his jacket, pushing images of Mandy out of his head. She had no place among the dark thoughts consuming him right now.

The police had finished their work, leaving him seeped in his mother's grief, his father's frozen stupor, and a clubhouse riddled with bullets and soaked in blood. "What happened?" He needed answers, and his parents were the only ones here. "Malcolm," he barked, shaking his father's shoulder. "What. Happened."

Malcolm glanced up, the dazed look in his eyes clearing. "We were shooting pool when the gunfire started. Cue, Scott, and me. I'd walked back to the kitchen to grab a beer, and then I heard it. It was automatic for sure." His jaw tightened. "I crawled back in on my hands and knees, but it stopped as fast as it started. Your brother was dead before I got to him."

A large pool of blood next to the table supported his version of events. The array of bullet holes along the front wall of the house and the interior did as well. There were too many for it to be anything less than automatic fire. "Who did this?" Either the Christian Soldiers or the Russians were behind it. Both groups would want Scott's head on a pike.

"Witnesses told the cops they saw a black van." With shaking hands, Malcolm poured a healthy dose of bourbon into a glass.

"Sergei," Kane growled. The Soldiers would have been on two wheels, not four.

"You tried to warn us." Malcolm gulped back the amber liquid. "We should have listened."

He wasn't interested in his father's self-pity. It was time for action, not words. "Call in the rest of the club. There's going to be a reckoning."

Malcolm had the men assembled in thirty minutes flat. Their reactions ranged from anger to heartbreak to fear.

"First thing we gotta do is be there for Cue." He turned to the prospect. "I need you to take Mama V and Desiree to the hospital. Use my mom's car."

The kid took the keys Malcolm held out, then led Mama out the front door.

Kane returned his focus to his brothers. "What do we know about where the Russians stay when they're here?"

Frank cracked his knuckles. "They've got a safe house in Mechanicsville. At least, they did a few years back. It's where we met with them the first time…me, Randy, and Scott."

Randy stroked his mostly gray beard, a frown wrinkling his leathery forehead. "Right. It was on Love Street. I remember Scott said he was gonna steal the street sign to hang over his bed. The Russians didn't think it was funny."

That sounded like Scott. He always—Kane's heart stuttered when he remembered his brother would never do anything again. No more corny puns or practical jokes. Scott's legacy was complete. It was all past tense now.

He shut down the rising tide of emotion. "Do you think you'd recognize the place if you saw it again?"

Randy's eyes narrowed. "No doubt."

Frank crossed his arms in front of his chest. "Me too. Plus, their van will stick out like a sore thumb. It's no Escalade, but it's nicer than anything else you're gonna see in the neighborhood."

"What are we going to do, Kane?" Scratch asked the question, but every eye in the room was on him. Funny how no one looked to Malcolm now. It wouldn't matter if they did. Nothing would stand in the way of his retribution.

Justice would be swift.

And it will be mine.

"We're going to pay them back, an eye for an eye. We're going to descend on the place where they feel safe, and we are going to kill every last fucking one of them."

A cheer went up in the room. Every voice bayed for blood.

"But we're gonna do it my way." He looked at the faces around him for any sign of a challenge. There was none. "We're not gonna drive by. We're gonna break in. This isn't business. It's personal," he snarled. "I want to look those bastards in the eye. I want my face to be the last thing they see when they take their last breaths. They will die knowing it's in my brother's fucking name."

The men murmured in agreement, and he handed out assignments for lookouts, drivers, and members of the hit squad. They split up, forgoing the bikes and piling into the Bronco and Pete's black Impala to keep a lower profile. Ten men in all would be part of the operation. Four would stay back with Malcolm at the clubhouse.

On the drive to the safehouse, the only sounds were the rumble of the Bronco's engine and clips sliding into various guns as the men readied for their attack. Pete parked a few houses down from their target, and the brothers split into their

308

assignments without prompting.

He led the hit squad with back-up from Frank, Randy, Bear, and Scratch. Randy and Scratch might be older guys, but they were ruthless and had shown no hesitation in taking a life, which was exactly what they needed right now.

Sure enough, the black van was parked in the carport, though it was half covered by a ratty tarp. Scratch snuck up behind the lookout, and Kane saw the flash of a blade a few seconds before the man's body hit the ground.

He and his men fanned out into positions at multiple points of entry and at Frank's shrill whistle busted in with guns blazing. Shouts and gunfire echoed through the house. Though it was impossible to know which Russian fired the fatal shots at his brother, he was looking for one man: the one in charge. He had no doubt Sergei gave the order.

The blond bastard was unloading a clip toward the front door when Kane shouldered his way in from the back. The fucker's normally slicked back hair had fallen over his forehead, his normally placid face twisted in rage.

He knocked the gun from his hand and shoved the barrel of his brother's Glock beneath the man's chin. All the screaming and violence around them fell away. Only Sergei's set jaw and his narrowed blue eyes remained. "You killed my brother."

Sergei raised one blond brow mockingly. It was covered in blood from a gash less than an inch below his hairline. "Nice to know my men can hit a target."

He pushed the Glock harder against the man's skin. "Your men are all dying or dead."

"There are more of us. We'll keep coming back. Besides, we are not your only enemy. We have the Soldiers with us now. You pissed off somebody very powerful, one who won't stop until your precious brothers are nothing more than a bloodstain on the ground."

It bothered him Sergei showed no fear, but in his blustering, at least the bastard had connected some important dots. The Skulls no longer had three separate enemies; now they were connected with Beau Griffin at the center of it all.

"Your brother was only the beginning," Sergei sneered.

With all the Russian's big talk, maybe the head wound was making him stupid. "I'll bet he died crying in a pile of his own shit." Maybe he was ready to meet his maker.

He pulled the trigger, and sound exploded in his ears as Sergei's brains splattered in an array of gore on the wall behind him.

He'd managed to go all these years without killing anyone. Pulling the trigger had been so much easier than he ever expected.

Turning on his heel, he surveyed the rest of the room. At least eight bodies littered the ground. Two were his own men. Bear was dead, the features on his face almost destroyed by bullets. Scratch wheezed a few feet away, his shirt soaked in blood. Frank stood upright, but he bled from a wound at his shoulder. None of the Russians survived.

"Randy, Frank, get Scratch to the car." Kane

squatted next to Bear and lifted the big man in a fireman's carry over his shoulder. Once he made it out of the house, one of the guys stationed as lookout helped him carry his burden to the Bronco.

By the time they made it to the hospital, Scratch had stopped breathing. Frank had come up with a story to tell the cops about a second attack from the men in the mysterious black van. Kane and Pete got out of the SUV at the edge of the parking lot, and Frank drove in the rest of the way alone. They didn't need to get tied up with questions from the cops.

It was too tight to squeeze any more men in the Impala, and too much blood covered Kane and Pete to call for a ride, so they started back to the clubhouse on foot, keeping to the shadows.

Their actions tonight were a start, but they still had enemies waiting to take another shot at them. The Christian Soldiers for one, and of course, Mandy's father. He had no doubt Beau Griffin was the powerful man Sergei was talking about. Hell, Mandy herself had warned him her father was a threat.

Mandy.

He'd made her so many promises, and he'd meant each one. They were supposed to have a future together, the one they'd both been dreaming about for years. But who were they kidding?

He was supposed to walk away from the club; no way could he do it now. His brother was dead, and only half the people responsible had paid the price. He owed it to Scott—to his parents and his remaining brothers—to make sure justice was served.

But he couldn't do it with Mandy at his side. He couldn't paint a target on her back. Besides, he was no longer the same man who made her those promises only hours ago. That man had never taken a life.

She deserved better than a killer fouling her bed.

And now, her father was now his enemy, more so than ever before.

He raked his hand through his tangled hair, no doubt coating it with Bear's blood. There could be no future with Mandy. No happiness or love. He had to let his dreams go. It was time to unleash a nightmare on his enemies.

CHAPTER TWENTY-FOUR

Kane

Kane stood in the shower with his head bowed, dried blood once again mingling with the water going down the drain. Dawn was already peeking over the horizon when they made it back to the clubhouse. The brothers were here, along with his dad, all crashed out; a few had snagged beds, others on the furniture, a few on the floor. Thank fuck, someone had cleaned up the spot where Scott had gone down.

Every muscle in his body clenched tight and tense. His head ached, and his fingers burned as they regained feeling after an hour in the cold. He needed to burn the clothes he'd been wearing. They all did. There was no telling whose blood was on there, a direct link to the death and destruction from the night before.

He grabbed the soap, rubbing the bar directly

onto his filthy skin. He'd never truly get clean, but at least he could get rid of the outward evidence of his sins. His hair needed attention too. As long and thick as it was, only God knew what DNA hid among the strands.

Ignoring the water he trailed across the floor, he climbed out of the still-running spray and stood naked before the mirror. Grabbing a thick handful of hair, he sawed through it with the knife he'd left on the sink. He did it one handful after another until the longest pieces hung right below his jaw.

Dropping the chunks of hair into the garbage bag with his clothes, he got back in the shower. Now it was easy to work up a lather with the shampoo. It hadn't been this simple to deal with in years.

And really, who gives a fuck what it looks like?

Once he got all the blood out from under his fingernails, he figured he was as clean as he was going to get. He wrapped a towel around his waist and finger-combed what was left of his hair. Too late, he realized he had no clothes here. But Scott did. Kane dressed in a pair of his brother's jeans and a flannel still carrying a hint of Scott's favorite cologne.

He carried the garbage bag into the backyard and tossed it into the big metal trash can. A quick squirt of lighter fluid, then he lit the contents ablaze. Neither the smoke nor the smell would turn any heads. This was the same way they'd burned leaves for years.

Ignoring the icy burn on his bare feet, Kane stayed outside until the bag and everything inside turned to ash. If only he could rid himself of the entire night the same way.

He trudged back into the house, exhaustion weighing on him like an anvil on his back. Spotting no soft place to lie down, he shuffled into the chapel and curled up on top of the table; his mother's favorite afghan became his pillow. He blacked out the second his eyes closed.

A gentle shake from Mama V brought him back to the surface. "KC?" she rasped. "Wake up, baby. Your father wants to meet."

"What time is it?" he mumbled. Or he tried to say it. It came out more like a mishmash of sounds.

Still, his mom seemed to understand. "It's three o'clock. C'mon in the kitchen. We've got some pizza."

His stomach growled. He hadn't eaten since…nope, he wasn't thinking about his meal at the Coopers. Nodding his head, he answered with a grunt.

She grasped his hand and led him toward the savory smell of the food. The men stood around the room, eating somberly. He grabbed a slice and downed it in silence.

Mama V stood behind Malcolm, who sat at the table. She kneaded his shoulders as she spoke. "Cue Ball is doing okay. The doctors had to do surgery this morning. One of the bullets punctured his intestine. They were really worried about infection, but they cut the bad piece out and put it back together again. They've got to watch him closely for signs of sepsis, but they think he's going to recover."

It didn't sound like he'd made it completely out

of the woods yet, but Cue Ball was a fighter. If anyone could pull through this, he could. "Is someone there with him? What about Frank?"

His mother kept her eyes on the back of Malcolm's head as she spoke. "Desiree hasn't left the hospital. She's staying as close as the doctors will let her. As for Frank, we're letting him get some sleep in one of the bedrooms. He only got back a couple of hours ago. The bullet went straight through, so the doctors patched him up pretty quick. He got tied up for a while dealing with the cops. I have a feeling they'll be by here before the day is up to ask some more questions."

Kane grabbed another lukewarm slice from the pizza box. "Did everyone burn their clothes? Ditch the guns?" There shouldn't be any other evidence in the clubhouse.

Malcolm nodded. "Those of us who stayed back last night took care of it all this morning."

"What about the safehouse? There could be something there linking back to us." There were too many variables.

Scratch spoke. "I lit it up before we left last night. Torched the van too. Cops will find the bodies, maybe some shell casings, but nothing will tie 'em back to the club."

"So, we have justice," Pete said grimly.

Kane pulled a water bottle out of the refrigerator. "No." He took a gulp, then wiped his mouth with the back of his hand. "David Bennett and Billy Meers. They've got a hand in this." He didn't mention Mandy's father. He wasn't ready to share every detail with the club.

316

Malcolm jumped to his feet, forcing Mama V to stumble back. "Meers? You know this for a fact?"

"It was the last thing Sergei said before his brains met the wall." He paused, waiting for the enormity of killing a man to hit him, but…nothing. "The Soldiers were in queue to take over the guns from us. They're the ones who tipped off the Russians we were selling to Ace."

"I'm gonna kill him." Malcolm's teeth clenched so tightly, his words were almost unintelligible. He stuck a cigarette between his lips and lit the end. After a deep drag, he laughed darkly. "No. I'm gonna gut his son right in front of him. Then I'm gonna kill him."

Kane had no objection. He wanted to burn the whole goddamn world.

Frank stumbled in, his left arm in a sling. "Whatever you guys are planning, I'm in."

"No offense, brother, but you look like a stiff wind could knock you over." He shook his head.

Frank opened his mouth to argue, then stood with his jaw hanging open. "The fuck you do to your hair, man?"

He ran his hand over the shaggy, uneven pieces. "Yeah, well, I guess I missed my chance at a modeling career." The scar on his cheek pulled tight with his mocking smile. "Last time I checked, though, I didn't need to be pretty to get justice for my brother's murder."

Mama V choked back a sob at the stark reminder. She looked like a ghostly shell of herself, her hair unteased and no make-up on her face. Without her high heels, she seemed so much smaller.

And, he realized grimly, this would be the first year she'd miss the after-Christmas sale to shop for his father.

"We need to strike before they realize we're onto them," he said briskly. "But first, we need a plan."

Maybe *plan* was too strong of a word. They only needed an alibi, a time, and a formation. The location of the club's headquarters was common knowledge. They were likely too cocky to be concerned about retaliation, but he didn't want to take chances with the brothers he had left standing.

"We cut the head off the dragon. Yes, we want to get them all, but Meers and Bennett are our priorities."

"Meers is mine," Malcolm seethed. "I'll make him pay, one president to another."

Kane ignored him. "First thing we need to do is be seen out and about. Preferably somewhere with cameras. The bank, the hospital parking garage. Maybe some of you can go light some candles at St. John's. Folks will remember seeing you there." The church wasn't far from the Soldiers' base in Druid Hills.

Everyone got an assignment, then agreed to meet back in the woods near the Soldiers' property around five-thirty. Frank and the prospect were the exceptions. They'd keep watch over Cue Ball in case he got any unexpected visitors at the hospital.

When they arrived on Meers' property, though, they found the house dark and deserted. So, they waited. It couldn't have gone smoother. Men arrived one at a time, and the Skulls picked them off like low-hanging fruit, hiding each body and bike behind the tree line. They took out six Soldiers in succession.

Meers, himself, showed up afterward, flanked by two big bastards. Two big bastards who dropped like flies thanks to Pete's unfailing aim. To his credit, Meers didn't try to run or even reach for his own weapon as his men fell at his feet.

Malcolm left the cover of darkness to face him in the driveway. Kane followed two steps behind. "You're lucky your boy isn't here," Malcolm rumbled.

Meers grimaced. "I heard about Scott. He wasn't the target."

"He was collateral damage, so it's okay he's dead?" Malcolm moved closer. "Tell me, Billy, who was the target? Me? My other son? My club?"

"You." Meers didn't hesitate. "You were supposed to be home. The idea was to cut the head off the snake."

Kane smiled grimly at the irony.

"We figured your death would drive the club into chaos. One son without the discipline to lead in your absence, the other without the desire." Meers looked meaningfully at Kane and the Glock clutched tightly in his hand. "Guess we were wrong about a lot of things." He folded his hands in front of him, like in prayer, closed his eyes, and dropped his chin to his chest.

Waiting.

Malcolm raised his gun and blew a hole in the center of the man's forehead.

They waited another hour, but no one else

showed up. The guys rolled up the bodies in tarps before tossing them in the back of Scott's old pick-up. Hopefully, there would be room in those barrels of sulfuric acid where they'd disposed of Sucre's crew a few weeks back.

He wasn't sure how long it took acid to eat through bones, but he had no doubt his brothers would figure something out. He lined all the bikes up behind the house, as if the owners had just parked them there for the night. Then he doubled back through the trees to where his bike waited about a mile away. They hadn't killed Bennett, but Kane would find him soon enough, and when he did, the man was dead.

**

Kane woke up the next morning to a gentle hand running over his hair. When he opened his eyes and saw Mandy, for a moment he forgot his resolve to leave her. He wrapped his hand around her slender arm and pulled her against his chest.

She smelled of hope and lavender. Her skin was silky and soft, her lips so close and irresistible.

Without thinking, he captured her mouth. She tasted like coffee and chocolate, delicious and warm and perfect. Her tongue curled around his own, coaxing his dick to attention.

Pulling away, she whispered, "Where have you been? I've been so worried."

And with her innocent question, the brief respite from his life crumbled into a puff of smoke. "Scott is dead." No use sugar-coating it.

Mandy gasped, her hand covering her mouth in horror. He didn't doubt her sincerity for a second. As much as she disliked his brother, she never wished for his death. "How?"

"How do you think?" he growled. "Your father made good on his promise. He made me pay."

"My father? He killed Scott?" She shook her head in disbelief.

"He didn't pull the trigger, but yeah. He set the wheels in motion." He climbed out of the bed and pulled on a pair of jeans over the boxers he'd slept in. "One of my other guys is dead too. Two are hurt. The shit's hitting the fan."

She rose to her knees on the mattress. "What can I do?"

Turning to the dresser, he started digging for a clean shirt, then froze. His face burned with the knowledge she could see her name inked across his back. Had she known it was there? He couldn't remember giving her his back before.

It was too late to hide it now. He turned back, the shirt clutched in his hand. She didn't mention it, though; she didn't say anything about his hair either. "You need to go. It's not safe to be around me right now."

She moved forward and put her palm over his heart. He flinched back at the contact. "What are you saying?" she whispered. "Are you in danger?"

He dragged the shirt over his head. "No. I *am* the danger."

She stood to face him. "I'm not afraid of you. You would never hurt me."

"I killed a man," he said harshly, and her eyes

widened. "After I left you. Merry fucking Christmas. You still want me now?"

"Always." She touched his arm, and he shook her off.

"You're not listening to me. I killed someone. I blew his fucking brains out, and I would do it again. I probably *will* do it again, if I can get my hands on the rest of the bastards responsible for what happened to Scott." He wrapped his hands around her upper arms and shook her gently. "You do not want me in your life, baby. Right now, I'm poison."

Her fingers clutched the necklace he gave her for Christmas. God, it felt like a lifetime ago. "But you love me," she whispered.

"God, woman, of course I love you. I always have and I probably always will." The words felt ripped from his chest. "It doesn't mean we can make this work. Sometimes, love isn't enough. Or maybe, I love you too much to let you near this toxic life of mine. Either way, the end result is the same."

"Don't do this, Kane." Her green eyes shone with unshed tears. "We're better together. We're *stronger* together."

"No." His voice was implacable.

She made a broken sound in the back of her throat. "It was supposed to be forever this time."

He walked past her into the living room, where he pulled on a jacket and stuffed his feet into the boots beside the door. "You can't be involved in this world, Mandy." He summoned the words that refused to leave his memory, even after years of trying to chase them away. "Don't call me; I won't answer. Don't try to see me. I love you, but you are no longer part of my life." He opened the door and spoke without looking back. "Leave the key under the mat on your way out."

Heart in his throat, he walked away and closed the door, leaving the love of his life behind him.

CHAPTER
TWENTY-FIVE

Amanda

Amanda managed to hold it together until Kane closed the door behind him. Only then did she walk woodenly back to his bed and curl up into a ball. His pillow still smelled like him. Would she have to go the rest of her life without smelling him again? Would the memory of it melt away as it had before?

Would she have to go back to the half-life she'd been living without him in it? The idea of it opened the floodgate of tears she'd held back in front of him. Clutching his pillow to her, she let her agony escape in heaving sobs.

It wasn't fair. They'd just found their way back to each other. And once again, her father was getting his way. He always did.

She cried for what felt like hours until all her tears ran dry. When she sat up, her insides felt hollow, like someone had scooped her out and left

324

only the shell in place. She'd hoped never to feel such emptiness again.

There had to be a way to stop all this. God knew Kane wouldn't listen to her, but maybe there was someone else who could get through to him. She picked up her phone and scrolled through her contacts until she found the name she was looking for.

Brick's voicemail picked up.

"Hi. This is Amanda Griffin. First, I want to thank you for your help at the site last week. If you and the other guys hadn't been there, I don't know what would have happened to me. I'm calling because I need your help again. Kane needs your help." She drew a shaky breath. "Someone killed his brother. I think my dad had something to do with it. Now, Kane—he's not himself—I'm afraid for him. And he wants nothing to do with me. I'm begging you. Please help him. He needs a friend. I'm going to go deal with my dad. Maybe between the two of us, we can keep this from getting worse."

She disconnected without saying goodbye. There was no way to know when Brick would get her message or if he'd take her seriously, but it was time to do her part.

Climbing from the bed, she stood in front of the mirror and put herself to rights. She wouldn't give her father the satisfaction of seeing her disheveled. Fresh lipstick and a comb through her hair left her looking almost as good as new.

She fought the urge to take the pillow with her when she walked out of the room. Instead, she stopped to scribble a short note and left it on the table. As he'd asked, she put the key under the mat on her way out.

***

No traffic slowed her down on the way to her father's house, so Amanda made it there in quick time. Normally he wouldn't be there during the week, but his office was closed between Christmas and New Year's.

She let herself in the front door, and Terrence scuttled over in dismay. "Miss Griffin. Is your father expecting you?"

"No. Where is he?" She hated putting the kind old man in the center of her family problems, but she knew him well enough to recognize he wouldn't simply leave her alone.

"He's in the study, ma'am, but—"

No longer listening, she marched straight back to the room her father used as an office. He was bent over the desk, rifling through some papers.

"What did you do, Dad?" She was proud her voice didn't waver at all.

He didn't pretend to misunderstand. Straightening, he looked at her coolly. "I did what needed to be done. Kane Hale has been a burr on the heel of this household since the day you met him. I tried to be patient. I tried to let you find your way on your own, but you couldn't see past your schoolgirl infatuation."

"It's not an infatuation. I love him. I always have. Your unwillingness to accept it doesn't make it any less true." All it did was reinforce her decision to cut her father out of her life.

"I still have the video, you know." He gestured vaguely toward his computer. "I warned you way back then there was no statute of limitations on murder. Did you think I was bluffing, darling? Obviously, Mr. Hale made it through the confrontation with his rival motorcycle gang. He's like a roach," he muttered. "So obviously, I need to come at this another way. The way I should have years ago. I'll turn the video over to the authorities."

"You'll do no such thing," she warned.

"Won't I?" He chuckled. "Tell me, dear daughter, why would I not? You have shown me your word is meaningless. You backed out on our agreement for you to stay away from him, not to mention how you reneged on our deal about Nathan." He looked over her shoulder. "And speak of the devil."

Fear pulling her muscles tight, she whirled to face the man she'd hoped never to see again.

"Amanda," he said smoothly. "So lovely to see you, pet." All signs of the bruising on his skin had faded to muted yellows and greens.

She took a step back and bumped into her father's desk. "Stay away from me. There's a restraining order against you." Her eyes flicked to her father. "He tried to kill me the last time we saw each other. I told you what happened!"

Nathan laughed and it was a chilling sound. "You do love to exaggerate. Obviously, you're fine."

Her dad picked up his keys from the desk. "You

two obviously have a lot to work out. I've got an appointment." He narrowed his eyes at Nathan. "I'm sure she'll still be breathing when I return."

"I think I can manage." Nathan patted her father's shoulder as he passed. "And you can count on my support next November, *Governor*."

The door clicked closed after her dad walked out, leaving her alone with the man who almost strangled her to death.

He advanced toward her. "You've been a very naughty girl, Amanda. I think it's time for a long overdue talk."

***

Kane

Kane stared, dumbstruck, at the small, wrapped package on the clubhouse kitchen table. His mother, even in the depths of her grief, found a way to buy Malcolm a birthday present.

How long had it been sitting there?

He wanted to hurl it against the wall just for existing. He wanted to shake his mother. Punch his father. What the fuck kind of circular pointless existence did they all live in where this shit never, ever changed?

His hand curled to snatch it, when someone beat on the front door. Was it the cops? David Bennett? The Russians? Only one way to find out.

He pulled open the door. "Brick? What are you doing here?"

"Repaying a favor." The big man barged in. "I

heard about your brother, man. I'm sorry."

He gaped. "How do you even know? How did you find me?"

"You forget I used to be part of this world," Brick scoffed. "You weren't really hard to find. Listen, your girl called me."

"Mandy?" An irrational jolt of jealousy shot through him.

"Don't look at me like I'm trying to steal her, dumbass. I have my own woman." Brick pushed his shoulder. "Listen, you came to me once when Olivia was scared for me. I was in a world of hurt, and you really helped me out. Now your girl is worried about you. You're in a dark place, a very dark place. The thing is, there's a bigger reason I'm here. I think you might need to be worried about *her*. She went to go confront her father."

He had cocked his arm back to return the forceful tap to Brick's shoulder, but he dropped his hand when the words registered. "He wouldn't hurt her."

Brick shrugged. "I wouldn't put anything past him." He rubbed his neck uneasily. "I didn't get into the details of this with you before because I didn't think it would help any. But after I dragged her ex off the build site—the day he hurt her—he was spouting off in the truck, saying the mayor was his bitch. Apparently, Amanda's dad wants to be governor, and he thinks her ex can give him the keys to the kingdom. The dude said flat out he could do anything he wanted to her as long as she was still breathing when he was done." His hands balled into fists. "Took all I had not to beat his ass all over again, but I thought he was only making noise, you know? Now your girl's walking back into her father's house. You trust him not to sell her out again?"

Not a chance.

"C'mon." Brick tilted his head toward the door. "I'll drive you."

***

Amanda

Amanda pulled the phone out of her coat pocket, holding it low behind her father's desk as she dialed 9-1-1. Putting it on speaker, she dropped it face down on the chair beside her. With the volume low, she couldn't be sure someone answered, but she could hope. "Stay back, Nathan. Leave me alone."

"Ah, pet, you know I can't. You've been a bad girl and you need to be punished." He took a menacing step toward her.

She backed away quickly, and he pursued. "My father is the mayor. We're in his house, for God's sake. You can't plan on hurting me here." Please, please God let the police figure out where to go.

Nathan snarled. "Your father is nothing to me. A political pawn. The only reason I have anything to do with him is that it gives me access to you." He bit his lip. "You and that sweet pussy of yours. Of mine, honestly. Because let's be real, you and I both know you belong to me."

She fumbled in her purse, then pulled out the same gun she'd displayed the night she broke things off. She'd gone nowhere without it since the day he'd strangled her. "I have a gun. I'm warning you. I won't let you put your hands on me again. Walk away. No one has to get hurt." She scurried around the desk, putting the heavy piece of furniture between them again.

"Someone does have to get hurt, but it's not going to be me. You and I both know you're not going to shoot me." With a sweep of his arm, he knocked everything from the top of the desk. The papers and files fluttered almost silently, but the lamp clattered onto the floor. "You wouldn't risk the scandal to your precious father. No. You're going to put the gun down and take your punishment like a big girl. I've waited for a taste of you long enough. When I'm done, you'll be lucky if you can walk again for days." He lunged forward, pushing her into the tall bookcase and tearing the sleeve of her coat.

Books tumbled down on top of them both, and the tall piece of furniture swayed, threatening to tip over.

"Get away from me. I said no!" She fired the gun twice.

The shock on his face was almost comical as blood bloomed on his left side. He dropped her arm and went down to his knees.

She pushed past him, back to the other side of the desk where she grabbed her phone, putting it to her ear. "Hello? Is anyone there? I need help."

A soothing male voice responded. "Yes, Miss Griffin, the police and an ambulance are on the way. Are you all right?"

The door flew open and two officers came in with their service-weapons drawn. She dropped her gun and the phone, raising her hands high in the air. "Don't shoot," she croaked.

"It's okay, Miss," the African American officer said, lowering his weapon. "We're here to help."

His partner, a middle-aged white guy with a mustache, approached Nathan. "Stay right there, sir. The medics are right behind us."

"H-how did you get here so fast?" It may have seemed like Nathan had her cornered in here forever, but it was probably only a few minutes.

"I called them, ma'am. As soon as I saw your father leave you two alone." Terrence kept his eyes on his feet as he passed the threshold. "Mr. Shaw said some terrible things to your father about what he would do to you the next time he saw you." He glanced at Nathan's prone form with distaste. "Folks like him tend not to see the help when we're around."

The medics rolled in behind him, making a beeline for Nathan. Kane and Brick were on their heels. Two men she didn't recognize rushed in last.

"Mandy!" Kane shouted. He looked crazed as he shouldered his way toward her. Her legs nearly gave out once she was inside his arms. "What's happening? What are the police doing here?"

"Mr. Hale? Is that you?" Terrence's eyes rounded like saucers.

Kane nodded. "It's been a long time, Terrence."

"Mr. Shaw tried to attack Miss Amanda, and she shot him." He pointed to the medics who were loading Nathan onto the gurney. "I'm so glad you're here, sir. I always thought you were the right man for her."

"This is the one you've been fucking? Does *everyone* know?" Nathan shouted, lunging off the gurney toward the white cop. "I'll kill you, you bitch." He grabbed for the gun in the officer's holster.

Kane spun Amanda in his arms, ready to use his body as a shield. But before Nathan could fire, the cop closest to her started shooting.

Pop. Pop. Pop.

She lifted her head from Kane's chest and craned her neck to see what happened. Nathan was on the floor, his sightless eyes staring up at the ceiling. Blood gushed from two fresh holes in his chest.

"Damn, Gleason," the white cop muttered, toeing the body with the tip of his shoe. "You shot Nathan Shaw. You know what kind of political nightmare this is going to cause?"

Gleason grunted, then tapped at his chest. "The hell it is. I've got my bodycam on. I don't care if he was the fucking pope. He went for your gun."

The medics loaded Nathan back on the gurney he had escaped. The female part of the pair stopped as her partner wheeled him out of the room. "I saw the whole thing. I'll testify if you need it."

"Do you need a statement from her?" Kane tilted his head toward Amanda. "Or can I take her home?"

Officer Gleason shook his head. "She can come in tomorrow. I have to warn you, though, once the media catches wind of this, you guys are not going to have a moment's peace."

"Thank you." She offered the cop her hand, and

the man looked a little surprised, but he shook it. "We're going to be okay."

The officer nodded thoughtfully. "Somehow, I don't doubt it for a minute."

CHAPTER TWENTY-SIX

Kane

Kane had never been so grateful for someone interfering in his life. He'd never be able to repay Brick for knocking at the clubhouse door. Though he realized his presence hadn't changed the end result, he would've never forgiven himself if Mandy would have had to face Nathan again all this on her own. God knew the bodyguards Mike hired hadn't done shit. They didn't even know anything had been going down until the cops showed up at her father's house, and they followed the cavalry inside. Then, when Nathan pulled the gun, who knew where they were. Needless to say, they no longer had a job.

He shook his friend's hand. "I don't know how to thank you, brother." The words felt inadequate.

Brick inhaled the cold air through his nose. "It feels good to be on the other side of the crazy shit for a change." He smiled ruefully. "Besides, that's what friends do. I didn't have any of those until you came around. If there's anything else you need, I'm only a phone call away."

He watched Brick's blue pick-up until it turned out of the driveway, then focused his gaze on Mandy. "You want me to drive?"

Slipping the keys into his hand, she climbed in the passenger seat of her car. She kept quiet for the entire drive, and he gave her the space she seemed to ask for without words. He took her to his place instead of hers.

Mumbling something about taking a shower, she disappeared into the bathroom.

He shrugged off his jacket, then sat at the table to tug off his socks. Instantly, his eyes caught on a note in Mandy's handwriting.

I know you're hurting, and you're scared. Even if you can't face it now, eventually you'll remember: we are stronger together. I'm willing to wait. As long it takes. I Love You. Forever.

She was right, of course. Losing Scott had broken his heart. Losing Mandy would have broken him entirely.

Stripping down as he walked, he dropped his shirt on the back of a chair. His jeans, he left in a pile on the floor. Then he joined her in the shower, circling her waist from behind. "I'm so sorry," he said hoarsely. "I've made such a mess of things." Breathing in the scent of her hair, he silently thanked God he hadn't lost her tonight.

She leaned her head back against his chest, giving him an unobstructed view of her perfect, creamy breasts. "You were grieving."

"Yeah." He kissed her shoulder. "But it wasn't your fault. None of this is your fault, but here you are, stuck in the middle between me and your father."

Mandy turned in his arms. "I'm not stuck between you. Fuck my father. The only thing I am to him is a bargaining chip, and I refuse to be one anymore." She lathered the soap in her hands and ran the foam over his chest. "We'll figure out how to deal with him, but not now, okay? Right now, I just want to feel you and forget about the rest of the world."

"Hell yeah." He ran his finger from the center of her chest, in a slow line down to her trim patch of auburn hair. "Get your ass in my bed. The condoms are in the top dresser drawer." He'd been sure to stock the place once he gave her a key.

She scampered out, and he rinsed quickly before facing himself in the mirror above the sink. He couldn't do much about his hair, but there was one thing he could do. Grabbing the razor he'd used to shape his beard, he got to work removing all the hair from his face. It was surreal to look at his reflection when he was done. If not for the scar, he'd look a lot like he did in college.

As he'd demanded, Mandy waited like a naked fucking goddess on top of his sheets, her red hair spread out like a fiery halo on the pillow. She gasped and sat up straight when he stepped out of the shadows into the dim light of the lamp.

He sat beside her, allowing her hands to smooth over his cheeks.

Her lower lip trembled. "I really have you back."

Leaning in, he caught her lip between his teeth before soothing it with his tongue, but Mandy had zero patience letting him take the lead. Her tongue shot out, tangling with his, pulling him into a kiss. There was nothing careful about it, no concern about any scratches to her tender skin.

She was passion incarnate, her kiss so consuming, he could almost forget they were both stark naked on his bed. Almost.

His thumb found her nipple, and he raked it gently with his nail. It pebbled instantly at the touch.

Mandy wasn't interested in the subtle approach. Rubbing her cheek against his, her mouth found his ear, and she traced the shell with her tongue. Her hot breath sent a wave of goosebumps prickling across his skin. "Seeing you like this makes me so hot," she whispered. Her hand tugged away his towel, then circled his erection. "Lie down for me, baby. Let me take the wheel for a while."

Hell, yes.

He settled on his back, and she straddled him. "More kisses," she murmured, licking, touching, and teasing his mouth before delving back inside with abandon. How did he ever think he could live without this woman?

All too soon she moved away. He very nearly

protested until he realized where she was headed. Thank God, she didn't tease him; she went straight for the prize. He almost came right then and there, the moment her tongue slid up his shaft. His hips lifted off the bed, and he made the mistake of looking down.

Her sultry green eyes stared up at him like a vision out of an amazing wet dream. Again, she licked him, root to tip, the flat of her tongue lapping over his skin as if he were favorite flavor popsicle. "You are so fucking sexy," he rumbled.

She gave him a knowing smile, then swallowed him whole. Her tongue twined around his cock as she sucked him back, then teasingly backed off. Again and again, she pleasured him in the way she knew he liked best until his orgasm was so close, he was on the verge of spilling in her mouth. "Let me suit up, baby. I need to be inside of you."

He reached for the condom the moment she came up for air. His body screamed for him to bury his cock in her pussy, but he forced himself to wait. She had to be ready for him first. "Get on your hands and knees."

His Mandy didn't hesitate, only did as he commanded. The position put her glistening sex on full display. Though part of him craved the intimacy of joining with her face to face, he needed to claim her, remind them both she was his in the most primal way.

Sliding his finger inside, he discovered her already slick and accommodating. She pushed back against the invasion. "Don't play with me. I need you too much. Please."

Who was he to deny her wishes? Spreading her open with his hands, he plunged his dick inside her in one long stroke. Her satisfied moan stoked the fire inside him even higher. Grabbing her shoulders, he forced her back to arch, giving him the perfect angle to hit the spot he knew always drove her crazy.

When she cried his name, he knew he'd found it. Snaking his hand around her hip, he sought the swollen bud at the top of her slit. He circled it with his finger in tandem with his thrusts inside her. Her soft mewls drove him crazy, emboldened him to strum her faster, ride her harder. She rewarded him with louder cries and a tighter grip from her internal muscles.

Finally, he felt her body tense, her breathing stop, and the ripples of her orgasm as it milked his cock. His balls drew up tight, and he came as she was still pulsing around him. They collapsed together on the bed.

Once his body started again obeying his commands, he unsheathed himself and tossed the condom in the trashcan by the bed. While he was turned away, Mandy's fingers traced over the letters of her name on his back. He stayed frozen until her hand fell away, and he settled back on the bed.

"When did you get it?" she asked, once she settled back into his arms.

He let out a breath. "The day after I got out of the hospital. I used some of the money I'd saved for your ring. I know it sounds stupid, but it made me feel like you were still with me in a way."

Her fingers ran through the hair on his chest in

soothing circles. "It's not stupid. It's romantic. It...makes me want to fly. And it makes me want to cry at the same time." She lifted her head. "Which is not your doing. It's mine. We lost so much time because of me."

She'd beat herself up forever if he let her, but he'd been about to make the same mistake. He'd be alone right now if it weren't for Brick's interference. "You thought you were protecting me."

"Yeah, well, it might have all been for nothing." She rubbed her eyes. "My father still has the video from back then. He's threatening to release it to the police all over again. He reminded me right before he left me in the room with Nathan."

How a man could do that to his daughter defied his understanding. "Your dad makes mine look like father of the year, which is saying something because my dad is a selfish dick."

She wrapped herself back around him with a sigh. "We've got to get rid of the video once and for all."

"We will." He kissed the top of her head. "Now get some sleep. I plan on loving you again when the sun comes up."

**

Amanda

Kane kept his promise, waking her with whispered words of love and a slow, languorous journey into pleasure. Her body was loose and

341

satisfied, but she had too much weighing on her mind to relax fully. Like her father's threats. The fallout from Nathan's death. The fucking motorcycle club.

She'd deal with it all, one step at a time.

When they were finally dressed and sharing some buttered toast at his kitchen table, she tackled problem number one. "What are we going to do about my dad?"

Kane swallowed his toast down with a sip of coffee. "I have an idea. Do you trust me?"

"With my life." Her face warmed, but she didn't regret saying it. The truth could set you free, right?

His smile made his entire face light up. God, he was beautiful. It should have been illegal to hide his face under all that fur so many years.

"It involves getting the club involved, and I'll need you to make some serious threats. You think you can manage it?"

"Threatening my father?" She laughed. "Yeah, I can manage it. After all he's done, the hard part will be keeping myself from following through."

He filled her in on a few more details before kissing her forehead and leaving to solicit his friends for help. If he was successful, they'd all meet at the Griffin house in an hour.

If she wanted, it gave her time to go back to her condo and change, but she felt safe at Kane's place, and safety mattered way more than what she was wearing. She had far more concern about coming face to face with the guys in the club again. None of them had ever liked her.

But Kane had faith in them, and she had faith in

him. If he said it would work out, she would believe him. In the meantime, she needed to get her shit together. She smoothed her hair into a tight ponytail and touched up her make-up. No way would she confront her father looking bedraggled.

Satisfied her appearance looked as good as it would get, she retrieved the key she'd left under the mat the morning before.

What a difference a day makes.

She arrived at the house at the agreed-upon time, and though she didn't see Kane, she had no doubt he was there. With a fortifying breath, she climbed out of her car, up to the front door and knocked twice.

Terrence opened the door, his face filled with apprehension. "Your father's on a tear in the study, Miss Amanda." His voice was pitched low. "It might not be the best time for a visit."

She squeezed his hand gently. "Thank you for looking out for me, Terrence. You probably saved my life yesterday." Now it was her turn to whisper. "Kane will be at the door in a few minutes. He's going to let himself in, and he'll be looking out for me. Maybe now would be a good idea for you to consult with cook about the menu for New Year's."

He nodded in understanding. "As you say, ma'am." The aging butler turned slowly and shuffled toward the kitchen.

Amanda confirmed the front door was unlocked before striding to her father's office for the second day in a row. The churning in her stomach reminded her of the feeling she'd had on the way to the hospital when her father demanded she break up with Kane. Dread, combined with the knowledge there was no way out; she had to see it through.

The door to the study hung partially ajar. Amanda didn't knock; she pushed the door until it was completely open and walked in. It looked like a hurricane had torn through the room. Books, files, and papers were strewn across the floor. All the desk drawers hung open, and a chair rested on its side. Her father stood at the center of it all, muttering to himself and pacing.

The room had looked bad when she left yesterday, but now the chaos was infinitely worse. "What are you doing, Dad?"

He stopped pacing at the sound of her voice and craned his neck to face her. "I don't recall inviting you today, Amanda. Perhaps you should call my secretary and make an appointment."

She swept her hand over the room, acknowledging the mess. "And miss all this?" She shook her head. "Tempting as it is, you and I have some unfinished business to attend to. Afterward, you can go fuck yourself for all I care, because we are done."

Her father tsked at her words. "Such language. Your pet thug is back in your life for a couple of weeks, and you already sound like you're rolling around in the gutter."

"The vilest man I've ever been with is the one you set me up with, Dad. Only, I guess it doesn't really matter if the guy can do something for you, right?"

His lip curled. "You do not want to talk about Nathan with me. The stunt you pulled last night could set back my gubernatorial run for years—if it's not derailed forever."

Like always, his eye was on the prize. "I don't care about your run for governor. In fact, this state would probably be better off with someone who's not willing to sell their own child for a networking connection." She held up her hand to stop whatever he'd been about to say. "But I didn't come here to talk about your political future. Let's be real: you and I, there is no relationship left. I only came here to get the video you've been holding over my head. Give it to me and we can go our separate ways."

He laughed, and menace poured off him. "I should have known. The Hale boy again. Tell me, my recalcitrant daughter, why on earth would I ever give you my ace in the hole?"

She pulled the small handgun from her purse. Time to bluff. "Because I'm asking you nicely."

Her father rolled his eyes. "I'm supposed to be afraid of you? As if you would shoot me if I didn't cooperate with your demands."

She didn't think it would work; her father never took the easy route. "No. You're right." She didn't turn, but she heard the footsteps enter the room behind her, and her father's eyes widened in response. "I wouldn't shoot you, but they would."

CHAPTER
TWENTY-SEVEN

Kane

Kane stepped up to Mandy's side, his father and friends filling the space behind him. She'd executed her part of the plan perfectly. Now, seeing the fear in her father's eyes satisfied him more than he'd imagined.

Of course, he'd seen Beau Griffin over the years; the man was the mayor. He was on TV all the time, and that wasn't counting all the billboards and flyers junking up his mailbox. In person, Mandy's father looked smaller than he remembered. Deep circles shadowed under his eyes, and his usually perfect hair looked like he'd been pulling it in different directions.

This small man had ruined his life. Stolen his love. Killed his brother.

He barely recognized the deep, gravelly voice coming from his own mouth. "You think I'm a thug. You can thank yourself for that." He moved closer, and Beau shrank back. "Thanks to you, I'm a killer. Thanks to you, I have a reason to seek revenge. So, tell me, Mr. Mayor, do you think I'm bluffing?"

Mandy's dad swallowed, swept his eyes over the room, then seemed to find his courage. He stood a little taller. "I don't have it."

"Bullshit," he barked.

"Check the house if you don't believe me." The man sounded all practiced and smooth again. "Look anywhere you want. There's nothing to find."

Malcolm put his hand on Kane's shoulder. "Take him up on it. Look for hidden safes, especially in his bedroom. I'll stay here with Mr. Griffin and talk father to father."

He wanted to argue, but the truth was, Malcolm hadn't just lost a brother in all of this; he'd lost a son. If he wanted to have it out with Mandy's dad, he deserved the chance. "Okay. Mandy, can you show us where to start?"

She clearly didn't like it, and she didn't try to hide it, but she also didn't argue. "Yeah. I have a couple of ideas, but we really need to go through the computers. Chances are, it's stored digitally somewhere." She took his hand. "He has a safe in his room upstairs. I know the combination."

***

Brick

From his hidden location in the hollow space

347

behind the study wall, Brick watched Amanda lead Kane and his club buddies out of the room. Only Kane and his girl knew he was here. His job was to watch and record everything he saw, in case they could catch her dad in an unguarded moment they could use against him. Well, if Kane's father didn't kill the guy first.

It would be one way to solve the problem.

Violence and death had been part of Brick's world for years, so it wasn't really a shocking proposition, especially since the man had set up his own daughter to be hurt. Low, even for the worst kind of sleazebag. The problem would be in covering it up. The mayor was a high-profile guy. His disappearance would be very noticeable, and after what happened yesterday, his connection to Kane was a matter of public record. No—there was no way to get rid of him quietly.

Malcolm's voice broke him out of his thoughts. "You've made trouble for my club for years, and I've let it go to avoid an all-out war. Harassment from the cops. Permits rejected. Bank loans denied. But this? There is no ignoring this. I should kill you right now and be done with it."

Beau scoffed. "You'll do no such thing. I stuck to our agreement to the letter."

"Our agreement," Malcolm hissed, "never said anything about you getting my son killed."

Brick's jaw dropped open.

"You and I both wanted our children away from each other. It's the entire reason you set up the video sting on your own son and sent it to me."

From his small peephole, Brick watched Beau

348

pick up the leather chair from the floor and settle into it. "It worked like a charm. Your son joined your gang, and my daughter moved on to run a business. But you and I both know there is no cop to testify to the veracity of the video. It wouldn't stand up for a second in court. So why are you here? Because of your oldest?"

Malcolm braced his hands on the arms of the chair and put his face less than an inch in front of Beau's. "You're damn right because of my oldest. You're the reason he's dead."

Beau shrugged. "Not true. He's dead because your club was foolish enough to cross a Russian syndicate."

"You are the one who tipped them off." Spittle flew from Malcolm's mouth as he hissed.

Beau wiped a droplet from his cheek with his thumb. "David Bennett tipped them off. And frankly, even if he hadn't, it was only a matter of time before they found out. Even you must see it."

"You can't weasel out of this, Beau. You know what you did, and so do I."

"But the kids don't." Beau's face broke out in a satisfied smile. "Your son has no idea you orchestrated everything that pushed him into your precious biker gang."

"We. We orchestrated it. Don't act like you're blameless."

The mayor shook his head. "But they already hate me. You can still play the injured party. Unless I tell the truth."

"And what does the truth get you? No leverage over your daughter—"

"That ship has sailed," he growled.

Malcolm made a show of cracking his knuckles. "But if you were to just disappear, it would be a win-win. My son would never know the truth. I get justice for Scott's death, and the whole fucking world would be rid of you."

Beau rolled his eyes. "How many witnesses saw you come in here? I'm the goddamn mayor of the city. You think no one would notice if I stopped coming to work one day? You think no one would wonder what a crew of dirty bikers was doing at my home the last time anyone saw me? Even you aren't so stupid, Mal."

"It would be worth it," Malcolm whispered. "To wipe the smug smile off your face."

"You're not going to kill me," Beau waved him off. "All we have to do is agree to walk out of here with the same story. I let you take a shot at me—maybe a shiner—for show, and I give you a copy of the video on a flash drive. We say it's the only copy, and you've threatened to kill me if I'm lying. You walk away a hero, and I wash my hands of the whole thing."

"And Scott? What about justice for my son?"

Beau folded his arms. "I guess you forfeited justice when you made a deal with the devil."

"I hate you," Malcolm seethed.

"Get in line." Beau flipped open his laptop and punched a few buttons. He pulled a flash drive out of a drawer and in minutes handed it over Malcolm. "Call them back." He stood and pointed to his cheek. "But first, make it look convincing." He grinned. "Here's your big chance."

Malcolm didn't hesitate. Rearing back, he clocked Beau so hard the man stumbled back. Then he pulled out his phone, presumably to call back the cavalry.

Kane and his girl were the first ones back in the room. Malcolm held up the flash drive. "I've got it. Let's get out of here."

Amanda wrinkled her forehead. "Just like that? What if he has another copy?"

Malcolm snarled. "Then he knows I'll kill him. Right, Mr. Mayor?"

Beau nodded in such apparent misery he deserved an Academy Award.

Without waiting for anyone to agree, Kane's father stomped out the door.

Amanda linked her hand with Kane's and shot her dad an inscrutable look. "He really will kill you, you know. Kane is the only child he has left. Meanwhile, you have none. We are finished, *Beau*. Good luck with your run for governor. You'll understand if you don't get my vote."

***

Amanda

Kane rode back to Amanda's condo in her car. He'd come in on the back of his friend's bike. It was a quiet drive; they both had a lot to process.

When they finally got inside her place, she was all too happy to change into some fresh clothes before offering to make them both lunch.

Kane flashed her a small smile. "I'm still getting

used to the idea you can cook. But let me do it. I need to take care of you."

He laid out the roast beef, mayo, and bread on the counter and began assembling their meal.

"What now?" Her voice didn't sound quite as casual as she would have liked, but it would have to do.

"What do you mean?" Carefully, he smeared the bread with a thin layer of mayonnaise, then piled the shaved meat on top.

"The danger to your club is over. You've got your revenge. We've got the video. So now what? For us? For you?"

He put the top layer of bread on the sandwich and handed her a plate.

She carried it to the table and sat down.

"You're asking about the club." He stayed standing at the counter and took a bite of his food. His shoulders hunched. "The million-dollar question, isn't it?" He bit into his sandwich again and chewed, a blank expression on his face. "I know how you feel about it. Part of me feels the same way. Even with the shit your dad pulled, he couldn't have done it if we hadn't given him the means ourselves."

She knew it was risky to ask about club business. It would be so easy to keep filling her mouth with food rather than cross the invisible line into MC territory. But either they were past this or they weren't. She opened her mouth to ask for more information, but Kane beat her to the punch.

He sighed. "The club is involved in some bad shit, babe. Guns. Drugs. Hell, we even did a murder for hire once."

Her stomach dropped.

"Not *me*. I mean, I didn't kill anyone for money. But I did kill the man who killed my brother. He's the only one. You need to understand, and you need to be sure it's something you can live with if we're going to make this work."

She didn't examine it too closely, but she could understand it.

After her nod, he continued. "I want to go straight. I want to marry you and be a part of your family." His cheeks darkened. "I want to have children with you and be the kind of dad our kids can respect and look up to."

"I want the same thing," she whispered.

"But how can I turn my back on my family right now?" He rubbed his eyes as he took the chair across from her. "My parents have already lost one son. If I patch out, it's like losing another."

Amanda shook her head. The whole line of reasoning was stupid. "Only if they choose to. It's on them."

He lifted one shoulder. "Maybe. I get where you're coming from. But the code is the code. To them, I'd be the one abandoning them, not the other way around." Pushing his plate away, he laced his fingers on the table in front of him. "It's not only my parents, either, it's also my friends. Cue Ball and Frank have been there for me more times than I can count. Walking away, I'm kicking them when they're down."

She got up to pour two glasses of iced tea, then rejoined Kane at the table. "I don't have the answers, baby. If those guys took care of you when I wasn't there, I'm grateful to them. If you love them, I don't want you to lose them. You know what I think of the club, but I can't tell you what to do. It has to be your decision."

They both started when his phone buzzed on the table. He glanced at the screen. "Brick wants to talk to us. Do you mind if he comes over?"

Brick. He was a friend she could get on board with. He had a sketchy history too, but by all accounts, he'd turned his life around and got engaged to a school teacher he was crazy about. "It's fine. He's always welcome here."

She called down to alert the doorman, and within minutes, Brick's heavy knock sounded at the door.

Kane ushered him in with a pat on the back. "Thanks again for helping out this morning, especially since you had to stuff yourself in such a tiny space for nothing." He hadn't had a chance to speak to his friend at all after Malcolm secured the video.

Brick rubbed at the back of his neck. "I wouldn't say it was for nothing. You learn a lot when no one knows you're listening." He gestured to the couch. "You'd better sit down, man. This isn't going to be easy to hear."

CHAPTER TWENTY-EIGHT

Kane

Kane hadn't been inside a hospital since he'd been stabbed all those years ago. Northside hadn't changed much in the time since. The smell, especially, threatened to take him back to one of the worst nights in his life. A pungent mix of antiseptic and death.

He'd successfully avoided returning like the plague, but the conversation he needed to have couldn't wait until his friend was discharged.

Frank was already in Cue Ball's room when Kane came in. "I heard everything went smoothly with your old lady's father yesterday. I'm happy for you."

Cue grunted. "You're really back with Mandy Griffin?" He shook his head. "How the hell did you end up there? She tossed you out like hot garbage."

He settled into the seat next to Frank on the left

355

side of the bed. "It wasn't what it seemed. She thought she was protecting me, but the whole thing was a set-up. One my dad and hers came up with together to keep us apart."

Frank frowned. "Your dad? You're saying Malcolm and the fucking mayor were working together just to make you break up with your girlfriend? You've got to know how ridiculous you sound."

"I heard them talking about it. My buddy recorded the whole thing. My dad told Scott to bring me along the day everything went down with the apartment fire." His fingers pressed hard into the wooden arms of the chair. "He fucking set it up so Mandy thought she was protecting me from prosecution for being there."

Cue groaned as he adjusted to face him more fully. "Why? Why would he?"

"Isn't it obvious?" Frank growled. "It's the only reason Kane joined the club. He got fucked-up, he lost his girl, and we were there to put him back together again." His friend faced him. "You were never going to patch in. It was all about college and getting married." Frank closed his eyes. "Fuck."

Cue Ball shook his head. "Her dad is the same guy who brought the Russians to our front door. He's the reason I'm in here…the reason Scott is dead. And Malcolm was working with him?"

He nodded. "Before, yeah. And keeping it a secret is why he's not pushing for revenge now." He put his hand on Cue's shoulder. "You know how much you guys mean to me. You're my brothers. I couldn't love you more if we were related by blood."

Frank sighed. "You're patching out."

Cue scowled. "No, he's—Kane?"

"I am."

His friends looked stricken. Tubes stuck in his hands, Cue rubbed tiredly over his bald head. Frank dropped his head into his hands.

"My father manipulated my entire life to get me into this club. I can't live with that. I don't want to sell drugs or guns; I never did, and you guys know it. My future is with Mandy. I want her to be my wife and the mother of my kids. This isn't the life I want; it never was."

"I get it," Frank said softly and looked up. "What your dad did was all kinds of fucked up. But the rest of us…we never betrayed you. You'd walk away from all of us?"

"I don't want to." He banged his head against the back of the chair. "I want to keep you both in my life. Fuck, my mom, too. But you are the ones who have to decide what the code means to you. I know what my mom's going to say, and it breaks my heart. Still, I've got to try, here, with you. I'm trying to tell you I want you both to be part of my future. But as for the club, as of today, I'm patching out."

Cue flinched. "You need to go now, brother."

Frank stared at his boots.

He respected his friend's wishes. "I'll always be your brother, man." His heart in his throat, he walked out of the room. His next stop wouldn't go any better.

***

The clubhouse had returned to its regular condition when Kane arrived. Someone had replaced the broken window and patched the bullet holes in the walls.

He found his parents together at the kitchen table, an open box of Papa John's between them. Mama V greeted him with a watery smile. "Hey, KC. Want to join your daddy and me for some pizza?"

Wordlessly, he dropped his cut on the table next to the box.

His father's eyes darkened. "What's this, boy?"

"I'm out."

His mother gasped.

Malcolm shot to his feet. "Bullshit. This club just stood at your back against your old lady's father, and this is how you repay us?"

His fingers curled in the front of Malcolm's shirt, the urge to hit him coursing hot like the blood in his veins. "Repay you? For setting me up in the first place?" He gestured to the scar on his face. "For this? For *conspiring with the man who got Scott killed*?"

Mama V tugged at his arms. "What are you talking about, Kane? Let your daddy go."

He released his grip, but he stepped further into Malcolm's space. "You gonna admit it, or are you gonna lie like a fucking coward?"

Malcolm shook his head tiredly. "Do what you want. I'm sick of fighting to hold this family together."

What a load of shit. "The only person you ever fought for was yourself." He turned to his mother, but her gaze was rooted to the floor. "Mama."

She shook her head, tears already falling down her cheeks. "I can't be your mama anymore."

"We're gonna lose everything," Malcolm muttered. "The deal with the Russians is gone. And you know Ace will only negotiate with you. You don't care. You don't care about anything except your precious piece of pussy."

He did hit his father then. A hard right-hook to the jaw. "You just showed the difference between you and me. I don't think of the woman who loves me as a piece of pussy. She's going to be my wife, and I will always put her first. Thank you, Malcolm, for teaching me what kind of husband and father I don't want to be. And Mom, if you ever decide you're worth more than this, my door is always open."

Breathing deep, he turned his back on his parents and left the Skulls MC in his rear-view mirror.

***

Amanda

Amanda traced her fingers nervously over the tattoos on Kane's forearm as they waited for his friends to arrive. Brick and his fiancé were coming over for drinks, and even though Kane promised she'd love Olivia, she didn't make friends easily. It was hard to simply be herself around strangers.

She jumped up when the bell rang.

Brick's broad shoulders filled the doorframe as Kane let them in. "I hope it's okay. I brought Robby along too."

"It's fine." Kane had told her he and Brick had sort-of adopted Xander's young assistant. "Come on in."

Brick's fiancé was a willowy blonde who greeted her with a hug. "It's so great to meet you. It's about time Kane got a little happiness in his life." She lowered her voice. "And great job with his new look. I barely recognized him without the beard and all the hair. What a lucky lady you are."

She chuckled. "Oh, I know. I'm reaping all the benefits of his makeover."

Kane was already handing out beers to the guys. "You want something, Liv? Beer? Wine?"

Her eyes sparkled. "Do I see zinfandel over there?"

Once everyone had a drink, Kane caught them up on what happened with the club. Robby made a noise of disgust and wrinkled his brow at her. "Your dad gets off scot-free? It doesn't feel right."

Kane shrugged. "No, it doesn't. But if it helps to know, Nathan Shaw's death at his house has ruined him politically. He'll never be governor of this state, and I doubt he stands a chance at re-election for mayor since David Bennett talked to the media." The new president of the Christian Soldiers gave a tell-all interview about his ties to the mayor, obviously worried keeping it a secret could provide a healthy motivation for making him disappear. He conveniently left out any details that could incriminate himself. "Beau will be lucky if he doesn't go to jail."

"And your club?" Robby pressed. "They've all turned their back on you?"

"Frank has called me a couple of times. I think he's willing to buck the rules, but otherwise, yeah. They're gone." It had been two weeks since he patched out, and from everyone else, it had been radio silence.

"I'm sorry." Robby tapped Kane's beer bottle with his own. "I know it's not the same, but you know you've got me. We're family, remember?"

"Yeah, man, I remember." Kane nodded gratefully, then turned to Brick. "Speaking of family, when are you two going to make it official?"

Liv snuggled in Brick's side. "Valentine's Day. It's going to be a small wedding, but it would mean the world to us if you were both there."

"What about you two?" Robby elbowed Kane in the arm.

Amanda grinned. "Kane's moving in this weekend. We could really use a few extra pairs of strong arms to help with the boxes."

"Count us in." Brick smiled.

Kane leaned over and whispered in her ear. "Not a bad little family we have here, huh, babe?"

She brushed her lips over his smooth cheek. "Not bad," she whispered. "Not bad at all."

EPILOGUE

Kane

Sliding into Gerry's chair at the Slipknot felt as familiar as breathing. The old tattoo artist had given Kane every piece of ink he'd ever gotten, including the bold letters of Mandy's name he wore on his back.

Other than his first tat, this would be the only art he wore that actually meant something.

The vinyl seat was cool against his bare back, as Gerry disinfected the skin of his left pectoral where Mandy had shaved him last night. At first, he'd considered putting the new tat on his hand, but in the end, it felt better to wear it over his heart.

They'd gone over the design last week, and the stencil was already done. The only thing left was making it a permanent part of his skin.

Mandy laced her fingers with his while Gerry worked, although the sting of the needle was barely a blip on his radar. She knew, of course. She was there for emotional support. Without her, it would be far too easy to fall back into memories that might break his heart.

Thank God for his wife. They'd quietly made it official after Brick—who went by Jonathan these days—and Olivia said their *I Do's*. There was no ceremony, just an exchange of gold bands and a justice of the peace to make it legal. Mike and Cindy grumbled about it, but in the end, they understood. Kane couldn't live another moment without tying her to him forever. He was blessed beyond measure she felt the same way.

Still no word from anyone but Frank in the club. It was better than he'd hoped, honestly. At least he kept one of his old friends, even if he missed Cue Ball every day.

The design on his chest was simple, but Gerry was a pro and took his time. It was a couple of hours before he held up the mirror and surveyed the scorpion so like the one Scott had drawn for them months ago.

"You happy with it?" the old guy asked gruffly.

He nodded, rather than dump his emotions all over the sterile field.

Gerry bandaged him up and carried off his credit card to settle the bill.

Mandy helped him button his shirt, then fidgeted with her own small bandage fitted over the inside of her wrist. When she told him she wanted her own tattoo, she could've knocked him over with a feather. Once he saw the design, though, he understood.

Just like the pendant he gave her for Christmas, it was two hearts woven together with the words *I*

Love You and *Forever* in script underneath. It was her way of marking him on her body as he'd done for her.

It was dark outside by the time they were finished, and they were only a few feet away from her car when she grabbed his wrist. Her head was tilted back, a smile curving across her beautiful face. "Kane, look. A shooting star. Make a wish."

He closed his eyes, but he was only playing along. There was nothing else he wanted.

All his wishes had already come true.

About the Author

Jen started her love affair with romance novels, first as a reader, then as a reviewer and blogger.

She is happily married to her high school sweetheart. Together, they're raising two kids, a cat, and a dog who is afraid of his own shadow.

Jen spends her days working as television journalist and her nights curled up with a good book.

Facebook:
https://www.facebook.com/jen.davis.author

Twitter:
http://twitter.com/redhotbooks

Website:
http://jendavis.net/

Join our Reader Group on Facebook and don't miss out on meeting our authors and entering epic giveaways!

Limitless Reading

Where reading a book
is your first step to becoming
limitless...

LIMITLESS PUBLISHING *Reader Group*

Join today! *"Where reading a book is your first step to becoming limitless..."*

https://www.facebook.com/groups/LimitlessReading/